THE FORSAKING OF THE BLIND

THE WING CYCLE, BOOK III

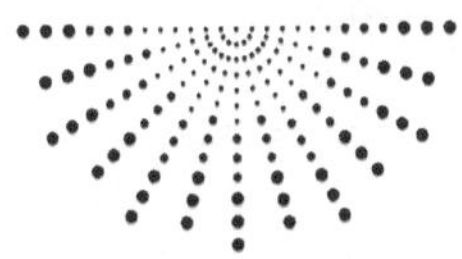

E.G. STONE

For the writers of stories,
Whose words shall endure

CONTENTS

PROLOGUE

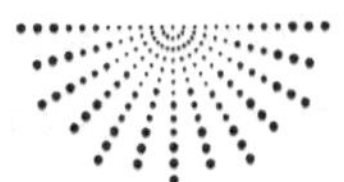

There was a reason that they were called Stormbringers. With every beat of a thousand wings, thunder heralded their arrival. They came with fear before them, driving it towards their enemies. They flew determined, meant to strike terror in the hearts of those who heard the oncoming storm. They were fierce. Dangerous. Deadly. They were sometimes called warmongers. They were sometimes called avenging angels. They were celebrated for their swift and decisive victories, leaving few standing in their wake.

Their purpose was not to cultivate war, though. Theirs was to end it.

Tiberius stood on the edge of their island, a haven in a world that feared their very presence. For every war they ended, for every warrior they sent back home, it seemed that thousands died. Of course the world feared them, Tiberius thought. How could they possibly do anything else? His wings hung limp at his sides, crippled some cycles before. He leaned on a staff, his wrinkled hand the colour of dark, nearly black ash. It trembled as he held the staff, his muscles weary from walking from the stone tower he and others no longer suited for war had built. A haven within the haven.

False peace, though it was.

Tiberius lifted his chin to the sky, watching the legion of Stormbringers head off into the rising sun. Their wings shone gold. Their features flashed in the light, too far away for him to make out the individual faces. They flew as one, the multitude of wings creating that distinctive sound. Still, he watched, some small part of him straining his eyes in the hopes that he could see one sylph amongst the storm.

"Fly thee well, my child," Tiberius said as the last of the sylphs winked out over the horizon, lost to the morning sun. He bowed his head and clutched his staff tighter. His *son*. Please, let his son live, he prayed. If anyone was still listening, that was.

"Come along, old greyfeathers," a young voice teased. Tiberius lifted his head and saw Mara, the youth charged with his care. She was strong and her wings mottled with shades of brown and gold. Her eyes shone like fire, bright against the charcoal-ash of her skin. She could have been Tiberius' mate, Ysa, dead in war these many cycles past. The same war that had crippled his wings.

"Watch who you're calling greyfeathers," Tiberius retorted, forcing a smile to his face. "I could still beat you in the Dalketh, whether you like it or not."

"As you say." Mara smiled and slid her arm through Tiberius', starting on the long walk back to the tower. It was a kindness, her willingness to stay with a grounded sylph when most of their people had flown off to war. Another war.

"Do you ever regret your decision?" Tiberius asked quietly. Mara's wings rustled, her feathers pulling together. Her expression, though, betrayed none of her anxiety or surprise. "Do not tell me that you have not considered the question, child. Nearly all sylphs of your age have since taken up the sword or the bow and the arrow. They have flown far and wide and seen the world even as they figh—"

"I am not alone in my thoughts on the matter," Mara murmured. She flicked her eyes to Tiberius and he saw a well of deep sadness there. "The Council has asked me to speak on the situation. Me and several others."

"I had not realised that such feelings ran so deeply," Tiberius said. He let out a slow breath, trying to lift his wings from trailing on the ground. There were several dead leaves hanging off the feathers. He gave up on the effort and let them gather what debris they would. It was a pointless battle. One of many. "The storm seemed so eager when they were preparing to fly yestereve."

Meritus had seemed so eager, his eyes the exact shade of his mother's. Tiberius had almost begged his son to remain, to not leave him behind. Sylphs bred with great difficulty and Meritus was all that Tiberius had left.

"Many wish for this journey to be the storm's last. Many others know that it will be, in one form or another," Mara breathed. The words hung in the air like moulted down, gently falling. Tiberius nearly stumbled, his feet catching on the tree roots as his mind gasped for relief.

"They cannot be so certain of such a thing," Tiberius said, pleading. Begging Mara to tell him something different, to tell him that it was not possible, not so. That the Watcher, that the spirits they praised could not be so cruel as to do what Mara was suggesting. To do this terrible thing, that others felt in their feathers.

He would not shed tears if the storm was to be dissolved, if they were to retreat from the world and let it fall to ruin. But what Mara suggested was far from the reasonable dissolution of their fighting forces. She, and others who had such feather-sense, were implying something far worse. The fall of the Stormbringers. The end of the storm.

Mara squeezed his arm, her wings brushing his. She knew he understood, and yet she still tried to shield him, her words merely politic. Gentle child.

"The High Council has… decided to bring the issue up with the Chosen King. We cannot survive if things continue this way. And our efforts are so wasted, so futile. Not one year has passed since we last flew to end one of the wars of the humans and here is another already raging and calling for our intervention. What can we do against a people who are so bent on violence?"

Tiberius hung his head. His wings drooped. How could he have missed this? How could he have not felt the oncoming doom in the pinions he still bore, despite their uselessness? Tiberius lifted his head, crying out.

"You save him! You bring him home! Or we shall never again fight against the tide. We shall never again end a war of their own making. Save them *all*!" Tiberius touched his forehead to the staff he bore, letting out a sob. Mara placed her hand on his back, just between the point where his wings began. She waited until Tiberius breathed steadily once more.

"Come, greyfeathers," Mara said, her voice quiet, the teasing gone. "We must go light candles for them. We have our vigil to hold."

It would prove to be the last.

CHAPTER ONE

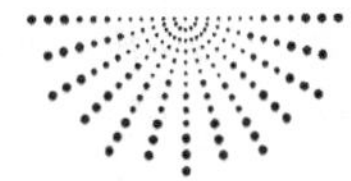

Ravenna stepped down the stairs into the lesser used parts of the Stone Tower. The stairs here were kept as clean and tidy as the rest of the parts of the tower, but she could see moss growing on the walls where the Intellecti rarely ventured, and their wings rarely brushed stone. This place was not kept so disused because of reverence at its contents, but out of a sort of primal fear. This was not one of their places of storage for the great tomes, able to be accessed by only the most senior Intellecti. This was not one of their round rooms of discussion, where they could debate and argue about history and facts as they pleased.

This was a place of death.

Ravenna passed a final turn on the stairs, then she entered into the lowest level attached to the tower. She was perhaps a hundred feet below the ground of Shinalea, in a cavernous and labyrinthine space little explored and oft forgotten. The floor was of that selfsame stone that formed the rest of the tower, but the walls and ceiling were of bone. Sylph bone. They were placed in intricate designs, with meaning hidden to all but the Intellecti, and even they had forgotten many of the designs over the generations. Or they had lost them on purpose, letting some things lie forever with the dead. The bones of many sylphs had been interred there. They were too numerous to count, but the chambers were vast and twisting, marking out the generations. Somewhere in there were her unborn nephew and her heart-father Tacitus, their bones pressed into the walls.

She understood why very few sylphs ever ventured down here, where their wings could not reach the sky. Ironic, given that it would be the final resting place for them all.

For the sylphs *she* was going to lead to war.

"This is not a good idea," Ravenna said to herself. She wrapped her shadow-dark wings closer to her body and thought of all of the sylphs waiting above ground in the Aerial City for her. That night they were with their families or celebrating being alive, preparing for the inevitable bloodshed that was to come in the following morning. Still, they would wait for Ravenna to appear back amongst them, amongst the living, among the warriors. They were waiting for the monster that would guide them from the peaceful people they used to be into the throes of history that perhaps should have been left behind.

They were up there, celebrating, waiting, not thinking about what was to come. Ravenna could do nothing but think.

The sylphs did not have beings to worship, as the humans did. They did not think that there was some divine presence watching over them, intervening in their lives, or looking out for either their welfare or their doom. They believed in facts and history and things that could be measured, things that were known. They had built their entire society on such a philosophy. At that moment, though, Ravenna really wished there was someone she could talk to that was greater than herself. Who knew what was coming.

"Tacitus," Ravenna said, passing her hands along the murals of bone. "This is not what you would have wanted for us. You never believed in any of the ancient stories about the Stormbringers or about the horrors that waited for us on the mainland. You never believed I came back compelled by violence to create more violence. Yet, tomorrow, I am going to destroy everything that you believe. I am going to lead our people into a war the likes of which we haven't seen in generations. I do not believe in the gods of humans, but I have to believe that you are out there somewhere, and that you understand why I did what I did. I have to believe that you understand what will happen to us after this…should we possibly survive.

"I know that there are ancestors out there who have survived worse and then died of long life. I hope they will give me strength. We have already lost one sylph too many. Itonus was one of the best of us. He was strong and good and…and he died because I was foolish enough not to trust my own people. Not to tell them my heart. I don't know if I'll ever return to Shinalea. Even if I do make it through what's coming, I don't think this is the place for me anymore. I was never one of these people. They never needed me until now. And they won't need me in the future. But if I ever was part of these beautiful people, if ever I was a true sylph, then please help me."

Ravenna ran her hands over the walls of bone, feeling the indentations in the skulls where eyes had once been. She felt the shape of the wings, the curve of the ribs. She wondered if Itonus was stripped bare of flesh before the sky, as he should be, or if Davorin had desecrated even that right. Would someone go to fetch his bones?

One shard of bone from a wing caught her finger, a single drop of blood spilling out and staining the wall. She put her finger to her mouth and sucked away the liquid. If that was a sign from her ancestors, she wasn't sure whether it was the forewarning or a message of purpose. Ravenna wasn't hopeful on the outcome.

Tomorrow she would lead the people to go fight the nightmares that haunted their history. Humans.

Davorin. It was her fault that he was aware of the sylphs at all. If it had not been for her foolishness, the human would have easily gone his whole life without ever knowing the truth about sylphs, or she about humans. If that were the case, though, she would never have met Miska and Lenore, the people to whom she had given her heart and her loyalty. She would never have understood herself. She would never have learned what it meant to be a warrior, what she was capable of. Or what it meant to find a family. Would she truly give up all that she had found just to save her people, if the choice were presented? She did not know. That terrified her more than the upcoming war.

The rustle of wing feathers startled her. Ravenna spun, reaching for the ever present blades at her back. She paused when she saw her sister Desarra, standing there in full battle regalia, with moulded leather armour, tight flying leathers, even a long knife at her waist. Her golden skin shone with health and with confidence and she had tied back her burnished gold hair in an elaborate twist, the crown of wings sitting on her brow. Her eyes glowed like the lamplight they reflected. Her posture was proud. Here was a queen, and Ravenna's first instinct had been to fight.

Kratos, the plump healer was beside her, wringing his hands together as though he hoped that all this could be avoided. His wings shuffled uncomfortably behind him.

Ravenna bowed low, her wings almost touching the ground. "My Queen," she said, the sound more biting than she would have liked. She straightened. "I'm sorry. Everything is a bit..."

"Your Stormbringers have requested that I call to pull out every container of mead that we have. I told them they can have half, so that their heads are not pounding tomorrow. I was informed, however, that you were not up there with them. Should I ask why you are instead keeping the dead company? Wings, Ravenna, this place is creepy. Pictures made from bone.

And not even a breeze to ruffle the feathers. What are you doing down here?"

Ravenna shrugged. Truthfully, she found the catacombs somewhat peaceful. Should she tell Desarra that the bones of her unborn son were down here? No, there was no need to bring back that haunted look to her sister's eyes. "I was looking for something I did not find," she said. "It seems the voices of our ancestors have left me long behind."

Desarra hesitated. She opened her wings once and closed them, uncertain. "Is this another one of your human things that you picked up? Like…well…"

"Like Miska My lover? My mate?" Ravenna had purposefully kept her relationship with Miska—a human—quiet, knowing that her people would not understand why it was that she gave her heart to him. First Crispinus then Desarra had found out. They, too, had kept it quiet, knowing that morale would be crushed if the other sylphs discovered that their leader, the one who was to have flown with them into an attack against the nightmares that were humans, loved one of those selfsame nightmares.

Desarra winced.

"The humans believe that there are gods and divine beings out there who watch them, who lend them their blessing if they worshiped them. These gods either love their followers uncon-ditionally or are more petty than the humans they bless. I sought a different sort of solution. I thought that maybe if humans have their gods, those of us who went before could perhaps lend their advice."

The wound on her finger throbbed.

"Our ancestors do not speak," Kratos said, a certain finality in his voice even as he attempted to temper it with sympathy. "Not with voices that you can hear. They left us their tomes, their wisdom. And I found something that you might be inter-ested in."

"Another discussion of warfare? Another suggestion on how I can go get my people slaughtered?" Ravenna turned to the bone on the wall, her fingers tracing the drops of blood she had left there.

"No, you have devoured all of those. You know more about warfare than anyone, perhaps living or dead. You shall see what good such knowledge does tomorrow and I cannot help you with that. No, this is something different, something for those of us who are staying behind. A vigil of candles to watch over the world. To keep spirits up. Apparently, when the last member of the Storm vanishes on the horizon, the sylphs left in the Aerial City and in the Stone Tower would light a whole fleet of candles. The largest to smallest, every candle in the city. The belief was that when the last candle went out, the Storm would return."

"And if they did not?" Ravenna asked.

Kratos smiled. He stretched his wings smugly and did his best not to preen. "There is no record of such a thing happening. I have had our candle makers preparing candles for a week now. Fear not, we will watch until you return."

"And yet the Storm disappeared from history," Ravenna murmured. The other two sylphs pretended not to have heard.

"*You* will watch," the Chosen Queen said, fluffing her wings. "I will be accompanying my sister to the mainland. I will not let my people go into battle without me."

Ravenna spread her wings wide, the feathers rustling. "Are you insane?!"

"Far from it, sister. I am simply doing what I said I would do those moons ago. Why else did you teach me to fight the Dalketh? I told you I would be on the battlefield. So do I intend to be."

"I taught you to fight because I feared what you would do if I did not. It was not right for the Chosen Queen of her people to be unfamiliar in the art of war when I was training most of the population to fight to the death. It would not do if you were to be ignorant of such things. The High Council would have taken that as a sign of your incompetence and made you even more than a puppet than you already are. But to actually appear on the battlefield?" Ravenna scoffed, shaking her head. "You would die. Swiftly."

Desarra straightened, her shoulders back, her wings wide, the golden tips nearly brushing the walls the way that Ravenna's never could. She looked every part the Chosen Queen. Had the world been a fair place, she would be the one leading people to battle, not Ravenna, the flightless sylph no one liked but they all seemed to need. Things were never fair. Ravenna had learned that a long time ago.

"You think me to be so incompetent you could just placate me? Lie to me and tell me that learning the Dalketh was worthwhile? That I was capable? Am I to watch my mate and my only sister, the only family I have left, go off without a chance of returning? You would have me sit here like a flightless wretch, unable to do anything but look pretty for the masses...I'm sorry. I didn't mean that—" Desarra's eyes widened, reflecting the torchlight even more. Ravenna noted that in the half-light of this place of death, the crown of wings and the colour of Desarra's eyes were one and the same.

She took a breath and broke gaze with her sister, placing a hand flat on the wall of bone. Perhaps if she could just get closer, then their ancestors might speak. Still, though, she was unsurprised when the only response was silence.

"Do not think I don't see the irony in this. The flightless one is Warlord, leading the Storm in the battle. No, I did not teach you Dalketh to placate you. Nor do I believe you incapable. You could easily match any of the others in battle. But the truth is that many of them are going to die. No, I don't want you there. Do you know what it would do to our people, our society, if you were killed? We do not have enough remaining for Choosing as it is, not with so many to go to battle. The High Council would take over. The Chosen Monarchy would be dismantled. People would lose the one thing they have left." Ravenna shook her head, dark hair obscuring her icy eyes. "They see me as a cruel sylph. As one who has seen death and encouraged it. I have blood on my hands and my wings are drenched. I am a killer. And that's what they *need* me to be. You? You are so much more. After this war, I will be nothing but a footnote in a tome. You will have to rebuild our society. Determine which direction we go. I can't do that. It's not my place. Even if I were in your wings, I could not do it. So don't go to the battlefield. I cannot order you. I am not your superior. But I as your warlord, as your sister, as the only one of us who has seen death and survived, I ask you not to go. I don't know what I would do if I lost you."

The catacombs echoed with silence. Desarra paced the rooms, studying each bone, each design made out of the remains of her people. She looked at the healer and she looked at her sister. She folded her wings, carefully, gently, with grace. Then, she lifted her chin. "I will go with you. I will not fight on the battlefield, but I will be there at the encampment with the healers prepared and charged to deal with the injuries of the battle. I will not put myself in danger, for your sake, not for theirs. Because you asked me."

Ravenna reached out and wrapped her arms around her sister, pulling her into a human hug. She had learned of this act from Miska, who had done the same to her and promised that all would be well. It was a testimony to that act that she still believed him. The sisters' wings touched, and Desarra relaxed in her arms.

"I don't want to do this," Ravenna whispered. "Wings, I would give anything to not have to do this. I'm scared."

"That is what makes you more than a monster," Desarra

breathed. She pulled back, and they were once more Chosen Queen and Warlord.

Ravenna turned to Kratos, who watched with the awkward embarrassment of an Intellecti witnessing an intimate and personal act. "Light your candles. Prepare your tomes. The Stormbringers fly on the morrow. And we *will* return."

CHAPTER TWO

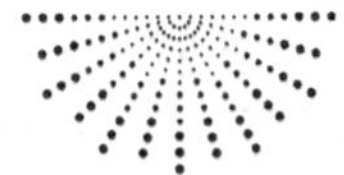

$\mathcal{I}$t had been three days since Miska had made his grand declaration to Cavaris and the Elders of Hull-gard that he would stand and fight without them, but his anger had not lessened. It was their fault that he was marching towards the Red Desert with nothing more than a magically enhanced bear as his familiar, and a young girl as his companion. He was not arriving with the army that he needed to help free his Queen and Ravenna. They had taken such hope from him and he had declared he would do battle alone, anger fuelling his path.

Of course, by the third day, he had discovered that anger did not count for a whole lot. It did not create soldiers to fight at his side. It did not lend his weapons or his magic any further deadliness or ability. The fact was that Miska was going to have to help his people on his own and he was vastly outnumbered. Yes, he had magic, but so did Davorin. And yes, Beringer was worth certainly a whole slew of warriors on his own, but there were more than that to fight against.

Miska would fight his battle, but he did not imagine it would last long.

"I think that Beringer is having a hard time," Allora said, her face tilted up to Miska. Her white-blonde hair blew around her eyes and she tucked it away in annoyance. He saw her words because she was riding backwards before him on the bear's shoulders, making sure that he could see her mouth and have a full conversation with her. After the first day of almost no talking, Allora had gotten bored and decided that this was far more entertaining. Now, he supposed that she was bored or hungry; there was little to do after three days march and she had not his fury. Why should she? Allora was but a child, indignant on his behalf but not fully understanding the cause.

Miska patted the bear's shoulders and sent him a mental command to stop. The two climbed down off his massive back and Miska saw that his young charge was right. The bear was panting more than he should have been given that they set a fairly easy pace for the day, having reached the foothills of the Iron Mountains. Beringer was able to move faster than a horse at a slow trot with just an ambling pace, but three days' worth of travel was taking its toll. Miska, too, had noticed that things were growing more difficult. It was harder to think, harder to stay awake while Beringer lumbered steadily on towards their potential doom. Part of that was because of the heat that the desert seemed to emit, even not being fully summer. After over-wintering in the Iron Mountains, returning to the familiar desert heat was more of a burden than Miska thought. He had abandoned his outer furs some thirty miles back.

Reaching out with his fingers, Miska tapped one of the colourful threads surrounding Beringer and sent his magic to the bear. Had he been a normal sorcerer, one who could hear, the magic would have sounded like a song, a myriad of notes and tunes that he could conduct. Being deaf, he instead had to weave the magic into place. This particular spell would have Beringer shed most of his undercoat so that he wouldn't be overburdened by the heat of the desert.

Miska almost wished he could do the same, but there was little more clothing he could shed and still remain decent. Allora alone seemed unbothered, though her white-blonde hair was darkened with sweat.

A cloud of fur erupted from the bear. Allora bounced with joy, having caught a face full of the fluff, and brushed it off of her. Beringer snorted, obviously not thrilled with this turn of events. He lumbered a few feet away and dug his claws into the ground, showing his displeasure.

"This will help, you great lout," Miska grumbled, following after his charge. Beringer huffed, halfway to a boulder where he could scratch the itch of his fur away, instead letting his humans approach. They spent the next hour brushing out his fur coat with their fingers as best they could, leaving a massive pile of hair off the side of the trail that they had been using.

After that, though, there was nothing else to do but to re-don their packs and prepare to move on. Even that brief respite had left Miska with a sour taste in his mouth. Would it be the last time they laughed together?

Allora looked at Miska and frowned, her pack still on the ground and already gathering a layer of red desert dust. "When are we going to get there?" she whined, brushing a dusting of fur out of her hair.

Instead of responding, Miska dug into his pack and pulled out some dried jerky and preserved fruits. He handed them to the young girl. She made a face, but scarfed down the food in any case. Their trail rations had been running a bit short since they started the journey, as Miska had thought that he would come upon small village or somewhere he could renew his supplies before meeting up with whatever remained of the Red Desert's army. Reality had not been quite so forthcoming.

"Are they going to be glad to see us?" Allora asked, her words muddled as she formed the words around the food. Miska made a face, which elicited a half-hearted smile. He leaned back against Beringer and shook his head.

"I do not know. Cavaris said that my queen was not dead, that the armies had not been decimated, that the desert was faring as well as could be expected under the circumstances. But after what he did, I don't know how much of that I can believe. I can only hope that things are not as bad as I imagine them to be, and that we get there in time. When we do get there, I think that Lenore and her people will be glad to see us. You would be glad to see us, wouldn't you?" Miska lifted Allora into his arms and spun her around before setting her back down. He couldn't hear the laughter, but he could see the smile and feel Beringer's rumbles of pleasure in the back of his mind. The bear was as fond of his heart-daughter as Miska was.

"I think anybody would be glad to see us. Especially Beringer," Allora said, brushing her tunic free from dirt and fur. She squinted up at Miska. "Except the enemy. They won't be pleased to see us. Especially Beringer."

The bear—easily twice the size of even the largest of that same species that roamed the Iron Mountains, due to his magical connection with Miska—rumbled in agreement. Miska had to privately agree; there was little more terrifying than being run down by a creature like Beringer.

"One of my friends is a queen," Miska said. "She was the leader of the Red Desert before the Salusian Empire came and took it over. You would like her. She was strong and proud and capable and kind. Just like you, but I think you might be prettier."

Allora scoffed. "Who cares how pretty she is. I just want to know if she will let me fight. Me and Beringer would take them all down!"

Miska sighed and chewed on one of the pieces of dried jerky so he would not answer right away. He handed the rest to Beringer. The bear could catch his own food, but the closer they got to the desert, the less he wanted his familiar far away from him. "We talked about this. I know you want to help. I know that you were there when Sisu and Asgeir helped to train me. I know that you want to help these people as if they were your own. But you are too young. You do not have the strength or the stamina to stand up against what we face. I expect you to be safe on the sidelines. And if anything should go wrong—"

"Nothing's going to go wrong. You told me so. And you have magic."

"If something should go wrong," Miska repeated, placing a hand on Allora's head, "then you are to return to Hullgard. Tell them what happened. Take shelter with Cavaris. You may not like it, but he will care for you."

Allora made a face, but nodded. Perhaps she understood more than Miska thought.

Miska didn't like it, either. His feelings for the interfering dragon were far from benevolent at the moment. Cavaris had been against the war from the beginning, and had even gone so far as to sabotage the meeting with the Elders so that Miska would be forced to fight alone. No, not alone. He had Allora to buoy his spirit from the edge of the battle, and Beringer's claws to fight beside him. And, with all hope, Ravenna and her sylphs. Together, they would free the Red Desert, Cavaris' interference or no.

A flash of emotion from Beringer's mind had Miska standing on the alert, threads of magic at the ready. Something had alarmed the bear, and Miska relied on his superior senses more than he had initially understood. He could hardly remember what it had been like before Beringer. How fragile, how empty his life had been.

Allora paused, looking around and reaching to the knife at her belt. She froze. Her eyes widened and she ran off towards the direction Beringer faced. Miska let out a shout of surprise and used his magic to hold her back.

Surely they couldn't have come upon Davorin's troops so early. Surely the Salusian Empire had not stretched so far in his absence.

Fear leapt into Miska's throat, making it hard to breathe.

A lumbering figure appeared before them, wearing the light furs that were common attire for the late mountain spring. Miska recognised the long black hair with tiny braids and beads, the beard that nearly covered the man's mouth. He recognised the height, the stature, the left hand that had been cut off and covered with a plate of metal. Sisu. He had thought that Sisu had remained behind in Hullgard, that the man wouldn't want anything to do with him since he had failed Cavaris' test and been unable to win the Elders' approval. But here he was.

"Sisu," Miska said. He released Allora from the magic and walked forward without thinking to greet the larger man, clasping arms. Beringer shuffled up and nosed Sisu in the shoulder, making the larger man stagger. "What are you doing here? Did…did they change their mind?"

The large man who had trained Miska in the Iron Mountains, who had taught him everything he knew about fighting and hunting, shook his head. "No, they did not change their mind. I am afraid that Cavaris has been too afraid for too long. I could not change his mind or even sway his opinion of you. But I would not stand by to see such an injustice done to you. Asgeir wanted to come also, but I persuaded him to stay behind and see if he could work on the conscience of the Elders. There is a fracture in our people, and I fear that this has only exacerbated it. My words with the Elders have certainly not helped at all. I doubt very much we will see any assistance from that quarter, but it is worth a try. Instead, I will make things better here as much as I can. So I came to help. Are you not glad to see me?"

"Of course I'm glad to see you," Miska said. "You are worth a battalion on your own. But…No it doesn't matter now. We will face what awaits us and that is the end of it."

To keep himself from having to hear more, to learn precisely how poorly he had fared in the eyes of the Elders, or how hopeless the situation was, Miska turned away so he wouldn't be able to read Sisu's mouth or his hands. Beringer rumbled quietly in the back of Miska's mind, the sound almost like words. It was so strange being able to hear inside his mind and not without, but he had grown somewhat used to it in the last seasons. The truth was, it was easier to focus on these mundane thoughts than was on what came ahead. If Cavaris had misreported anything, then Miska could be walking into a devastating aftermath of a war that had already been fought. He could be walking into the end of things. He could be walking into a trap. Who knew if his magic would stand up against the blood magic that Davorin wielded? There was too much uncertainty, and even having Sisu to fight at his side, Miska's stomach turned.

Sisu touched Miska's shoulder and turned him so that the big man could be understood. "How much farther is it to your homeland?"

Miska turned and surveyed the land around him. It was disturbingly familiar, even though he was mostly certain he had never before ventured into the foothills surrounding the Iron Mountains. A memory flashed in his mind and he saw the face of his childhood tormentor, the one who had ganged up on Miska and, with the help of his friends, beat him until he could hear no more. His village. The nightmare of his childhood. His village had been located in the cliffs just at the edge of the foothills. It was where the mountain met the desert, and it was a place that he had thought long forgotten. This place looked exactly like the hills surrounding his former childhood home. Miska had no idea of how far it was to there, or where he would have to go to find Lenore, but he was back home.

The word burned in Miska's mind more than he thought it would. It wasn't home without his friends, without Lenore, without Ravenna. Would he see her again? The winged being who had haunted his dreams. Would she meet him in battle and fight at his side?

Miska turned to Sisu, who had lifted Allora onto his shoulders. "Half a day's journey at most. There will be a village soon, and from there we can determine where it is that we need to go."

"Okay," Sisu said. He lifted Allora to Beringer's shoulders, the bear still dropping clumps of fur, but moving far easier in the heat. Sisu nodded at Miska. "This is your terrain. Lead the way."

"You may want to leave your furs behind," Miska said with a wry chuckle that he did not feel. "It's only going to get hotter."

Sisu frowned, but did as Miska suggested. The man muttered something, which Miska understood simply because he was paying attention to the shape of his mouth. "It's not even full summer yet. How could it possibly get any hotter and not be summer?"

"At least it's not snowing," Miska said. Without another word, he turned and marched off. Beringer, Allora, and Sisu followed behind. Like it or not, Miska was going home. To the village of his youth, but also to the Red Desert. He didn't know what he would face, but he would face it.

He just hoped he would survive.

CHAPTER THREE

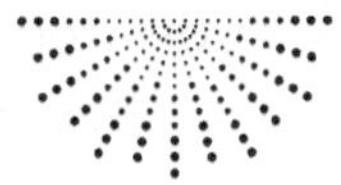

$\mathcal{L}$enore paced the cramped central room of the wood-and-mud house, one hand pressed against her protruding belly, the other against her back. Being pregnant was not an easy task. Being pregnant whilst conferring with the rebellion to try and remove her husband and his empire from her lands was far worse. And her bladder was feeling full. Again.

Lenore huffed and turned, pacing in the other direction in the vague hope for relief.

"My Queen," Vareis said, watching Lenore nervously from where she sat at the table with two other resistance leaders. Vareis had once been Lenore's training master, whipping the recruits into the army of the Red Desert into shape, and impressing upon them the duty which they were sworn to uphold. Now, she was ragged, worn, and conspiring with many of the other displaced peoples that the Salusian Empire had created when they took over the Red Desert and other surrounding kingdoms. Lenore was unsure whether the transition had been a good one for Vareis, whether she was as capable at helping to lead a rebellion as she had been at training an army. "Perhaps you should sit down, get some weight off of your feet. The talks might take some time."

"I only have a short amount of time before my husband returns from his cloak making efforts," Lenore said. "You are fortunate that he is more interested in wearing a cloak of feathers than he is in keeping an eye on me. Tell me what it is that you have to say and move on."

A squirrelly man sitting across from Vareis tapped his fingers nervously on the table. The resistance was meeting in one of the larger houses in the village where the army was currently camped. Davorin had been leading Lenore and most of the army on a grand progress throughout his new kingdom, to show off his wife and their pregnancy, as well as to inspect the people. What he had been doing in actuality was inspecting things and issuing orders that made no sense. As far as Lenore could tell, this grand progress was beginning to tear her beloved kingdom apart. Davorin was having weaving towns start mining, having olive growers start herding goats. None of it made any sense, and the people had been turning to Lenore to explain. She had no answers. And she knew that this could not last much longer, though, or her sacrifice to marry Davorin and protect the people of the Red Desert would be pointless. Her people would die without her help.

The man swallowed nervously and took a drink of some precious water drawn from a well nearby. "We do not have sufficient numbers to take on the army. Our forces are busy with trying to get supplies together. We are attempting to gather weapons. There were rumours that the slave markets had been made into a weapons forge. That Jazer had vanished and the slaves had taken over and were preparing a rebellion of their own. But we can get no confirmation on this. Our supplies are—"

"You have been prevaricating about getting supplies for moons now," Lenore snapped. Under other circumstances, she would have tried to be more polite, more understanding, more subtle in her need to get the people to do what she wanted. But she was pregnant. And tired. She had just witnessed Davorin murder a sylph. The sylph had tried to kill Davorin, yes, but the way in which he had died, with magic choking the life from him, was too cruel to wish upon anybody. Lenore had hoped that this was not Ravenna's only foray against Davorin. That the flightless sylph she had come to call friend would return and fight and help Lenore with her people. Perhaps she shouldn't hope. Perhaps she should find another way to fight. But the resistance was reluctant to commit any forces. And now, that dead sylph was having his wings plucked and the feathers sewn into a cloak for Davorin.

"It is true that we have not moved as quickly as we would have liked," Vareis said carefully. She took the pitcher of water on the table and poured Lenore a glass. Lenore drank it gratefully, some of the water spilling upon her golden-brown skin. She wiped her mouth with the back of her hand, not caring one jot if it was anything but queenly. Vareis coughed nervously and continued. "However, many now under the thumb of the Salusian Empire would rather keep their heads down and obey their new masters. Their lives were not severely disrupted by the changing regime. Well, not until recently. Dagan had begun stripping the lands bare for his own purposes. Davorin initially seemed to have halted that, but things have changed once again and we do not know what it is that he wants. Under these circumstances, gathering food and weapons for a prolonged attack has been difficult."

"If you do not fight with the few scattered pieces that my army has remaining, then Davorin will be left to his own devices," Lenore said flatly. The two resistance leaders winced, but said nothing. Vareis would not even meet Lenore's eyes. Lenore pressed both hands into the small of her back, hoping to relieve some of the pressure. It did not work. She sat, giving up on trying to reduce the discomfort.

"I placed all my resources with you," Lenore said. "Everything I could possibly have access to under Davorin's careful watch has been put at your control. Are you telling me now that it was wasted? That you are going to stand by and do nothing while Davorin's madness spreads?"

"Is he truly mad?" the squirrelly man asked. He looked at the walls as though they were closing in on him, or they were listening to every word they said. Lenore had been assured that this place was safe, that Davorin was occupied and that no one would be worried about her when she was not found immediately. Still, their time was short. "It is well known that he has obtained some sort of foul magic. But the thought was that this would simply make him more powerful. And he *is* powerful at that. Many of our people are afraid to cross him. But not simply because of the magic. His actions make no sense to us. It is like he is playing a chess game where he has control of most of the board and we only have a piece and can see but one move ahead. He is either incredibly intelligent and playing us all for fools, or..."

"His moves make no sense to me either," Lenore said. She sighed and ran a hand through her hair. Before her unwelcome nuptials, she had kept her auburn copper hair in tiny braids. Now it was loose, and while she had grown somewhat used to the style, she still did not recognise the person who looked back at her in the silver mirror. Her fingers fumbled with the strands, loosely braiding a small section. She gave up a few moments later. Lenore sat back in the chair and sighed. "I have learned and studied statecraft my entire life. I have dealt with bureaucrats and with warlords and tribal leaders from farther away than I will ever go. I understand what it is to run an empire, a country, a kingdom. I understand economics and how the news travels. But I do not understand what it is that Davorin is doing.

He is moving resources about as though we were preparing for a long siege in one part of the Empire and had a surplus in another. Except the place preparing for the siege has a surplus, the place preparing for the surplus has a famine. It's like he's dismantling everything that his ancestors built—and my ancestors and yours—as quickly as possible and with as little bloodshed as possible. It does not make any sense."

"So he is mad," Vareis breathed. The former training master looked hopefully up at Lenore. "If he is, then we could maybe... maybe we won't need to fight his army."

"Have you not been paying attention?" Lenore asked. She scoffed and folded her arms, resting them across her belly. The child within kicked viciously and she hissed in pain. After three deep breaths, Lenore sank deeper into the chair. "We have been parading the main portion of our forces around for the last moon. This is not some show. This was not a simple declaration of power. Davorin does nothing unless he intends to follow through. He gathered the army together. He armed them. He took pieces from ten different peoples and stitched them together into a cohesive force. He would not have done so if he did not intend to use them."

"For what?" Vareis whispered. "There is little left to conquer but the Iron Mountains, and the Wastelands beyond. There is nothing there."

The man nodded. A slight smile touched his mouth and he relaxed ever so slightly. "He said that he intended to find the Stormbringers. Find the angels, so that they could show divine favour for his rule. That is what his army is for. A children's story. Thought is not some sign of madness, then I don't know what is."

Lenore closed her eyes and sucked a deep breath in through her nose. The child kicked again, this time more gently. She pressed her hand against her side. "Did you not see the sylph? The angel that came here yesterday intending to slaughter him?

They are no child's story. They are history. Separated from us for generations, but they are returning. I only hope they can do it in time. Before Davorin's madness...before it can destroy our whole world."

Vareis reached out and grabbed Lenore's hand. "Don't worry my Queen," she started. A quick rap on the door interrupted them all. Lenore surged to her feet, holding her shoulders back and ignoring the weight that settled and caused pain on her hips and in her feet. The door opened a crack, revealing Blodwen, the Salusian maid that Davorin had assigned to Lenore. Unbeknownst to him, she had seen past his charming exterior, past the power that he commanded. Her loyalties lay now with Lenore and the resistance.

Where the loyalties of the so-called resistance lay was another matter entirely.

"The demon Dagan has just returned," Blodwen said, curtseying slightly to Lenore. "I would suggest you return to your tenants, unless you wish for the demon to come looking for you."

"No," Lenore said. She pressed a hand to her forehead. "I would rather not have to deal with that monster at the moment." She turned to the two resistance leaders waiting at the table. Nothing had been accomplished in that meeting except discovering that nothing more had been accomplished since their last meeting. Things were moving too slowly, and at this rate it would not be ready to fight until Lenore was an old woman. "I don't care what it takes, but you will arm your people. Or you will return my resources to me and I will put them elsewhere."

Without a glance backward, Lenore strode from the tiny house and into the dusty streets of this pitiful village. It was one at the edge of the Red Desert, where the foothills from the Iron Mountains abutted the sands and scrub. They managed to scrape out a decent living growing olives, and producing oil.

But the people were thin, the village was falling apart, and olive trees had been neglected due to Davorin's orders. It was dismal, and Lenore should have been able to prevent it.

She had failed.

"Things are not getting any better, Blodwen," Lenore said. Her friend slipped an arm through Lenore's and the two walked slowly back to the ostentatious tent that Davorin had set aside for her. Villagers bowed and curtsied dutifully, their eyes hollow and hopeless.

"Do you think that…that the angel that came yesterday was the end of it? That perhaps your Ravenna was only ever planning to send the one?" Blodwen asked cautiously keeping her voice low in case anyone would overhear and report.

Lenore held her breath and looked at the blue, cloudless sky. She let her shoulders slump ever so slightly, knowing that she still needed to keep up appearances. Davorin was not above having the villagers report on her. "I am hoping that he was simply a scout who got carried away. I am hoping that Ravenna will come. That sylph was proof that she has not forgotten us at least. She made it back to her people, and told them about us. I know no more than that, but I can hope. No, it is our own forces which are making things worse."

Blodwen nodded in understanding. The two had discussed of the reluctance of the resistance to actually take action. No matter how desperate they seemed to become, the people were happier to keep their heads down and to suffer. Bloodshed was not a great improvement on such matters, but at least they could take a stand and do something. Disrupt supply chains. Continue working the land in a way that made sense. Not follow these ridiculous, mad commands blindly. The reality was, though, that Lenore was likely on her own. That the resistance would do nothing and that Ravenna, after the death of her sylph, would never come.

Lenore sighed. Perhaps, after her child was born, she could

see about finding an assassin to kill Davorin for her. Or perhaps his madness would tear the Red Desert and the Salusian Empire apart before even that could happen. No, she would have to resign herself to this new existence. Perhaps that was all she could accomplish, after all.

The two had almost reached Lenore's tent when a creature stopped them. Its figure was female, having the body of the former captain of Davorin's army, Nadezhda. But the skin was blistered pink, with scales of bread around its eyes and interspersed over its body. It claimed to be the spirit of a dragon, the embodiment of magic, returned from the grave to possess Nadezhda's body and serve. Davorin called it after his dead brother, Dagan, and he said the name with a sneer each time he uttered it. Rumour was that Davorin had killed Dagan, but nothing could be proven. Lenore had heard from Seraphina, Davorin's sister, that the rumour was true. The fact changed nothing. Not Davorin, not this monster that stood before her. As far as Lenore was concerned, this creature was evil incarnate. It was powerful and bloodthirsty and had no conscience. It only followed Davorin's orders and took pleasure in the mayhem that its presence caused.

"And how is the pregnancy going?" it asked, flashing razor-sharp teeth. Lenore drew up short. Blodwen stepped halfway in front of her, as if the girl could possibly protect her. Lenore put her hand on Blodwen's arm, pushing her loyal servant aside. She straightened her shoulders, and put on all of the airs that the Queen of the Red Desert could manage.

"As you are not a human female," she said, looking down her nose at the creature, "I do not see what interest it would be to you. You know as well as I that it has two or three more moons to go. Until then, you shall just have to be patient and wait, as Davorin does."

"I can be patient," the creature said. It reached out a hand and hovered it above Lenore's belly, never quite touching, never quite getting close enough to cause distress or to complain to Davorin. "I am very fond of children."

"You are the cause of Davorin's madness," Lenore said, lifting her chin. "By the time my child comes, you will be long gone, or I will want to know why."

"And what makes you say that, pretty lady?" The creature sniffed. It leered at Blodwen, then watched as two soldiers walked by, its eyes tracking their movements like a predator hunting prey.

"Because his madness will kill him, and then you will be gone," Lenore said. This was not a theory, was not a wish. She knew it as surely as she knew that her heart beat. Davorin's madness would be his downfall. And she would happily stand by and watch while it happened. She could only pray to The One Who Watches that it was not her downfall, too.

"The illustrious Davorin has madness and power both within him. He must go through one to achieve the other. I have nothing to do with it. Nothing at all." The creature cackled, head tilted back and fangs flashing. Without a further word, it raced off, leaving Lenore and Blodwen standing at the entrance to the tent, a chill on the back of both of their necks.

CHAPTER FOUR

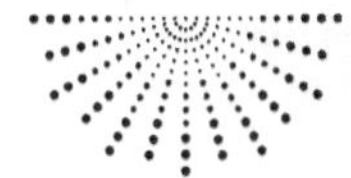

The next morning at the plateau, Ravenna was faced with two thousand sylphs, arrayed in formation, seemingly ready to face down an army of monsters. For her. Yet Ravenna knew that most of them had residual headaches or hadn't slept off their celebrations from the night before. Many of them were perfectly capable to fly, but fighting would be more difficult. Or perhaps that was just her fears whispering into the back of her mind. She didn't know how many of her people would hold up well in an actual battle. The most that they had done was participate in fierce skirmishes between each company. Itonus' death two days before had made this impending war a reality for many of them. Some of them were going to die. They would know the names of those who did not return.

Ravenna would have prepared them for their deaths.

Yet now they were all gathered, standing on the plateau above the Aerial City, wearing their will as blatantly as their armour, carrying weapons and supplies and still talking amiably and almost cheerfully with each other. Proud and prepared. Or so they believed.

Most of the weapons and armour had come from the former slave camp where Ravenna had first been taken when she was captured by humans all those seasons ago. Some of the sylphs didn't much care for having weapons and armour made by humans—seeing as they had been told all humans were their enemies—but they would rather have steel in their hands than sticks. Ravenna's throat tightened slightly at the memory of steel slicing into the narrow space on her back between her wings.

Wings, what was she doing?

Ravenna stood at the edge of the plateau, Desarra at her side. Crispinus and Brianna, her generals, were doing last checks on the various sylphs and the supplies. Brianna appeared first, her massive wings folded neatly against her back, a long sword at her waist and a bow clutched in her fist.

"Everyone is set," she said. "The last of my checks are done. The healers will be escorted by the Wing Dancers. And then… we fight a war."

Ravenna snapped her wings once, a sign that she was not pleased with Brianna's words. "No," she said doing her best not to pace out her nerves, to show how difficult it was to keep her feathers smooth and still. "We set up an encampment. We gather all of our forces together on the mainland near enough to Davorin's army so that we will not have to fly far to reach him. Then, we set up healing tents and places for us to sleep. We set up our supplies we do our best to make sure that the camp is properly done. Food, scouts, everything. We need to be prepared and well-rested before we fly into battle."

"They won't like it," Brianna said. "They have been waiting for this war for moons. They all think they're ready. Then you're telling them that they need to set up camp first? I thought you wanted the element of surprise."

Ravenna wanted to draw one of the swords from the sheaths on her back, if nothing more than to emphasise her seriousness.

She settled instead for spreading her wings wider, the feathers bristling, her hands low and ready to strike at her side. The few sylphs that were close enough to see her stepped back. They were not used to the Warlord showing so much emotion, and certainly not rage. Ravenna lifted her right wing high into the air and sliced down, a signal for all the sylphs to come together and hear her speak. The companies, neatly arranged and just checked over by Crispinus and Brianna, took to the air, getting as close as possible without overlapping and being sure that everyone could hear.

"Don't alienate them. Not now, when they're scared," Desarra breathed quietly to her sister. Ravenna closed her eyes and took in a deep breath.

"They must understand. This is not some game we're flying into. We're going to die. Some of us, all of us, I don't know. But if we don't do this right, then none of us will come back at all."

Desarra ducked her head. "I will support you, whatever you do. Just be careful."

Ravenna nodded firmly and then stepped away from her sister and queen. The wing beats around her quieted as the sylphs hovered in place to hear her speak. "You want to fly directly to war, don't you?"

There was a resounding cheer.

Ravenna sneered. "And when one of you gets cut down? When an arrow hits your wings and you cannot fly? When you are forced to the ground there is nothing but blood on your hands and your weapons are gone and you face yet more humans ready to kill you? Where will we go to treat your injuries? How are we to collect your body? What if this battle lasts more than a day and you require sleep?"

The air seemed to grow thicker, the wing beats loud in their discomfort. Ravenna took a deep breath, expanding her chest until her own leathers would let her draw in no more air. She let it out, slowly.

"I understand how eager you are. I want nothing more than for this to be over. We have already lost Itonus. He was my *friend*. I want to tear them into pieces. I want to face Davorin and remove his head for ever threatening us and our way of life. But I will not do so at the expense of my people. I will not do so at *your* expense. You are my friends too. My family. If it takes one more day to do things properly? To be rested and ready to go without having to fly to the mainland and search for Davorin's army? Then I will do what it takes to be sure that you survive.

"If none of those arguments persuade you, then do not forget that I am your Warlord. If you disobey my orders then I will have your wings clipped. You will be barred from flying into battle. You will be relegated to keep watching the healers, or sending messages back to Shinalea. Even if it cripples my force, I will not let to one single soul fly unless they obey my orders. My orders are to take to the sky, to follow Crispinus to the appropriate encampment spot, and set up. We will not approach any humans, we will not seek them out until the time is right. Am I clear?"

There was a slight hesitation, and then another clear acknowledgement from her people. Ravenna nodded, though the tension in her neck would not be abated by a simple agreement. The sylphs went back into formation on the ground, and she felt a strange stirring in her belly. She pressed a hand to her stomach and felt it squirm. Pride, she realised. It was pride that her people were here fighting a battle that had been made theirs by no fault of their own. They were strong and capable and they followed her without question.

Ravenna placed a hand on her chest and spread her wings wide before pulling them tight, a traditional sylph sign of mutual respect. Crispin and Brianna, the only ones to actually see the gesture, copied it. Desarra lay a hand on her shoulder and squeezed gently.

Everything between Ravenna, Desarra, and Crispinus—a childhood of misery, cycles of wing-weariness, a family fractured by Ravenna's black wings, pale skin and icy eyes, even her falling for a human—was gone. None of that mattered, now. None of them cared about Desarra's anger at her lost child, or Crispin's fury at Ravenna for her silence on the matter. Ravenna's inability to fly, her Intellecti upbringing, none of that mattered. All that remained was one people.

"Alright, Stormbringers!" Ravenna shouted at the top of her lungs. The sound echoed over the whole plateau. Those waiting in the Aerial City built out of the cliffs below probably heard it and prepared to light their candles for the vigil. She stepped over to a wooden platform that two sylphs would carry through the air. It was the easiest way for her to get to where they needed to be, though it was far from elegant. Ravenna grabbed the ropes and handed them to the two that had been designated to carry her. It felt a little strange, but apparently sylphs had fought over the honour.

"Let's fly!" Ravenna said, the words a croak.

In a flurry of wings, the synchronised flapping causing the air to ripple and warp around them, the army of sylphs took to the sky. The sound of all of them flying at once, in formation and swift as hawks, was enough to make Ravenna want to cover her ears. She had flown on her platform with several companies, to witness aerial manoeuvres. She had witnessed in-flight skirmishes between the groups from the ground. But never had all two thousand sylphs flown in formation at once. The sound was...it was like thunder. They were truly the Storm.

Crispin took the lead, having been the only one to witness where Davorin's army was currently stationed. He would be the one to have the sylphs fly to their battle site. Ravenna wished that they were going instead to the Red Palace, to the oasis there, the place that she considered a home. Or even to the No Man's Land, the former slave markets that she had liberated.

They would be fighting instead on unfamiliar ground. It was the desert—there would not be much to obstruct them—but it would be unfamiliar all the same. With fear now ever present in her belly, Ravenna wanted familiar.

The wing beats of the sylphs evened out as they flew over the turbulent air currents that came with the water separating Shinalea from the mainland. The sound of thunder lessened until it was a quiet rumble. When they hit the hot air rising from the desert, the stillness forcing many of them to flap all the harder, the sound increased, until they reached the thermals that would carry them in an easy glide. They were flying high enough so that they wouldn't be spotted by humans except as a fast-moving cloud, but there was no doubt in Ravenna's mind that word would spread quickly. The Storm was coming.

Brianna broke off from formation and flew back to the two sylphs who were carrying Ravenna's platform. She had her golden wings spread high and beating low so that she could maintain pace with the Storm and still be able to talk with Ravenna.

"Crispin says it's not too far now to the place where Itonus died. He thinks that another hour's flight and we should settle," Brianna said.

"How are the healers coping?" Ravenna asked. The healers had not trained with the army of sylphs but with the Intellecti, and their flight would not be nearly as powerful or as enduring as the others'. Brianna gave a wing-shrug, an impressive manoeuvre in mid-air, and shook her head.

"Most of the supplies are being carried by the Wing Dancers. The healers are struggling a bit, but they're keeping up."

Ravenna nodded and tightened her grip on the rope suspending her from the platforms. "If they need to stop tell me. I don't want all of us to stop early, but I can spare a company to keep them safe while they rest."

Brianna gave a dry laugh. "You underestimate your powers

of motivation. They will not be stopping anytime soon, for fear of disappointing you. Even Desarra is keeping up with Crispin without even breaking a sweat. You don't know the sort of morale boost it has been to have our Chosen Queen at the head of the army. That you trust her enough for that. I know there was some question of her staying behind, but...thank you, Warlord."

She did not wait for a dismissal, only flew back into formation once the report was given. Ravenna settled in for the remainder of the flight, torn between apprehension and relief that it would soon be over. One of the sylphs carrying her called down, his charcoal-dark skin made lightless shadow against the desert sun.

"Are we going to make it out of here alright? This place seems to be forsaken entirely." Ravenna heard the male try to keep the wobble from his voice.

"The humans believe in ancient beings powerful enough to shake the stars. If anyone has forsaken this land, it is they. But they have forsaken it for humans. There are no trees for them to hide underneath. There are no caves for them to scramble into. In this land, a force with flight shall win. Remember that, and you will be well."

The male said nothing more, just tightened his grip on the rope and exchanged glances with his flying companion. This surged upwards, flying above the Storm. Below, a myriad of backs in shades of gold, mixed evenly with charcoal dark shadows, with wings that ranged from gilded to brown, moved beneath them. It was a sea, a show of force greater than had been seen in generations. To the humans, it would be a legend come to life. It would be the story from their childhood to come to tear the safe world they knew to pieces. It would strike fear in the hearts of their enemies and joy in the minds of their allies. And Ravenna realised, as she watched the people she had trained so ferociously, even perhaps with a touch of cruelty for fear that they would not take the lessons to heart…she realised she loved them. All of them.

So she would reassure them and talk with them until the sun vanished beyond the horizon and the dawn returned. She would face her fears to take on theirs. She wouldn't let them down.

THEY DID INDEED SETTLE into the proposed encampment spot within an hour. It was a slight dip in the ground surrounded by low hills and rocky scrubland. They were close enough to the foothills of the Iron Mountains to be able to see a tinge of green upon their slopes. And they were far enough from any humans that no one would stumble upon them in the dark. It was not perhaps strategically wise to give up higher ground in favour of this shallow dip, but with beings that could fly, there was little use in high ground. Ravenna was surprised at the efficiency with which her people set up the camp. The healers had tents erected before the sun started to set. The army would be content to sleep out in the open, the warm desert air already unexpectedly hot for the time of year, warming and soothing their feathers. Ravenna knew from experience they would only get hotter.

As she walked through the camp, inspecting her people's gear and pausing to chat with them, to reassure their fears, she was stopped by Crispin and Desarra who had obviously been making similar rounds.

"We have been instructed by about seven different sylphs to make you stop worrying," Crispin said. "Your concerns are beginning to show. Your people are worried."

"I was concerned earlier, perhaps," Ravenna murmured, looking at the clusters of sylphs around her. "We will be facing something the likes of which you have never before seen. Every trick that I have taught you, every battle move and strategy will fall to pieces as soon as the war actually starts. I was concerned that everything would be for nothing, that as soon as blood was spilled, all our training and preparation would be lost. But there is something powerful in watching the flight of the Stormbringers."

"As long as you remember that," Desarra said, wrapping Ravenna in a very human hug," then we will come out of this in one piece."

"I'm sorry for getting you all into this," Ravenna said softly. It was perhaps the first time that she had actually said the words out loud to her family. "This is all my doing. This impending death is my fault."

"No," Crispinus said. "This is the doing of humans. If you had not encountered them, we would have happily lost a part of our heritage forever. And you would have wasted away to nothing under the life you led before. Look at us now. *All* of us. Strong and capable and willing to take on the world so that we may live free. And you brought that about. Do not apologise for that. Never apologise for that."

Strong, yes. Fighting for freedom, yes. But all Crispin's words told Ravenna was that they did not fully understand the cost. She rubbed the four parallel scars across her left shoulder. That naïve innocence, one way or another, would vanish the next morning.

CHAPTER FIVE

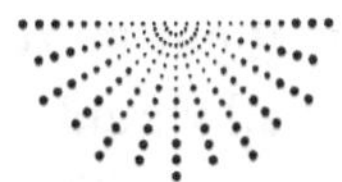

"*A*rchers!" Ravenna was directing the formation of her people, as though they hadn't prepared for this very moment for moons. "You will fly front formation. Our heavy battle-ax and staff wielders will follow behind and punch through whatever lines remain. After that, it will be a matter of fighting sword-to-sword and hand-to-hand. This is going to get messy. It will be nothing like what you know. But remember, we are fighting for our people. We are fighting for a way of life. We are fighting to remind the world that we are not something that should be treated as an object to be bought or sold. We are not just a legend. We are alive and free. You have my utmost faith and respect. May you fly high, and soar free."

Ravenna raised her arms and spread her wings wide. Without hesitation, the first wave of companies took to the sky. She stepped back onto the wooden platform and it too was lifted into the air by sylphs rearing to go to war. It had been quieter this morning, before everyone flew, not sure if the waiting had calmed them or made them more nervous. But when Ravenna looked back and saw Desarra and the other healers standing there, wings raised in a salute, she knew that whatever came of this, her people would never let her down.

Flying to battle was nothing like flying to set up the encampment. For one, the weapons were drawn and at the ready. Armour was worn and tightened. There was no conversation, no aerial games, even the formations seemed stiffer and perhaps more prepared.

Ravenna wanted to shout out more commands, more things to reassure her people that all would be well, but she knew that the time for such things was past. There was nothing left but to fly onwards. The sun was barely rising over the horizon and it would be in the eyes of their enemies. She hoped that they were caught unawares and that this could end before it really began. Something told her that was not be the case.

It took little time to reach the site of Davorin's army, and that sight frightened Ravenna more than she could say. This was nothing like the mercenary army that she had traveled with back when she had been bought by Davorin. This was something far more organised and massive. The tents were arrayed in neat lines and soldiers were already up, armoured, and prepared do whatever was required of them. What they did not expect, though, was that their enemy would bear down on them from the sky.

The sound arrived first. The Storm of beating wings and bodies moving air alerted the warriors on the ground before a single sylph dropped down to low enough to be seen. When they did drop, each of the archers drawing their bowstrings, arrows aimed, loosing in perfect synchronicity and with the numbers of the sylphs at their sides, the army seemed terrified. Or perhaps scattered. Shouts from a dozen tongues filled the air. Those soldiers still sleeping or off performing other duties quickly gathered into place and did their best to prepare for the attack that was bearing down on them.

The first volley of arrows dispensed, the larger sylphs

bearing the heaviest weapons bore down, ready to punch through the humans that stood in their way. Ravenna was with the third wave, those that would be fighting hand to hand with humans. She looked around for Davorin, but she couldn't see him. She did not know if that was because she was higher up in the air or if it was because he was not there. She wanted nothing more than to tear his head from his shoulders, but she would settle for his people. For those who had taken her friends, who had forced her to leave a place that she loved.

Finally, it seemed that the fear in her belly was replaced with that comforting icy fire that flowed through her veins. She grasped the anger willingly and prepared for the onslaught.

All too soon, it was her turn to fall to the ground. The sylphs holding her platform released it a good thirty feet into the air. Then, there was nothing to catch her as she plummeted towards the ground. This was familiar to Ravenna, that feeling of falling. No other sylph would dare to do it, unable to face the fear of falling with no wings to catch them. Ravenna had been falling her whole life.

She drew the two swords from her back as she angled her wings to lessen the impact of the fall. When she slammed into the ground, crouching to reduce the kinetic force, her swords were drawn, her lips curled in a sneer, and she was ready for whatever came her way. What came her way was a face she recognised.

"You," the mercenary woman said. This was the woman that Davorin had made the new head of his mercenary army after he had maimed the old, second only to Nadezhda and himself. Ravenna did not know this woman's name, but she recognised hatred in her eyes.

"Did you think that I had gone for good?" Ravenna asked, straightening and spreading her arms wide, blades at the ready. She shifted into the Dalketh stance that would serve her best, and waited for this mercenary to attack her. "You think that your master had frightened me off? Or that I was going to fetch an army to fight at his side? Well I have brought the army. And we are here to fight. But I do not think that you will like who we choose as our enemy."

The woman didn't bother with responding, just let out a guttural cry and lunged forward. Ravenna's blades moved swiftly, motions so ingrained in her after moons and moons of practice that it was like a familiar dance. One that she had missed. She did not have time to see whether her warriors were faring well or if some of the dying screams came from them. She simply fought.

The mercenary in front of her was a fairly skilled opponent, but she had been unprepared for a battle, and fighting against an army of legendary beings who were using a fighting technique that had not been seen by humans in countless generations, she was doomed to fail. As with Jazer, Ravenna did not hesitate to deliver the killing blow. The tip of her swords crossed and uncrossed at the woman's neck, leaving the body falling to the ground, the head not quite severed. There was no doubt the woman was dead.

Ravenna quashed all emotion and bile that rose up with the act. This was not the time for sentiment. This was the time for her to become everything that she had been working towards. Cold, cruel, deadly. She was going to be the nightmare these humans screamed about. So she turned and sought her next opponent.

SURPRISE WAS one of the few things that the sylphs had on their side that day. Once the humans got over their shock, and managed to rally their forces, the sylphs were in for a pitched battle that caused more damage than perhaps it should have done. Ravenna herself was injured mildly, a few scratches across her armour being the worst of it. She had a small, shallow cut on her right thigh that dripped annoyingly. A few of her feathers had been tweaked out of place when she used them to beat humans back, but on the whole she was more tired than injured. Her people, on the other hand, were struggling. Many of them had done well, cutting down their enemies without hesitation. Their injuries were more numerous, perhaps, but that was simply because they were not used to fighting an enemy that fought back with the intent to kill. Some of them, though, did not take to fighting as well they would have liked. They hesitated in the moment when they should have swung through. They jumped back into the arms of waiting soldiers. Their wings got in the way in the midst of a crowd of people trying to cut them down. Still, despite being outnumbered three to one, the sylphs were doing remarkably well.

"I knew that you would come," Davorin said.

Ravenna wheeled around, pulling her sword from where it had lodged in the shoulder of an opponent, leaving the man bleeding on the ground, whimpering in pain.

Davorin was before her, astride a massive horse in armour. He wore—Ravenna nearly vomited at the sight—a cloak of feathers. Unmistakeable feathers. He wore the wings of Itonus. All this time had passed, time she spent training her people to face down nightmares, to fight impossible battles. So many moons, and yet the very sight of Davorin sent her reeling. Her stomach clenched, her breath caught, her throat closed into hoarseness. But the cloak he wore sent rage thrumming through her body, loosening the horror wrapped around her bones. She wanted to kill him. For everything he had done to her, for everything he had done to Itonus, for everything he had done to Lenore and Miska. She was going to plunge her swords through his heart, sever his head. She was going to kill him.

Ravenna let out a shriek, like an eagle after prey, and surged forward. Her wings folded at her side so she could have speed, cutting through the air. The horse reared up, striking at her with its hoofs. Ravenna leapt out of the way, snapping open her right wing for balance. She sliced at the horse's belly, but the creature was too well-trained. It tried to nip at her with massive teeth, catching one of her primary feathers. Ravenna pulled her wing back, barely wincing at the pain of a feather being torn from its socket. She had done that before, too, and was used to such pain.

Hatred blinding her, Ravenna beat her wings against the ground so that she might get some lift and reached for Davorin. He wheeled the horse around so that she could only scratch her swords uselessly against the armour on the creature's back. It was leather with metal plates on it, some unwieldy thing that creature had obviously been trained to bear.

"I do not like it when my property runs from me," Davorin sneered. His voice was off. It sounded as though he had shifted fundamentally in his personality, that he was something other than what Ravenna remembered of the angry, cunning heir to the Salusian Empire.

The horse was Ravenna's immediate enemy. Davorin was smiling down at her as though he had some secret he wanted to share. He didn't even have a sword to wield. He just turned the horse and watched her try to take it down. What he did not count on was that Ravenna was not alone.

Another sylph, Ravenna didn't recognise who amongst the dirt and the blood, slammed into the horse's side, beating its wings about the horse's face. The creature let out a scream and toppled to the ground, unable to combat the weight of something so strong. Davorin, appearing to be lighter than a feather, floated to the ground. Was the cloak he wore giving him some sort of strange power?

Ravenna lunged forward, leaping over the horse's body as if it were not even there. Davorin extended a hand and she paused mid-air. Some invisible force wrapped itself around her, keeping her from moving up or down. She wasn't flying—that was impossible. But she was immobile. Frozen. Terror clutched her throat.

Davorin cackled like a giddy child of death, first stretching its demonic hands into the realm of destruction. Ravenna swiped her sword through the air, hoping to cut whatever invisible ties held her.

Davorin swung his hand and Ravenna flew backwards, slamming into the ground with her wings bent awkwardly beneath her. She rose to her feet as swiftly as she could manage, stretching her wings and eyeing Davorin warily.

"What?" Davorin asked, wiping off some of the dirt that had smudged on his skin from the flailing horse. "Do you not like my new weapon? Do you not like the magic that sings through my veins? Oh, Stormbringer, you should have *stayed* with me. I would have given you the world. I would have stretched your wings so that you could fly through the sky. You would have been my messenger and I would be a *god*. And now you have thrown all of that away. But at least you brought me toys to play with."

Davorin flexed his fingers and a sword made of some bizarre, crackling red energy appeared in his hand. He swung it through the air at the sylph that was moving towards him, the same one that had barrelled over the horse. With a wide smile and madness in his eyes, Davorin swung his blade through the outstretched wing of the sylph. Ravenna's screaming matched that of her companion. Davorin laughed louder and swung his blade through the other side, slicing that wing neatly off, too. The sylph fell to the ground, catatonic with pain. Ravenna surged forward and ended her warrior's misery with her own blade, screams echoing in her ears.

What was this horrid thing that he controlled? It could not surely be magic. Magic was impossible. It was something that hadn't been seen in this land since the Fire Wars. Was this how he had killed Itonus? Ravenna remembered that Crispinus had told her that Itonus's death seemed impossible, twisted. Yet here he was, doing things that were indeed impossible, and killing her people in the process. Ravenna did not know how to combat this. She could not kill him and she could not fight him. And if she were lost, where would her people be?

"Coward," she snarled. "To fight me with this nebulous thing. You cannot even use a real weapon to defend yourself anymore! Are you afraid to fight me? Are you afraid that this slave that you bought like some animal could possibly stand against you?"

Davorin giggled. Not a chuckle, not a laugh, a giggle. He held his free hand to his mouth and giggled again. The red blade in his hand crackled ominously.

"I have nothing to fear from you," he said. "I have conquered the Red Queen. I have taken the Red Desert for my own. I have unlocked secrets of this land that have been dormant since before the dragons slept. I am making things *better*. You are the one who has been forgotten and left behind. If you want to fight me with your little sticks, feel free. I have better things to do. I will conquer everything. You will see my genius. And you will realise your mistake. I want you to live as you watch your people get slaughtered. I want you to be at my side when it becomes time for me to take my rightful place among the stars. So no, my dear Ravenna, I'm not going to fight you. I'm not going to let you die. I'm going to see to it that you live."

There was a blinding red flash, and then Davorin was gone. Ravenna blinked the afterimage from her eyes. In the few moments that it had taken her to recover, another soldier in Davorin's army converged upon her. She did not have time to process what had just happened, to understand what Davorin was demanding from her. She didn't have time to understand the magic, or how she could have failed so magnificently in her only goal. She did not have the luxury to understand anything.

She just fought.

Time wore on. She gained new injuries, watching her people

do the same. Sometimes they rallied and it seemed as though they would win, and then a new wave of soldiers would appear, seemingly untouched by battle. Davorin was flitting in and out of the edges of her focus, slicing down one of her people there, accidentally hitting his own person somewhere else. He seemed to revel in the atrocities of the battlefield. But she could never get close enough to do anything about it. And so, as he had said, she watched as he slaughtered her people.

And yet, they made progress. Some of the human warriors seem to put up less resistance than others; was this the remnants of Lenore's warriors, pressed into Davorin's service?.

Ravenna was dancing her way closer to Davorin, trying to catch him unawares. Maybe she could kill him from behind. Maybe she could still remove his head from his shoulders. He did not seem to have a strong focus, but he sought and killed ferociously, avoiding her at every step of the way. And then, something shifted.

At the edge of the battle, where the desert met the hills that came off the mountains, something was stirring. Warriors' screams and cries that had so far punctuated the battle grew pitched and sharp, the tang of fear filling the air. Ravenna fought her way closer to the edge, her breaths coming in quick pants. She had trained her people well, but even they were growing tired. And she was also. But whatever it was that was edging closer, a hulking shadow that seemed to make no sense in this landscape, it was fighting on their side. It was a monster, its shoulders half-a-hand again higher than any horse. On its back, two figures sat, wrapped in unfamiliar clothing. One of them was so massive that he seemed to blot out the light, his left hand missing. The other...

"It can't be," Ravenna said. She fought harder to move closer, to be sure that her vision was correct. Her heart leapt into her throat. The soldiers moved around the creature, weapons high. She couldn't get close enough to stop what was about to happen.

The figure slipped off the back of his mount, that monstrous creature. He pulled out some sort of large knife and lifted his hand in the air as if preparing to draw figures in the sky. No less than four soldiers converged on him, two of those sneaking around behind him so that he could not see.

Ravenna sliced the sword in her left hand through the exposed leg of her current opponent, cutting her to the ground. She turned and ran for this new figure, desperation pounding in her ears. The fight fell away except for this who blocked her path. She had to reach him. She had to get there before he, too, fell. She could not run fast enough.

Ravenna screamed. "*MISKA!*"

CHAPTER SIX

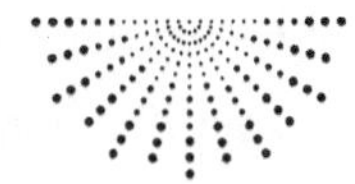

Miska had not expected to arrive back in the Red Desert with a fervent battle already wreaking havoc on his home. He had led Beringer, Allora, and Sisu down the hills and past a far too familiar village, trying not to think of the implications of his memory. Neither Sisu nor Allora had tried to engage him in conversation, either talking with each other or remaining silent. Miska did not bother to see which. Then, just as they passed the village, they saw it.

Stretched out before them on the plain of sand and scrub grass, rock and grit, was a field of tents surrounded by two armies, doing their very best to tear each other to pieces. Miska wanted to surge forwards, to help his people, when he stiffened atop Beringer's back, his hands frozen in his familiar's fur. Even Beringer paused when they saw that one of the armies was comprised of beings with golden or night-dark colouring, bearing great wings.

Ravenna's people. They *came*. Miska signalled to Beringer and they stopped a short distance away from ongoing battle, long enough for Miska to instruct Allora to get off of the bear. He shot her a significant look. Allora scowled, but nodded. She shot a desperate look to Sisu before acquiescing and taking the pack that Miska handed her.

"I will stay out of sight," she said, her expression flat. Miska raised a brow and said nothing. "I promise," Allora said, this time looking contrite. Miska smiled, despite the urgent need to go to battle roaring in the back of his mind. He leaned over and ruffled Allora's hair so that some of the strands stood on end.

"I love you, heart-daughter," Miska said. Allora returned his smile, even as she tried to tame her hair. Miska coughed pointedly and she looked up at him, then over to Sisu. It was time for them to go. She huffed and stalked off to go hide in the village cowering behind the hills, not sparing them a backwards glance. She would be safe, Miska told himself. She had to be. He wondered for half a moment if his old enemy Qilas was there in that village from his past, or on the battlefield. He had not thought about boy who stole his hearing for cycles. Now was not the time for that. Now was the time to help his people.

Miska turned back towards the battle. Sisu clambered onto Beringer's back; the bear was large enough to carry them both, but not for far. Sisu was too large for long distance riding with Miska. But he could go into battle and take advantage of that small help that being on Beringer's shoulders provided. Judging by what lay ahead, Miska would happily take any advantage he or Sisu could possibly manage.

Davorin's army was vast and the sylphs were outnumbered. They were using that same fighting style that Miska had seen Ravenna use, but they did not all seem as confident or as capable. Who could know how long the battle had been raging on, but the sylphs seemed worn. Winged bodies were visible, lying still even as their brethren fought on. Those that remained, in the air or on the ground, all bore wounds of some sort. Still, they fought on. Davorin's army had also taken a beating; there were bodies of armoured humans strewn about, but there were more to face.

Yet, the humans fought legends. Creatures from a time long past, long forgotten that flew at them like deadly raptors. That was enough, perhaps for an advantage. Where though, among all of these ferocious creatures, was Ravenna? Surely she would not have sent her people alone. Surely she would have come to save Lenore, and even himself.

Miska reached the battlefield. Soldiers turned and looked at him, not even wondering if he was fighting on their side. Their swords gleamed with blood and their faces were twisted into vicious snarls; those still surviving were the ones to fear. Without turning to ask Sisu's advice, Miska slipped from Beringer's back and prepared to do battle with the hunting knife and his magic. It was all he had. He prayed it would be enough.

Threads wove around his vision, their colours bright, pulsating. They seemed stronger, more intense, here amongst the fields of sand and blood. He reached up and grabbed hold of two strands, aiming for two of the soldiers that were moving in his direction. He waved his hand sharply. Threads exploded outwards, shredding through an advancing soldier's armour. For once, Miska was more than glad he could not hear. He did not want the screams to linger in his mind.

Alarm coiled up the back of his neck, a thought from Beringer enough to have Miska fearing for his massive familiar and turning to face this threat against his companion. Instead, Miska saw two soldiers bearing down on him from behind, swords raised and deadly. They were too close for him to gather magic and retaliate. Miska was going to die before he could even join this battle.

Then, something shifted.

Miska could not hear the sound, but he felt the pressure of the air change as he was thrown backwards. By a sylph. He beat his wings once before facing down those two soldiers with a sword already worn in battle. The sylph's wings stretched wide, feathers a mottled golden brown. The sylph's dark skin was shiny with gore, though the blood was hard to see.

Miska's heart beat faster. It was not Ravenna, but one of her people had come to his—a human's—rescue. Why? He did not know. What he knew was that the sylph was defending him, dispatching the enemy soldiers with a quick flick of his sword. The sylph turned back to Miska and held out his hand. In the back of Miska's mind, Beringer grumbled, unsure if this being was friend or foe. Silently, Miska reassured his familiar, and then he took the hand offered him.

The sylph said something a language that he could not understand, his lips moving with that same grace that Ravenna often displayed, though these words were more unfamiliar. It was the sylph language that had diverged from his own generations ago. Miska shook his head, then put a hand on his chest. "Miska," he said

The sylph nodded in understanding and repeated the gesture, his wings folding inwards, his hand flat on his chest. "Crispinus," the sylph said.

Miska repeated the word a couple of times to be sure that he had read the sylph's mouth correctly. He nodded. Then, when Beringer let out another roar in the back of his mind, they turned to the battle at hand. Miska and Sisu had arrived at the edge of the battle, but with this sylph at his side, Sisu at the other, and a massive bear behind, they pressed further inwards, doing their best to make headway against an enemy that wanted them more than gone, that wanted them subdued and subservient.

Miska soon discovered that all of the fighting lessons and hunting techniques and hand-to-hand combat that Sisu had taught him during his time in Hullgard was meant for a rather different sort of fighting. Those techniques were meant for pitched skirmishes where the enemy was close at hand, their weapons matched against yours. Armed with hunting knife and no armour except the few furs he had retained, against swords and battle axes and staffs, their bearers wearing leather armour, and occasionally armour of leather with metal plates attached to it, Miska was outmatched. His hunting knife was hardly long enough to get around the guard of a sword. He was constantly having to dance back to avoid being cut down. He was physically weaker than his enemy. But the soldiers had not counted him having magic.

The threads in Miska's vision seemed brighter, more vibrant the more time he spent on this battlefield. Flickers of energy seemed to pass into the threads from the dying or the dead around him. He grabbed a thread and in preparing to use it, he received a shock, something that never happened before. A memory of Cavaris talking about gathering energy from life for magic whispered in the back of his mind, but he shut out all thoughts of the traitorous dragon. Miska ignored the unusual happenings—there was no time to investigate or understand now—and shaped the magic into the form of a wolf. The construct came to life and lunged for an opponent that was advancing on his position. The soldier's blade cut through the construct's shoulder, but the wolf snagged its teeth on the woman's arm and tore it visibly from her socket. She screamed and fell to the ground.

Sisu stepped forward and finished her off, a mercy killing. He turned back to Miska with wariness.

"I've never seen you do that before," he said. Miska shrugged and shook his head.

"I have never before been in battle. I did not even know it was possible." Should he be concerned at the strange emptiness he felt about having just killed somebody?

"Well, it better be more than just a one-time thing. Because it's about to get a whole lot messier."

Sisu was right. The fighting moved to meet them, the warriors taking Miska and his companions more seriously after witnessing the death of one of their own. They managed to separate Miska from Sisu and from Beringer. He could feel his familiar in the back of his head, fighting so that his claws tore flesh like loam, his teeth dripping gore. But there was no way Miska could see his bear through the fighting, even massive as Beringer was. Sisu also had diverged, stopping to take on an opponent with his massive axe, deflecting blows with the metal plate on his stump of a left hand, or sometimes deflecting it with his body, taking the gashes as they would come. Sisu had obviously fought this sort of war before.

Thankfully, the mysterious sylph Crispinus had managed to stay by Miska's side, using his wings and his weapon and that selfsame graceful dance that Ravenna had displayed all those moons ago. But this was not the time for musing about the art of war. Miska only had time for the battle.

It became easier for Miska to use magic to kill as he moved along. He would wrap a thread around the soldier's throat and tighten until the head was nearly severed. He would create constructs of wolves or desert lions that would last for moments, long enough to open a wound on the thigh that would have the person bleeding out, or tearing into the throat. Some managed to get close enough to wound him, but if he could get inside their guard then he could stop them with his knife or beat them back with his fists as Sisu had taught him. He would worry about the blood on his hands later.

It seemed days since he had first arrived, but eventually he noticed that progress was being made. His appearance had changed the pitch of battle in the sylphs' favour. Soldiers were distracted by his magic, by the ferocious and massive bear, by the giant that he brought with him. They were afraid of the sylphs. It was enough to push the tide back. Miska almost felt it was enough to go and see if he could seek out Ravenna, to fight at her side, and be sure that she was safe.

And then he felt a tap on his mind.

I remember you, a voice said, dark and giddy and mad. Miska whirled, looking for the source. He should not have been surprised; he had trained in magic for this very purpose. He had begged Cavaris to come with him for the same reason. But the touch of another person's magic—Davorin's magic—against his mind was like being able to feel sorrow after moons of emptiness. Miska's stomach leapt up into his throat and he forced down bile. Then, he saw Davorin.

The man was standing in the midst of carnage, his own wounded soldiers at his feet, the body of a beautiful sylph female at his left side. He wore no armour, but had instead a cloak that was drenched with blood. Was it made of feathers? Miska hoped beyond hope that they were not black feathers, the feathers of Ravenna.

The strangest part was that Davorin had no weapon, either. He was far from defenceless; the crimson magic that he had awoken wrapped around him in a multitude of threads, a pulsating shield. Miska hurriedly did the same with his own magic, weaving a pulsing barrier to protect against Davorin's deadly magic.

You're that servant that was so fond of my dear Ravenna. I remember you were there the night I threatened her. I thought you couldn't hear. Now look at you. Fate has an interesting sense of humour, to give you magic to battle mine. We shall see who is the stronger.

Had Miska not experienced the strange sounds of mind-to-mind speech with Cavaris, then he would have been on the ground screaming, oblivious to whatever soldiers were trying to get in his way. As it was, Davorin's voice sounded nothing like he had expected. Back when Miska served under Lenore, before all of this began, he had thought Davorin a cruel, dark man with a voice to match. This was something else entirely. This was like a shadow laughing in the face of the sun, mad and glorious.

"I'm going to kill you," Miska said, in his thoughts and out loud. "I'm going to dismantle everything you have built."

Davorin tossed back his head and laughed. He grinned at Miska, showing his teeth like a desert jackal. He bowed spreading the cloak wide. *You are more than welcome to try.*

Miska did not hesitate as he thought he would have when he finally faced Davorin. He reached for his magic and wrapped it around the man, trying to bind the blood magic into place and prevent its use. Davorin laughed all the harder and waved a hand, attempting to shake it off. Sweat beaded on Miska's brow and he could feel his back splitting open in pain. The price of his magic when he fuelled it with his life force instead of from the world around him usually sent him reeling. It was not as bad as he would have thought, the energy from the fallen around him helping some. It was not nearly enough. He knew that the dark ridges forming a labyrinth of shadow on his back would fade if he had time to rest, would allow him his full range of motion again, but he wasn't sure if he would be able to do that before defeating Davorin. The binding was taking too much energy. Miska released it.

Davorin chuckled.

How can a man who cannot hear, manipulate the song? Does the singing pulse in your blood? Does it make your bones tremble? Or is it some mystery that you do not even understand? One must appreciate irony.

Miska did not answer the goading. He did not know how to answer. It did not make sense to him either, but there it was. Nor did he wish to banter with a mad man. Madness, insanity, the cracking of his mind must have been the price of Davorin's magic.

Miska twisted threads of magic—some of the few remaining that he had access to—into the shape of a massive wolf that hunted the forests surrounding Hullgard, and that selfsame desert lion that Ravenna had defended him against so many moons ago. They lunged for Davorin.

Why did the man not jump out of the way when he saw the constructs coming? The wolf snapped its jaws onto his leg, biting through some of the blood magic wrapped around him. The damage to the man was minimal, but the magical shield started unravelling. The desert lion stalked around Davorin to attack him from the side.

The world shifted just as something jumped between Davorin and the constructs. It defended him, a desperate pet defending its master. The desert lion's fangs sank deep into the new creature, this monster that Davorin summoned. Miska instantly recognised it is as the creature that had slaughtered his friends during the fight to control the Red Desert. This was the demon Davorin had created from Nadezhda, the captain of his army. It had pinkish red skin, veins as black as Ravenna's wings pulsing through, red scales around its eyes.

The desert lion bit harder.

The creature opened its mouth in a desperate scream, all its viciousness impotent against Miska's magical constructs. It would die defending its master, its summoner, its terrible purpose wasted on something so pointless.

Then, reality fractured.

Miska fell to the ground, piercing pain like he had never felt splitting through his head. The creature had gotten in the way, so Davorin might live. Was it intentional or just the requirement of a summoned being? Had he summoned the creature there to sacrifice itself? Was that the reason he carried no weapons?

The world around Miska fell away into a narrow field, that too fading into mist. He no longer saw the fighting, no longer felt Beringer in the back of his mind. He no longer sensed the wing beats of the sylph behind him, nor did he feel anything but earth shattering pain. He could see only directly before him.

And he saw Davorin fall to the ground in the same way as himself, blood dripping from his eyes and from his ears.

The constructs tore Davorin's demonic creature to shreds even as they faded, the last of Miska's energy reserves gone.

Black shadows spotted at the edge of his vision, creeping closer. The last thing he saw before he fell into unconsciousness was a familiar sylph, stepping over him to where the creature writhed on the ground. Her boots were worn and grimy, her pale-as-moon skin smeared with dirt and with blood. Her wings, black, hung weakly at her side as though she were more than exhausted. She took one of the swords in her hand and sank it into the dying demon. A shriek filled Miska's mind and he let out a desperate gasp as reality fractured further.

"Ravenna," he breathed. She turned and sank next to him. The last sensation he had was her hand on his cheek. Then, shadows and silence.

CHAPTER SEVEN

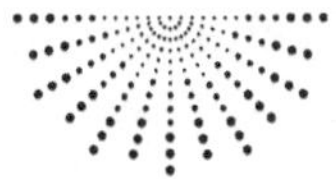

The battle raged far enough from Lenore's tent that she had not felt herself in any danger. She and Blodwen watched as the sylphs descended upon Davorin's army and wrought chaos. They had not said one word. They just watched as a horde of winged beings came to fight a battle that should never have been theirs. And when Vareis and that other resistance leader appeared out of the hills like some herald to victory, Lenore had wanted nothing but to show them their folly.

"Do you see what you have done? You have decided to let your freedom lie in the hands of others. They came. Oh, yes, they came. But only because Ravenna knew that Davorin would come for her eventually and wanted to get there first. They did not come for *you*. They did not come for *me*. Are you content with that?"

"If she can achieve victory, then yes," Vareis said flatly. Lenore hissed and withdrew from the entrance to the tent where she had been watching. Victory was all but certain at this point. She had seen the flashes that told some other magic user

—one of the sylphs perhaps?—had fought against Davorin. The sylphs were outnumbered, but they were deadly and they had the advantage that the humans could not counter: they could fly.

So Lenore would wait and ignore the carnage and the resistance fighters that she was meant to be leading, or at least encouraging as they watched someone else fight their battles. Was that what she had been doing this whole time? Had she been waiting for Ravenna to fight her battle against Davorin? Lenore had thought that she was protecting her people by wedding the heir to the Salusian Empire, preventing their obvious destruction and murder by giving herself in their place. Now she bore a madman's child inside her and she was as yet unsure whether or not her sacrifice had been at all worth it.

"Lenore," Blodwen said, her voice shaking.

"Yes?"

"Something's happened," she said. Her hands fluttered at her side, tugging at the Salusian style dress that she still wore despite her loyalties to the desert. "The soldiers…they are laying down arms, or running. The fighting seems to have stopped but nothing is yet resolved. Perhaps we should send someone to go see what was happening?"

Lenore rested her hands on her stomach. "I will go," she said firmly. Immediately, the two resistance leaders argued for her to remain, to stay far away from the aftermath of her war.

"You are still their queen," Vareis snapped. "You are too valuable. Send your servant. Send one of us. But—"

"No." Lenore straightened her shoulders and stared down her former training captain. After a few seconds, Vareis blinked and looked away, the lines around her mouth deepening. "I have had enough of standing by and letting others take the risks for me because I was too powerful or too important to lose. These are my people at stake. My lands. Everything I have worked for stands to be destroyed if I do not do this. So I will go and if you make one comment about the fact that I am pregnant or a queen or even a female, unable to defend myself, then I will have you slaughtered by those sylphs who came to rescue us."

Without another word, Lenore strode from the tent and into the mayhem that awaited her. Her dress was another unsuitable ensemble picked out for her by Davorin. He had seemed to enjoy making her wear the most absurd things and since she had willingly taken the role as his wife to save her people, she did not see the need to battle over clothing. It was a dress, not some food shipment or trade deal. This one was long and cumbersome, dragging on the sand and scrub behind her and catching rocks in its wake. The fabric was almost sheer and gathered in several different areas so that modesty might be maintained. She looked like some great statute from an age long past. It was entirely unsuitable for going out to battle.

She did not care.

The ground beneath her sandalled feet turned to sludge before she actually met any remaining warriors. Those that did remain, of human or sylph persuasion, stood aside and lowered their weapons as she walked past. Lenore kept her chin high and walked on, looking for someone she recognised—Ravenna perhaps—to declare that things were officially over.

She walked around bodies and over splashes of blood. She did not differentiate between the sylphs and the human dead, but she did note that a good portion of both sides still seemed to be alive, if wounded. Though, many of the human soldiers were fleeing into the desert or the hills. Davorin's army was scattering.

"You are alive," a voice said. Lenore turned and found Ravenna standing there with two sylphs at her side and a large giant of a man carrying an unconscious, maybe dead figure. It was Miska. Lenore had known that Ravenna would return, that she would be here amongst her people, but seeing her in person still had the air escaping Lenore's lungs.

"Ravenna," Lenore breathed. "You came back."

"I came back," the sylph agreed, her voice hard and cold. "The cost was great."

"I can never thank you enough. Is it...is it over?"

"It is only the beginning," Ravenna said. She gestured behind her where a score or more of the sylphs were advancing on their position. One of them bore another prone figure in her arms, blood dripping from his eyes from his nose. Lenore wanted to recoil, but she forced herself to stand her ground. Davorin. And from the breath moving his lungs in his chest, he was alive.

"I think we have much to catch up on. Perhaps we should see to the wounded and then hold a council?"

Ravenna turned to one of the sylphs at her side and said something in a slightly unfamiliar tongue. The sylph responded in the same tongue, sounding more upset or annoyed than anything. Ravenna spoke again, this time her voice sharper, harsher. The sylph bowed his head, exchanged words with the female carrying Davorin, and then they turned and strode away. A few moments later, a few words exchanged with many of the sylphs, and they took to the skies.

Lenore's mouth fell open. She had never seen anything so beautiful, so absolutely impossible and magnificent. Even carrying weapons and covered in gore, it was hard to look away. She knew they were not the messengers of the divine that so many stories claimed, but they were still a being declared impossible for so long. They had been forgotten and yet were here, darkening the skies and making her heart beat faster.

"We have an encampment not far from here. We will take our wounded there. See to your wounded and we can talk tomorrow. Determine the consequences of these events." Ravenna's voice cut through Lenore's reverie.

"What of him?" Lenore asked, nodding her head at Miska. "Will you take him also?"

Ravenna shook her head, her icy eyes showing more weariness than before. "My people would not tolerate such a thing. I would prefer to keep him close, but…"

"Has he been with you this whole time? Since I sent him away?" She wanted to know because he looked so different, his hair long with tiny braids and even a few feathers and beads throughout. He wore clothing that was unlike anything she had ever seen; furs and thicker fabrics that would be horrid in the desert heat. And then there was the giant of a man at his side, his hair as dark as Ravenna's, his expression just as grim.

"Now is not the time," Ravenna said. She looked back over her shoulder and the shadow of a smile flashed over her features. "No, he has not been with me, but I am more than glad that he is not dead."

"I am more than glad that *both* of you are well. Go, see to your people. We will talk in the morning."

Ravenna nodded. Without another word, the two women turned and went to direct their people accordingly.

Lenore worked to help the healers tend to the wounded into the wee hours of the morning, unable to do much more than that. Her people, the remains of the army, did not need a queen directing their movements. They needed someone to tend their wounds. She stopped only when Blodwen tapped her on her shoulder and demanded that Lenore sleep.

"Your Ravenna has already gone back to her own people. The healers are doing everything they can. It is late. You are pregnant. You need sleep," Blodwen said, fisting her hands on her hips. She grabbed Lenore's hand and practically dragged her away from the remains of the battlefield, ignoring the arguments that lingered on her tongue. Only when Lenore felt the tremors in her hands did she give in.

She would have preferred to sleep somewhere else, not near

a field of blood, not when everything was so uncertain, but she allowed her friend to take her back to her tent where she washed the grime from her hands and, trembling, fell asleep with her palms splayed flat on her belly. She dreamt little, the only remaining impression a thought of wondering why Davorin was still alive. And the fear of Ravenna's words: it was only the beginning.

Morning came all too swiftly, with Lenore being woken by Blodwen, and the inpatient Vareis standing in the entrance to the tent. Lenore hobbled to the washbasin and splashed her face and neck with a damp cloth. In this remote part of the land, water was scarce enough that a full bath was a rarity. She missed the oasis of the Red Palace. She ruled a desert kingdom, and had still grown far too accustomed to oasis plants. Maybe that was why her kingdom had so easily succumbed to Davorin.

"Are you just going to let the sylphs control this whole situation?" Vareis demanded as Blodwen helped Lenore into a dress.

"You don't get a say in any of this," Blodwen snapped, glaring at Vareis. "You did nothing to help. The sylphs were the ones who defeated Davorin's army. So if they want to be in charge, then that is their right."

"His army is not defeated," Lenore said. She braided her hair into a single strand and tossed it over her shoulder. A glare followed, fixing both friend and former training master into its depths. "They are scattered. Yes, many of them lie dead, many of them are wounded, but the rest are scattered. There is no formal surrender, no declaration of victory. That will come later. There still remains the fact that Davorin lives."

"As his wife, though, you have every right to declare the loss. To secede from the Salusian Empire under the presumption that the sylphs demanded it." A flicker of grim pleasure crossed Vareis' features. Had Lenore not been pregnant and moving slowly after her late night, she would have happily slapped the woman. As it was, she simply turned her back on her and strode towards the entrance to the tent, ready to go meet with Ravenna and the others.

"I am his wife. And I am still the Queen of the Red Desert. You would do well to remember that, Vareis. You would do well to remember that you and your supposed resistance did nothing. I am going to meet with Ravenna. You will wait here until I return."

"Lenore—"Vareis started, clenching her fists at her side. Lenore rounded on the other woman, who was still thin from her time running from Davorin and his people, but grown stronger as she had taken up a leading position in the resistance. Lenore held Vareis' gaze, proving her authority to the other woman. As if there could be a question.

"You. Will. Obey."

She turned again and was gone.

"My people do not yet speak your language, though they are learning," Ravenna said, pacing around the long table that had been set up inside one of the remaining tents from Davorin's army. "I will translate accordingly."

The sylphs—the two that had accompanied Ravenna the day before as well as a third with a diadem of golden wings on her brow—had flown in from their encampment. Everyone wanted this meeting to be well away from both armies so that no tempers might rise. Also there was the large man that had carried Miska's form to the healers the day before. Miska was still with them. Accompanying this other man was a young girl, her hair nearly white, resting in the paws of the giant bear that had apparently participated in the battle. Lenore had too many questions, all of them spinning inside her head trying to vie for their importance. As a result, she said nothing.

"I should like to know how you came to be here," Lenore

finally managed, taking a seat and tearing up the piece of bread provided for her. "We had no hope that anyone would come."

Ravenna let out a slow breath through her nose, her eyes sharp. "I went to warn my people. We trained. We came. Did you really think that I would leave you?"

Lenore lowered her gaze. Shame filled her throat at the realisation that she had imagined just that. That same shame grew stronger at the thought that she had placed all her hopes in Ravenna and not herself. "I believed you would. Now that you have returned, I am not certain I know the next step forwards."

"I wish to know all that has happened since my absence. You are pregnant. Miska…he was wielding magic. And accompanied by these…people."

The black haired man who had accompanied Miska said something. Lenore thought she recognised some of the words, but it was not her tongue. Sylphs broke out chattering, obviously astonished, in that same language. Ravenna raised a hand, her wings spreading slightly at the tension in the air. She said something that cut across all the other words. Silence descended.

The man spoke, this time slower.

Ravenna translated as he did. "He says his name is Sisu. He comes from a place called Hullgard in the Iron Mountains. He will not say how he knows our language. Sylph language. He has…he has been the one to train Miska in these last moons. And something called Cavaris?"

"Hullgard!" Lenore leaned back in her seat and rested an arm across her stomach. "Hullgard is the main coalition of peoples in the mountains. They are essentially the capital of what is a loosely aligned collection of people. We haven't had dealings with Hullgard for nearly a generation."

Ravenna shook her head. She sat in one of the chairs and spread her wings wearily. The other sylphs copied her, shifting uncomfortably as the backs of the chairs cut into their wings.

"We will have time to discuss trade relations later. I wish to know what has happened since my absence. Perhaps then I can answer some of the obvious questions which now face us."

Those words lifted burden from Lenore's shoulders that she did not know she had been carrying. A moment later and it returned, along with the thought she was perhaps giving Ravenna too much power, too much agency in their combined futures. She trusted the sylph, yes, but there were more circumstances and dealings involved than before. Many more.

Well, there was nothing for it. Even if Lenore were to take full accountability for everything that was going to happen, then she still required Ravenna's input. She took a sip of the goblet of water someone had placed before her and began to speak. She told Ravenna everything, from the conquering of the Red Desert, to her wedding, to the resistance and their failure to act, to her pregnancy, to wondering what happened to Ravenna and Miska, to Davorin's madness and his strange governing of the people. It was nearly an hour later when her voice finally gave out in a croak. The large man, Sisu, refilled her water. Lenore accepted the goblet with a smile.

"I have missed much," Ravenna said after she finished her own translation. "There is much to understand and to apologise for. And I am sorry from many things that happened. But that will have to come later. We must still deal with the matter at hand: Davorin lives. His army is scattered. But it is possible that they will regroup and return. What are we to do with him? If he truly does bear magic, then Miska is the only one who could contain him. And if he is mad, that I do not know..."

"Contain him?" Lenore scoffed. "Are we not going to kill him? After everything that he has done?"

There was more discussion amongst the sylphs, as Ravenna relayed the words. An argument seemed to be breaking out, growing louder, with wings flaring and feathers rustling. Finally, the man from Hullgard slammed his metal plated left hand onto the table, ending the argument with a crack. He said something, his voice deep and angry. Ravenna retaliated. The golden sylph with the diadem said something sharper in return. Ravenna retaliated to that, too. Then, silence.

"Davorin has committed many crimes. Truthfully, I would wish him beaten and left in the desert to die. But, our society demands more. If he were able and sane, that would be one thing. He would simply stand trial and be executed. But he is not in possession of his faculties. Before, yes, when he bought me and did his best to control the desert. But once he awoke that magic, we can trust nothing that he has done to have been done in a sane mind. After all, he told me he was going to be a god. If that is not proof…without command of his mind, he cannot stand trial for what he has done. It goes against everything that we believe."

"They are alright with this?!" Lenore jabbed her finger at the other sylphs. The dark one, the male, straightened and beat his wings once. "This is absurd. Davorin deserves death."

"Do you not have similar provisions under your laws?" Ravenna asked.

Lenore did not remember Ravenna being this cold. Yes, she had been depressed, lonely, even furious at the world. But never cold. Now, she looked at Lenore with emotionless eyes, reflecting shards of ice. She did not appear to be kind or good or anything that Lenore had remembered. Just hard.

"What has happened to you?"

"What was necessary," was the reply. "Do you or do you not have similar provisions under your own laws?"

Lenore took a breath, wincing as she felt her child kick in her womb. *Her* child. *Davorin's* child. She wanted her husband dead. She wanted to see him suffer for everything that he had done. But if Ravenna was correct, if Lenore was correct and the magic had caused Davorin's madness, then there was nothing to be done.

"When Miska wakes, we shall have to find some way to contain Davorin. We will have to determine what to do with him then. And may The Watcher forgive us all."

Ravenna had been right. The end of the battle was only the beginning of the war.

CHAPTER EIGHT

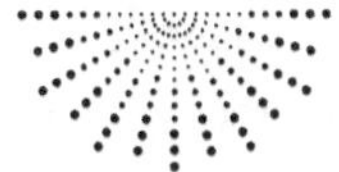

The sun was setting by the time Ravenna returned to the tent where Miska was resting. The healers had said he was not seriously injured, but that he had merely used up a great amount of energy. This was apparent only in the sweat on his brow and the black ridges on his back. The healers could do nothing for either affliction, their knowledge of magic limited to stories. So they left Ravenna to tend to him, assuring her in half-hearted tones that he would wake. Eventually.

She perched on a stool by his cot, dipping a rag into a precious basin of water and dabbing it across his forehead. Her mate still slept on.

"He talked about you," a voice said. Ravenna lifted her eyes to gaze at the large human who had accompanied Miska from Hullgard. He, the small girl child that Sisu claimed was Miska's heart-daughter Allora, and the massive animal that Sisu called Beringer, came into the tent. Allora ran to Miska and immediately took over from Ravenna, pushing the sylph out of the way as though she had not earned the right to be there.

Ravenna rose and wandered to the other side of the tent, folding her wings closer around herself as she watched Miska sleep. She took a breath and looked away from Miska and the human child, focusing her attention on Sisu, standing tall beside her.

"I did not ask it today because it was not the time or the place, but you shall answer me now: where did you learn our language?" Ravenna watched the man for some sign of deception or anger. He was hard to read with the thick black hair and the small braids, his beard cut close but still full.

"Now that is quite the story." Sisu looked at Ravenna, his gaze taking her in, not in an interested way that would indicate an attraction, but with a mere curiosity. His eyes glimmered in understanding. "I lost my hand some, oh twenty-five, twenty-six cycles ago. I was hunting Great-wolves in the gap between mountains. It was a rite of passage, one that would elevate me from an average hunter to a leader amongst our people. Only, the wolves were far cleverer than I. Instead of falling for my trap, I was lured into it. My hand was lost in the process. I was three days from any civilisation, anyone who would help me, delirious and wounded. On the second night, I dreamed about a woman with wings of spun gold."

Ravenna scoffed, but she pulled her wings closer. "It is forbidden for us to come to the mainland. Anyone who does is banished."

Sisu ignored Ravenna's protests, and she knew they were ridiculous, too. How else would he know their tongue? The explanation only served to awaken more questions in her.

"I thought she was only a delusion. But she came every night for a moon. She tended to my hand while I was feverish and could not walk, and she taught me this tongue. She lay with me once, under the light of the new moon. I never saw her again after that."

"She must have realised her folly," Ravenna snapped. There was no other way for this man to know their language, but she didn't want to hear the truth. She didn't want to hear that others before her and ventured into the human realms and returned with no consequences. They had returned with no scars, no broken spirit.

"You look surprisingly like her. You and that Desarra from today's council. The two of you are sisters, are you not? And yet the fact is that you look nothing like the other sylphs. If it were not for the wings, you would be a battle maiden in Hullgard."

In a flash of movement so swift that no one in the tent reacted before it was done, Ravenna had drawn both her swords and put them against Sisu's neck. She bared her teeth. She ignored the way that the monster Beringer moved up behind her, rumbling deep in his chest. Sisu held up his right hand and stared at Ravenna, smirking.

"Did you think it was just some strange abnormality? That you are so different from the others? I will be honest, when Miska described you, I did not believe that my mystery woman was more than a delusion. I thought he was drawing on some lost poetry. Then I came here and heard your tongue and I saw your people. Can you deny these things? Will you deny the truth?"

Ravenna was silent for a moment, sword tips trembling as she did her best to control her muscles. She took two deep breaths. Then, she cut a thin line on Sisu's neck, just below his beard. "The words that you have just uttered will never again cross your lips. Do you understand me?"

Sisu nodded, the smirk wider. She lowered her blades and turned around. The bear was standing on its hind legs, its paws outstretched and ready to strike. It growled deep in its chest, menacing and dangerous. Ravenna spread her wings and beat them twice, the feather tips brushing against the bear's nose. It snorted and moved back.

"Beringer...fears that you will hurt Sisu." Miska licked his lips and turned to Ravenna, his eyes half-lidded but clear. The child let out a squeal of joy and chattered at Miska, making sure that he looked closely at her as she spoke, her hands waving rhythmically through the air. Ravenna did not recognise the language. But she was more astonished when Miska responded in that same language, his fingers twitching in those same motions. She pulled her wings close.

"Allora tells me that you have been watching me. She says you are angry." He coughed. In an instant, Ravenna was at his side with a small cup of water to press against his lips. He drank slowly and still spluttered. She helped him to sit up, her fingers brushing against the ridges on his back. He winced.

"*Are* you angry?" Miska turned his head to look at Ravenna, his eyes meeting hers instead of watching her mouth move. Ravenna smiled, the motion slight. It was enough for him to blush, his reddish skin becoming burnished, even in the darkened light of the tent.

"I missed you," Ravenna said in the human tongue that she and Miska shared. The tongue of the Red Desert. Miska smiled and reached out a hand, brushing his fingers against her cheek. His fingers trembled, but when Ravenna leaned into the touch, the trembling vanished, as if he only ever needed her to heal him. It was a foolish thought, and one she wished she could keep.

"I missed you, too," he said. Ravenna was going to say more, going to tell him all that had happened since they had parted, but Allora pushed into his line of sight again and started speaking, her words rapid and her movements swift. Sisu broke in, his words gravelled and directed more at Allora than at Miska. And then the bear nudged his head forward, nose brushing against Miska's shoulder.

Ravenna pulled back. She let the others have their reunion with him. That moment of affection, of soft heartedness, was perhaps all she should allow herself. She had many things to be tending to. She had to stop her sylphs from killing every remaining human. She had to explain the state of things as they were now, being sure that Desarra and Crispinus and Brianna understood that this war was not yet over. They had argued earlier that the danger to their people had passed and that they should be returning home, victorious. Some of the wounded sylphs who could still fly were already on their way back to Shinalea. It would have to be enough, Ravenna had argued. One battle did not a victory make. Once she had described the magical atrocities that Lenore spoke of, Desarra had finally agreed, but the others were still wary.

Then Ravenna had to go see to the death counts. She had to determine who was wounded and who still was healthy enough to continue on. This was one duty as Warlord that she dreaded more than others; the reduction of everything that her people had worked for into cold numbers. How many lived. How many died. How many could fight. How many must return home. She then had to talk with Lenore about the future of the Red Desert. She had to understand how Miska came to bear his own magic so that he might deal with Davorin—who was luckily still asleep after all of the trauma that Ravenna killing his pet demon and battling with magic, not to mention his madness, had caused.

Something brushed against Ravenna's mind, a soft touch that felt as though it should have been familiar. Instead, she recoiled, both in thought and in body. Her wings were spread low, her crouch defensive. Her mind was sharp, defending itself with icy shards.

It took her a moment to realise that the discussion in the tent had fallen silent. Everyone was looking at her, eyes wide or wary. Even Beringer was frozen, his breath shallow. But Miska's eyes, those rich deep green depths that Ravenna was so fascinated with, wounded her most. They were wide, shocked, and a little afraid. He reached out a gentle hand and she felt that same brush against her mind. It was him. His magic.

Taking a deep breath and forcing her feathers to flatten, and

Ravenna closed her eyes and let down whatever mental barriers she had instinctively constructed.

I did not mean to frighten you. I only wanted for you to stay.

Ravenna shook her head. "I have many things to attend to. Talk with your…family. I will return later. We can discuss things then."

Before she could hear his response or feel another brush against her mind, she fled the tent.

Crispin found her some distance away, crouching against a boulder, her wings wrapped around her.

"Desarra said you went to visit your…mate? To see if he fared well. I told her that you would not be returning to the encampment tonight. You will have to return tomorrow, so that the people can hear you discuss the state of our future. They are not settling for gossip. Many of them expected to be home already. I have tried to explain why it is that we are remaining, but—"

"I will be there in the morning. I will provide a sufficiently rousing speech so that the people do not worry about why we are remaining with these humans. Is that all?"

"For the Warlord, yes." Crispin sat on the ground beside her, wrapping one wing around her own. Ravenna stiffened, but Crispin did not retreat. After a moment or two, she relaxed enough to be able to take in the sights around her instead of focusing on the touch of another person. The camp was still bustling with people dismantling tents or moving supplies, seeing to the wounded and burying the dead. No one cast a second glance at her or Crispin, or the several dozen sylphs that mingled amongst the humans. Things were winding down now that the sun was set and the stars and the moon were the only illumination in the desert. There was still enough activity, but it was almost peaceful. If they could forget that this place had been in a battle. Had been stained with blood.

"You seem sharper, harder than usual," Crispin said. "Desarra was a little surprised at your attitude earlier in today's meeting, considering that she had expected you to show some camaraderie with your human friends. She did not want to ask, so I have come to do so. What bothers you?"

She tilted her head back so that she could gaze at the stars. "After all that we have been through, you think you have the right to ask me that?"

"I have the right to ask you that because of all that we have been through."

Ravenna reached down and grabbed a handful of sand and grit. She let it flow through her fingers, watching the smaller pieces fly away on the slight wind. There was too much in her mind to explain. Too much to unravel.

"I have him back. And he has found a family of his own. How can I have him back and still feel as though I have lost him?"

Crispin chuckled. He tapped Ravenna on the head with his wing. "You have your own family. You are no longer the isolated Intellecti that you were. Tacitus may be dead, but you have Desarra. You have me. Even Brianna would give grudging acceptance of your relationship. You are our beloved Warlord. Not one sylph on Shinalea would let you be without a family. Do you think all of this makes it so he has lost you? It is no crime to find comfort in relationships where you can. You do not know what he went through all those moons."

"Do you think I don't know that? Do you think I don't know I am being selfish in my desires? I am fully aware of my faults. Which is why I left him to his family. I will go and be with him later."

"Then what is really bothering you?" Crispin asked. In that moment, Ravenna hated him for knowing her so well. She wanted to go back to those days when they could barely understand what motivated the other, when they were enemies, when she was waiting for him to trip her on the stairs to the Aerial City. Even the ability to go back to before, when she had kept

Desarra's miscarriage from him, when he had been furious at her decision to keep silent, that would have been a boon. Now, she could not push him away. She could not flee. For he knew her. Him and Desarra.

"That large human. The one from Hullgard. Who speaks our language? Sisu, is his name." Ravenna lowered her gaze to the sand, tracing out mindless patterns with her fingers. Crispin reached out and put a hand atop hers, stilling the nervous motion.

"I recall. He was quite a shock during the meeting," Crispin said. "Desarra speculated on how he knew our tongue for nearly an hour. She believes he must have learned from his ancestors, who maybe kept the language alive for the generations without the Stormbringers."

She knew that the words were said to make her laugh, a joke, for such things surely could not be possible. She wished they were. "He said he learned from a winged woman some twenty-six cycles ago. He says that she taught him our language and that they lay together. He says that her features are similar to those of Desarra. And of me."

Crispin was silent for a moment. Ravenna wanted to watch his expression to see whether disgust or horror lingered there. To see whether the shadows of hate that haunted her childhood would reappear. She had intended on keeping that news quiet. To learn of her origins now, when she had no reason to doubt, was a blow crueler than many she had been dealt. She may have given her heart to a human, but she had always been a sylph. And now she was not even that.

"I cannot say it surprises me. Your colouring is remarkably similar. And you have always been an oddity amongst a generally uniform people. But it does not matter. You are ours, no matter where you came from. No matter whether you can fly or not."

Ravenna sucked in a breath. The desert air was cooling

rapidly with the loss of the sun and she revelled in the bite of the air in her lungs. "We have gone to war against the humans. And here I am, sharing their blood."

"You love a human. You said it yourself back when we dealt with those former human slaves: they are not all out for blood. Humans are as varied a people as sylphs, perhaps even more so. And you are still sylph, no matter what else you are. However, I can see why it would upset you. It shouldn't. I just told you you are our Warlord and our family. You are Desarra's beloved sister. You are even my friend, though it took much to convince you of that. If you wish to keep quiet about your being half-human, then that is your right. I would suggest that many would not care. You're not alone anymore, Ravenna."

"Why don't you hate me?" she breathed. Crispin's wings tightened around her. He stared at the camp straight ahead, the fire in his eyes a little sad.

"Why would I hate you?"

"For everything I've done. For bringing these humans into our lives. For destroying everything we were only to remake us into a people of war. For being the cause of so many deaths. For...for Silvius, for everything," Ravenna said. There was much to be laid at her feet. The weight of many responsibilities on her wings. Crispin just shook his head, his dark brown hair falling across his forehead, making the distinguished sylph, a Lord of the Wind, her general, look like everyone else.

"You've also made us into so much more," Crispin said. He flicked his eyes to hers and Ravenna forced herself to not look away. "Silvius, my son, was not your fault. It was not Desarra's fault. It was just the wrong time. You have nothing to be blamed for in that. You gave him the death rites, after all. You gave him a name. Wings, Ravenna, I should be *thanking* you for everything you've done for us. For Shinalea."

"I'm not so sure."

Crispin kissed her head, smoothing out her hair with a hand. "I am."

Her chest shook as she took in a deep breath. Her eyes, though, were dry. She looked up at the stars again and said nothing. Crispin's wing tightened around her and she leaned into the embrace. She closed her eyes.

That brief instant of peace was shattered a few moments later when a commotion sounded from the collection of tents the healers were using. A young healer ran past, shouting frantically. Ravenna stood and strode over to her, ready to draw her swords at a moment's notice.

"What has happened?"

"Lady!" The healer fell to her knees before Ravenna, eyes wide and terrified. Ravenna lifted her to her feet.

"What has happened?" she repeated, this time her words a snarl.

"He has escaped. Lord Davorin is gone."

CHAPTER NINE

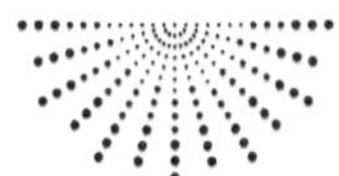

$\mathcal{E}$ven another day of resting after waking found Miska tired and unable to move fully. The ridges on his back were fading, but still present. His movement felt stiff, when he could bring himself to move at all. He had overextended himself. Badly. Annoyingly, he had gotten hardly any more time to talk with Ravenna since waking. Since she had fled. He had wanted to introduce her to Allora and to Sisu, to tell her all about his adventures in the Iron Mountains, but she had only appeared once more in his tent, minutes before he fell asleep. There always seemed to be someone calling for her attention or demanding his.

Miska had learned from Lenore that morning that Davorin had escaped. She had questioned him extensively on his magical abilities, pushing to see if he could track Davorin, bring him back, or kill him. He wanted to weep for the state he found Lenore in; she was weary and pregnant and her spirit had been beaten down. She had simply looked at him and said, "You did exactly as I asked. You came to save us all."

That had not helped Miska at all.

He gestured to Beringer, signalling the bear to come help

him out of bed. He was tired of lying around, no matter that he was still exhausted and couldn't use his magic fully. If he pushed himself too hard, the damage would be permanent. Still, Beringer complied and lifted his muzzle under Miska's arm, giving him purchase to stand. Bear and sorcerer tottered over to a washbasin where Miska splashed his face. He put on a fresh sleeveless tunic, perfect for the desert heat, and some loose trousers. He rubbed his hand over the stubble on his chin and felt the long hair on his shoulders. He was not truly what he was before. He was still changed. Clothes would not fix that.

Miska put his shoulder around Beringer's neck again and turned towards the entrance to the tent. He might not be able to perform magic well, but he could at least lend a hand. He halted, blushing furiously when he saw Ravenna standing in the entrance to the tent, her arms folded and a skeptical look on her face.

"Were you planning on going somewhere?" she asked, the scorn playing in the twist of her mouth.

"I remember you being a particularly poor patient back when you got attacked by that lion. I can hardly stand just sitting in here and doing nothing. There's too much to do. There is a war to finish. Order to restore. Davorin to—"

"Davorin is not your responsibility, despite what the others say. Just because you have magic does not mean you have to chase after him." She took a tentative step forward and reached out her hand to Miska's familiar. Beringer snuffled, searching for a hint of food. He did not find it, but he nuzzled her hand the same. A brief flicker of delight flashed across her features. Miska smiled.

"He likes you. Possible he likes you because I like you, but I think he would like you all the same."

"How did you come to tame such a creature?" Ravenna asked, brushing her hand over Beringer's forehead. Miska felt a rumble of appreciation in the back of his mind from the bear.

"That is a long story and involves a bad hunting trip and a dragon. I would tell it to you, but I don't know if you would sit still long enough to listen." He had not intended his words to wound, but when Ravenna turned her head so he would not see the flash of emotion, he knew that they had done just that.

She rustled her wings, folding them tightly against her back. "It is not that I do not wish to spend time with you. I want nothing more. But...I hold an obligation to my people to see this through, and there is too much to do for me to—Why is this so much harder than it was before?"

"It's only harder because you think it is," Miska said. He reached out a hand and, to his surprise, she stepped forward and took it. They said nothing for a moment, just letting the familiar touch between them rekindle whatever connection they had. "I know you are busy. And I do not blame you for it. Lenore has explained some of the obligations you hold to me. She was not here long enough to do a thorough job. Don't apologise for being there for your people. I will not apologise for being there for mine. Nor will I apologise for the events that have transpired. We both know that this is far from over. Especially with Davorin escaped. If nothing else, we need him to bring about an end to this. If such a thing is even possible."

Ravenna lifted her eyes to meet his and he was surprised by the sheer depth of emotion he saw there. She had been so cold and distant before. He squeezed her fingers.

"It's not your obligation to follow after Davorin. You're perfectly welcome to rest and recover. None of the healers here know the correct treatment for magical exhaustion."

"Finding Davorin is as much my pleasure as it is my obligation. I saw what he did to Lenore and our people. I know what more he would have done to you, after all the suffering he truly caused you. And, yes, I am the only one here with magic and so it is my duty to follow after him. Before he gathers more power, more forces, enough to defeat even your sylphs. Enough to tear this world to pieces. I felt...*reality* fracture when you killed that demon of his. The cracks are already there; if he is allowed to remain free, they will get worse."

"I have told Lenore, my sister, and the others that I will not support his killing. He is mad. His actions were not his."

Miska closed his eyes and shuddered as he recalled the giddy voice that had speared through his mind during their battle. Beringer grumbled deep in his chest, the sound enough for Miska to feel through the bear's fur. Ravenna squeezed his fingers in return. "Yes," he said opening his eyes. "He is insane. I don't know if that means that he should live or die, but he cannot run free. He needs to be contained. There is something more at work than his desire to take the place of his brother, to win glory and honour for the Salusian Empire."

"What would you suggest?" Ravenna asked, the ice back in her eyes. This was part of the war, not part of their relationship, and she was obviously determined to keep the two separate. To keep from feeling too much as she did what was required of her. He could see that she had already done more than enough of that in bringing her people here. The scars ran deep.

"I would not send people after him. We do not know where he has gone. I can track him, but...I do not want for anyone to get hurt. Sisu, Allora, they would be injured beyond repair if they went with me."

"You care for them," Ravenna said. There was no anger in her expression, no nor surprise or even distance. Just knowledge.

"They are my family. As much as you are. Allora was abandoned and Sisu came when I returned here. They would follow me to the ends of the earth, and yet I will leave them behind."

Ravenna lifted her chin and spread her wings. "And will you leave me behind? Obviously you mean to go alone."

Miska broke out into a grin, feeling more alive than he had felt for a while. He had missed her. Before he could answer, or before she could move her beautiful mouth to make more conversation, he pulled her into a hug. This time, Ravenna did not even stiffen at the embrace. She just wrapped her arms and her wings around him and held on. After a while, they both pulled back. Miska was still grinning. Ravenna was still calm and stoic.

"I could never leave you again. And I think that you would stand up to the trials that lie ahead better than anyone else I've ever met. It would be my honour to travel with you."

"So, what, we just go off into the desert some night and try to find Davorin?" Ravenna flexed her wings. A glimmer of uncertainty flashed in her ice blue eyes. It was gone a moment later, so quick that had Miska not been paying close attention, he would have missed it.

"We will go to finish this before it begins. Before more people die and before the world we know is changed forever."

Ravenna reached out and ran her fingers through his hair, catching on one of the small braids mixed amongst the other strands. Something in her seemed to shadow, growing melancholy. "I think it is too late for that. But we will do what we can."

—

* * *

THE DECISION TO go off into the desert and find Davorin was perhaps more easily decided than achieved. Sylphs and human riders on horses had already gone after the missing man to no avail. He was either dead and picked apart by jackals and carrion birds or he was hiding himself with magic. Miska assured Ravenna that he could track Davorin, but there was still some doubt. She left Miska to gather supplies while she went to seek out Desarra.

There was always a sylph stationed near her in case she

needed to send a message back to the encampment. It was meant to be a convenience, but Ravenna rarely found it that way. It felt too much like being watched, to be certain she did not grow too attached to the humans. Now though, it was but a matter of requesting her sister's presence and watching the sylph warrior off. Ravenna wound her way through the tents of humans until she came to the tent that had been set aside for her use and that of Lenore and whatever other meetings needed to be held.

She waited.

"I do not expect to receive a summons this late at night," Desarra said as she arrived. She slipped into the tent with her wings clearing the way before her, stretching after their flight. She wore the looser fitting clothes that were common to the sylphs and to the desert people in the heat, as opposed to the tighter fitting warrior garb that Ravenna favoured. "I thought you would be with your Miska this night."

"There are more pressing matters that he and I must tend to."

Desarra rubbed her brow, just below the winged crown. She had taken to wearing it whenever she encountered the humans, just to make things easier for the purpose of identification. Ravenna could see that it was wearying her sister, though. "The people are having a difficult time remaining behind and doing nothing. There has been no sighting of this Davorin and they are not entirely sure why it is that we should remain to help the humans. The battle has been fought and won. Yes, there are many warriors still at large, but surely our part in this is done. I will admit that, even knowing your affection for them and the potential ramifications that our interactions with them hold, I see little reason to remain. They still do not know where Shinalea is. Perhaps it would be better to return there and resume our life."

"And do what?" Ravenna asked. She settled into one of the chairs at the table, ignoring the way that the back pressed into her wings. Desarra fluttered her own wings at the sight and wrinkled her nose. None of the other sylphs had grown used to such uncomfortable human accoutrements. "Whether the people realise it or not, I have created a warrior race out of something bent on peace. Do you think it would be so easy to discard our weapons again and return to the life of art and philosophy and playing games in the sky? They know now what it is to be Stormbringers. Even if we were to isolate ourselves again, that remains. It is not my decision as to whether we should go back to our life of solitude, but I fear the consequences have already been meted out."

Desarra scoffed and shook her head. She fisted her hands on her hips and spread her wings wide, in show of annoyance or dominance. Ravenna was not sure which. "I thought we were going to deal with this question once we returned. But if you wish to talk philosophy now, who am I to stop you?"

Ravenna ran a hand over her face, rubbing away some of the exhaustion that had plagued her since this began. "I did not call you here to discuss philosophy. I called you here to inform you that Miska and I will be going into the desert to find Davorin and return with him."

This time, when Desarra's mottled gold wings flared, it was obviously a sign of dominion. Ravenna simply raised an eyebrow. "You are as crazy as the human you chase! What makes you think that you will have success where others fail? And even if you know where he has gone, then send someone else. You are too valuable to send on a fool's errand alone with a human."

"Even if that human is my mate?" Ravenna stood and walked to the entrance of the tent where she looked out on the desert sand. The sun had set, but shards of light still spilled over the horizon, changing everything a to pinkish red. The first hint of stars were beginning to glimmer overhead. The heat of the desert remained, though Ravenna knew from experience it would get much worse in the coming moons. "I called you here, sister, to inform you as a courtesy, rather than disappearing into the desert myself. Crispinus and Brianna are perfectly capable of taking my position once I am gone. And I will return. But I do not think that sending out a war party to go fetch him would do us any good. Miska is the only one who can track and contain him. I will not send him alone. You may protest however you like, but I am going. And when I return, I am going to finish this war and set the world to rights."

"And if your Queen demands that you remain?" Desarra asked, disbelief widening her eyes and dropping her wings.

Ravenna shrugged casually. "I am sure that Crispin has told you of my mixed heritage. Being only half-sylph, I feel perfectly justified in disobeying."

She did not wait for whatever argument her sister would provide, nor did she wait to see the expression Desarra would wear when she realised the truth of Ravenna's existence, a truth that she herself was still grappling with. Ravenna simply strode from the tent and, with her dark wings wrapped around her, blended into the twilight. She didn't hear anyone calling after her.

With Beringer as a mount, Ravenna and Miska could travel farther during that night than they could on horse or on foot. The bear's shoulders were massive enough for both Miska and Ravenna, though Miska said that they would have to rest him frequently enough. He was used to the mountain climate, not the desert. And while Miska had thinned his fur, there was still some struggle ahead. But, the bear was larger and stronger than a horse, and had some sort of strange magic running through him that made his pace fast enough to traverse the desert far more swiftly than Ravenna would have expected.

They set off into the dark, Miska plucking a thread from the sky and setting it before them like a guide, pulsing faintly in the dark. Magic. It was slightly unsettling, to see Miska wield this unfathomable power with a few waves of his fingers. Then, he had said that he learned from a dragon, and he was not one to give falsehoods. Considering that sylphs had been a legend to these people, considered divine messengers to their mysterious gods, Ravenna should not have doubted the existence of magic or dragons. In fact, every tome and history that she had read containing some unbelievable fact was swiftly reconsidered.

As Beringer lumbered into the darkness, Miska spoke to Ravenna's mind so that they could have a conversation without him needing to read her lips. He told her tales and shared images of his time in Iron Mountains, revealing how terrified he had been when he first came upon Cavaris, the harsh but necessary lessons that Sisu had taught him. He showed her Allora laughing in the snow. And with each word and emotion and image, the gaps that had risen between the two during their moons-long separation lessened.

"Sisu claims to be my father," Ravenna said in both thought and spoken word. She felt Miska stiffen in shock before her. She wanted to pull away and see what it was that his features would show her, but instead she wrapped her wings tighter around them both, ostensibly to keep off the desert chill.

"He told me about a dream that he once had, when he was delirious and lost his hand. But he didn't believe it. And I never would have expected that you..."

"How else would he know my language? And it is quite apparent that his features are similar to mine. You said it yourself, how our hair and my wings match. And it would explain why I am so different from the other sylphs. Everything makes sense, and yet I do not believe it."

"Do you feel this changes you?" Miska asked. He squeezed Ravenna's hand where she was wrapping her arms around his waist. Ravenna leaned her head against his back.

"I am who I have ever been. Yet...how can the knowledge not shape me?"

"You are the same to me. You are still Ravenna. Strong and stubborn and kinder than you know."

Ravenna was about to change the subject, to move away from her supposed attributes and suggest that they stop for the day as dawn peeked over the horizon. They had been traveling for many hours, the magical enhancements that Beringer received from being connected to Miska allowing them to travel swiftly. The time had passed swiftly with Miska's stories. But, even as Ravenna breathed in, ready to voice her thoughts on resting, two things happened. One was that a tinge of moisture, familiar with the scent of flowers attached to it, hit her mouth and her nose. The second was that a high-pitched, unstable giggle filled the air, causing both Ravenna and Beringer to stiffen and lift their heads. The thread they had been following pulsated. And then, with a flare, the sun rose above the horizon.

Before them was a sight that Ravenna had longed to see, though this came from her nightmares. The oasis of the Red Palace. A place that she had learned to call home, a place where she felt she belonged. It was a beautiful sight, and yet it was terrible, too. An army—borne on horses from the plains and far more massive than the army that the sylphs had faced but a few days before—had overrun the palace. And staggering towards this army, never in a straight line and moving slowly, twirling and stopping to pick up stones, laughing gleefully, was Davorin. The intruders welcomed him with bows drawn and staffs raised. Davorin was consumed and taken away, leaving Ravenna and Miska and Beringer exposed against the desert.

The word floated into Ravenna's mind, tinged with shock and horror from Miska. "Seraphina."

CHAPTER TEN

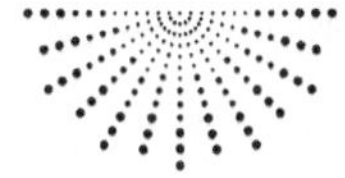

"We have to hide!" Miska speared his heels into Beringer's side, turning the bear far from the wandering eyes of the invading army. Ravenna tightened her grip on his waist. He felt the words in her mind, an impression of confusion and lack of understanding, but he was too busy turning to run and hide to answer her. Beringer took them to an outcropping of rock, one of the red spurs that stuck out of the desert. The same stone from which the Red Palace was made. They hid in its shadow as the sun rose to fully illuminate the desert. Judging by the lack of shouts, they had not been spotted, saved by the beginnings of dawn and by Davorin walking freely into their arms. There was some relief in being safe, for the time being, but the situation had just grown more complex than he or Ravenna had anticipated.

Miska clambered off Beringer's back and Ravenna followed after him, albeit far more gracefully. Her wings spread slightly for balance. Miska wished he could admire them, but things were far too serious for that.

"What is going on?" Ravenna asked, spinning him around so

he could read her lips and be sure to understand. She let her hand linger on his. "What is Seraphina?"

"Not what. Who. The Lady Seraphina is Davorin's sister. She is wife to the Warlord Baldur of Southron." Miska saw that Ravenna did not understand anything beyond being Davorin's sister. And even that did little to mar the calm collectedness of the sylph. "Southron used to be a coalition of warrior tribes, loosely allied, but they have united under Baldur's flag and Seraphina leads them as their queen. If you think Davorin was dangerous, then you have far worse ahead of you. There are stories told about her cruelty. She is cunning and malicious and dangerous. Davorin—our whole reason for being out here—is now lost to us."

Ravenna furrowed her brows, extending her wings and folding them tight. She did this twice, each time looking as though she would rather turn than just stand there, her expression solemn. "We must bring Davorin back. Without his presence the war cannot end."

"I don't think you understand. The war that we were trying to end, the one against Davorin and his madness and everything that he stood for, that is *over*. We now face something far, far worse." Miska grabbed Ravenna's other hand and squeezed it tightly, trying to be reassured by her touch. He failed. "Venturing into the desert to go capture Davorin and bring him back would have ended everything we faced...except we did not account for Seraphina. She is not in the Red Palace by chance."

"How can you know? How can you be sure that she hasn't come for the same reason that we have?" Ravenna peered around the outcropping of rock to examine the oasis and to the overrun Red Palace. Miska pulled her back, his hand tightening around her wrist. He released her a moment later.

"I...I cannot be certain. But everything I know about Seraphina tells this to be true. We are in far more danger now than we ever were."

How to impress on Ravenna the truth of the situation? Miska had been terrified in times past. He had faced down a furious bear, had discovered magic, had argued with a *dragon*. He had been to battle against a sorcerer and had blood on his hands that even Ravenna couldn't deny. He wasn't that same cheerful and trusted servant of the Red Palace that she had known. But Miska knew that some part of her still saw him that way. Still saw him as someone to protect against the world. Well, he didn't need protection any longer. And even with that in mind, Seraphina terrified him in such a way that his blood seemed to freeze, even in the rapidly warming desert.

Ravenna frowned. She folded her arms across her chest and paced a small circle in the shadow of the rock. Beringer watched her, interest from the bear pricking the back of Miska's mind. He pushed the thought away. Ravenna took another thirty seconds, considering the options.

He did not know how to make her understand that having Seraphina here—a woman who did nothing by halves, whose mere presence was enough to have people fearing to look over their shoulders—was so much worse than even the fiery ambitions of Davorin. *He* had terrified Miska, even before he had magic. Facing him down had nearly killed Miska; he still had the ridges on his back preventing his wider use of magic and limiting his motion. Seraphina was a nightmare to a nightmare. Contained in Southron before, now she was loose. With an army.

"We must figure out what it is that she wants. Perhaps she is just here to find her brother. Can you sneak in there and find out? You know the palace better than I. And I stand out."

Miska shook his head, the braids swinging against his chin. "I am not one to easily blend in, though perhaps easier than you. My skin marks me as someone who does not fit in easily. And their armour is not one I could replicate. There may be a way to send my mind in by magic, to see what it is that they are planning. To follow Davorin and determine the extent of his sister's plan."

Ravenna considered. "Can you send me? I might be able to hear more, to be sure that we catch everything."

Miska nodded. He wasn't entirely sure if that were the case, but he was willing to give it a try. Cavaris had warned him about using magic on others, but surely it was possible. He gestured for Ravenna to sit, and she did, remaining close to the rock. He sat behind her, pressing his hands flat against her back, his fingers brushing against the feathers of her wings. The sensation seemed to ignite some sort of fire inside him, and his vision swam with magical threads of all colours. With his thoughts, he reached for threads that would push someone's mind into an unfamiliar space, to allow Ravenna to see that which was happening in the Red Palace without her actually having to be there.

He took a breath, plucked the strings, and opened his eyes, aghast. He was *in* Ravenna's mind. He could see through her eyes, see her body sitting on the ground and hidden beside it. Was that how she saw him? It was tinged with affection and admiration and pride. Had he been corporeal, Miska would have blushed.

But what else was there, pressing against him, was the noise that started to sing in Miska's mind the more he connected with hers. He was somewhat used to these noises inside his mind now that he was proficient with mind-to-mind communication, but it was strange to feel it this deeply inside his being. These were not just the words of someone else, their voice ringing in his mind as though he were actually able to hear them. This was constant noise, ambient sounds that Miska had hardly even noticed before he could not hear. The wind over the sand. The call of the birds that lived in the oasis of the Red Palace. The whisper of leaves on leaves and moisture making everything sound different. Beneath his hands, Ravenna sucked in a breath.

When she spoke, it echoed doubly in his mind. "Is this…It feels strange. I can see you and I can feel you inside my mind."

Miska nodded and closed his eyes again. After overextending himself during the battle, he was not sure how long he could maintain this. So far he felt but a negligible energy drain, as though he were just walking casually. But it would not be long before that changed. Ravenna seemed to sense this and turned, her formless self gliding gracefully across the desert, as if she could fly. Miska went with her in thought.

Ravenna's mind was an unusual place to be. She did not focus on the greenery or the smells of the Red Desert and the oasis. She did not focus on the beauty of the plants that Miska always sought or the impressive styling of the Red Palace's architecture. Things that he considered perfectly normal to notice, she ignored as if they were not even there. She did notice, however, the places that predators could hide. She felt a tingle in the back of her neck when she passed the spot where she had been attacked by the desert lion. Her eyes tracked the movement of the warriors from the southern plains, when she noted the weapons they bore, suited for long distance hunting, for battling on horseback. She did not stop to linger over these sentries or the gathering of the army, though she noted their tactical details.

Miska physically shifted in the sand, having to grab another thread to strengthen the connection the farther away she got.

"I see Davorin," Ravenna whispered to his mind. Indeed, Miska saw him, too. His arms were being held by two of Seraphina's soldiers. They had long hair plaited down their backs, almost like Ravenna's, and at least three knives on their belts, bows slung across their backs. Davorin was dusty from walking through the desert and smiling deliriously. He did not seem to be struggling at all, despite his arms being held in restraint.

Through Ravenna's mind, Miska was not as aware of magic

as he usually was, but he did notice that the red threads that had surrounded Davorin were fading, pulsating, unraveling. Was it Miska's mind causing the strangeness or was it Davorin?

"Hello dear brother," a voice pierced through Ravenna's mind, sweet and smooth and dark and dangerous. Following it was a woman with that same tawny brown skin of Davorin and long brown hair. Her hair was, however, done up with beading of burnished gold, the tips gilded and clanking together. She wore what seemed to be robes spun from that same metal, draping over her as though the weight were substantial and yet simple to bear. Her fingers were tipped in golden claws, decorated with whorls and jewels. She was gaudy and outrageous and somehow impressed upon Ravenna and Miska more than just those things; she showed her power overtly and was no less frightening for it.

"Seraphina," Davorin said, giggling as he said her name. In Miska's mind, Ravenna winced. "You look silly."

"My courtiers do not seem to complain," Seraphina said with a smile. She stepped forward and peered at Davorin, lifting her right hand and running one of those claw-tipped fingers down his face. "You seem to have gotten yourself into rather a lot of trouble brother mine. My spies tell me that your army has been torn to shreds by sylphs."

"Angels," Davorin said. "I found *angels*. They will sing me to godhood."

"You sound like Dagan," Seraphina said. She pulled back a step and considered her brother. "What happened to that silly little creature that you called after our brother? I would have expected it to come with you. Even if it were not some real Dagan".

"The funny dragon is dead." Davorin tossed his head back and laughed. The two soldiers holding him had to shake him to get him sensible again. "Dead! The angel killed it. Beautiful angel. Full of such stunning rage. Dead, dead, dead, is Dagan! I'm supposed to tell you that it splintered my mind. Broke my magic. Lost my shoes."

"I had hopes that this conversation would be more entertaining. That I could gloat in front of you how far you had fallen. That you failed to see that I was unwilling to settle for Southron. I had hoped that you would realise that all of this time, I was the one who would be ruling the Salusian Empire. I had hoped to prove you and all of your scheming wrong. To hold Dagan's failures and successes over you. To show that you have always underestimated me." Seraphina watched her brother to see if any of her words struck true. As far as Miska could tell, through Ravenna's keen observation, Davorin was perfectly oblivious to the goading. "You don't understand any of this, do you? *I* am the one history will remember. *Me*. It will be *my* glory, not yours or Dagan's."

"Glory. Gloooooorrrry. Such a funny word. Means nothing with no people to define it," Davorin said, a smile splitting his face. Seraphina hissed and turned aside.

"Taunting a madman, though, is no fun at all. You just spit my words back at me as though they don't hold any meaning."

"Do they?" Davorin's question was sincere. He seemed genuinely curious. Seraphina clicked her tongue and turned aside.

"What am I going to do with you? You were such a good puppet. And now you are broken. What good was your magic?"

"I see the fractures in reality. I see the shape of the world as it *should* be. We are just living shadows compared to the reality that I am making. That will be brought into existence. Your funny self won't matter at all once the sky falls."

Seraphina clenched her fingers into fists, those claws digging into her skin and dripping blood on the red floor of the Great Hall. This was where Lenore used to preside over her people, the place of fairness and justice and righteous power. And it was being defiled by an army that did not belong there.

Miska felt the revulsion rise in his throat just as much as he felt it in Ravenna's mind. He also felt sweat trickling down his back, the droplets stinging and lingering on those ridges that were forming. His time was running out.

"I am so tired of living in your shadow. Seraphina, daughter of the Empire, sold to Southron for what? A trifle. A trade route. And then there was Dagan, the great conquerer, killed by my other useless brother. I was seen as *nothing*! Yet here I am, holding the Red Palace, commanding all of Southron! You are the one who is nothing. You are the one who won't matter. Yet you still have the gall to spout nonsense at me?"

Seraphina dripped blood closer to Davorin as she approached, seemingly ignorant of the wounds that her claws had caused. Davorin just inhaled deeply and looked around the room as if admiring the view. "I think I danced here, once," he said, a wistful look on his face. Seraphina roared her fury.

"Bring forward the child," Seraphina demanded, turning her back on her brother. She took several heaving breaths before turning to face Davorin again. A young woman cradling a babe in her arms, her clothes simple and practical, stepped forwards. Seraphina plucked the child from the girl's arms and held it up to Davorin. He leaned forward, frowning.

"I sense something," he said. "She is important. Something about her..."

"So, your mind is not completely gone," Seraphina said, smiling. She handed the child back to the girl. "She is yours. Scion of your liaison with my servant girl Nadira. Your firstborn. Under Salusian law, under Southron law—even, I believe, under the law of the Red Desert—she is your heir. And she *belongs to me.*"

"She is a key," Davorin said, the giggle back again.

Seraphina struck out, her claws raking down his cheek until three bloodied gouges shone there. Davorin's blood mixed with his sister's on the floor. Ravenna's mind roiled and Miska's control slipped for one moment, the image of sand appearing where there should have been palatial stone. He took a deep breath and tightened his mental grip on the threads that seemed to so easily slip through his grasp.

Seraphina leered at Davorin. "You have ruined my sport. But I am not done yet. I am going to tear down everything that you have worked so hard for all these moons. I'm going to finish what those 'angels' started, and then I am going to take them for myself. To have the Stormbringers under my command, can you imagine? I am going to raise your child and I'm going to rule the Salusian Empire as soon as our father dies, which should be soon from the reports I've received. This whole land, from the western edge of the Empire to the sea, stretching all the way to the Iron Mountains, it will be *mine*. I never cared about godhood like Dagan did, or showing him up like you were so intent on doing. I knew myself to be more capable and now you know it, too. Madness or not, you know it's true."

"Capability means nothing and it means everything." Davorin looked at Seraphina, as if taking her in for the first time. "Why believe yourself more capable than any other?"

Seraphina bared her teeth and lifted her chin. The golden beads in her hair swayed with the movement. "Take him to a dungeon."

This last command was directed to the two guards at Davorin's arms. They straightened and bowed their heads. They turned, their prisoner still smiling, but silent as he stood between them. He did not resist, even in word, as they tightened their grips on his arms and all but dragged him to the doors.

Miska felt the control over Ravenna's mind slipping, its time projecting her into the Red Palace coming to an end. His back flared in pain. The image of the Red Palace, with blood on the floor of the Great Hall, with its new mistress sneering at her mad brother, the infant child that was Davorin's spawn squirming in agitation, began to fade away until Miska saw nothing but blurs through Ravenna's eyes. He could feel the connection fading, but it was long enough to hear one last thing from Seraphina.

"Prepare for his execution."

CHAPTER ELEVEN

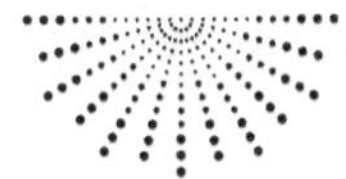

Ravenna was pulled back to her body with a jolt, the feeling of flying and freedom and openness that had come with walking with only her mind, vanished. She felt a deep seated loss, as though she had just experienced something she had never before experienced and would never again feel and her memories would soon fade, leaving nothing behind but melancholy. She rubbed at her chest, trying to unknot the despair that lingered there, leeching energy from her lungs. She blinked a few times and then stretched her wings experimentally to be sure that everything was working precisely as intended. She took a deep breath.

Still shaky, Ravenna recalled Miska and turned. He was still behind her, but crawling slowly towards Beringer, his hands pulling him backwards across the sand while he faced Ravenna, watching her. He seemed stiff, unable to move properly. His legs jerked against the sand, providing ineffectual aid to his movements. Had the magic done something to harm Miska? Had they been attacked while she was not in her body? Or perhaps he was feeling the same strangeness that she felt.

"What has happened?" Ravenna asked kneeling beside Miska. He shook his head, smiling. It did not reach his eyes.

"It's nothing," he said. "I just used too much magic after the battle."

"You can barely move," Ravenna said trying not to sound like a scolding aunt. She appraised him more closely, noting the tension in his shoulders, the trembling in his fingers. "What has happened? You should tell me now before I ask you to do something that you cannot do."

"It is...It is the price of using my magic without taking life from something else." Miska turned, dislodging sand as he did. The day was bright enough even in the shade of the rock outcropping to see the labyrinth of black ridges that had formed over Miska's back, showing through his light tunic. Ravenna remembered those ridges from when he was healing, but they had faded. Hadn't they? She ran a finger over one of them, pulling back when Miska flinched. They seemed artificial, strange, like some ancient language that had long been forgotten written upon his skin. And they seemed to restrict his movement. "I will be perfectly fine in a while, provided I'm allowed to rest."

"Can you walk?" Ravenna asked. She stood and held out her hand. Miska took it and she lifted him to his feet, watching the image of pain flashed across his features, furrowing his brow. She held up a wing to steady him and he tottered over to Beringer, leaning on the bear for support.

"I will be fine. There are other matters to attend," Miska said. Ravenna took a deep, calming breath. She wanted to beat him over the head with her wings like she would one of her other sylphs who lied to her. But this was Miska, not one of her warriors. She did not know if she had that authority here. If the distance between them all these moons had created barriers. She let the matter rest.

"We're going to have to do something about Davorin,"

Ravenna said, breaching the topic that both seemed to be avoiding. But after seeing what they had, she was in no more doubt than she had been before. This changed nothing. And it changed everything. Miska coughed, wide-eyed, leaning against Beringer, twining his fingers into the bear's fur. Ravenna flared her wings, unimpressed.

"You cannot be serious. After what we just saw? Seraphina is on her way to where our people are camped. She is going to complete everything that Davorin set out to do, and she's far more dangerous than he. You saw the size of her forces. They are not mercenaries or conscripted men and women from conquered kingdoms. They are people whose very lives revolve around battle. No wonder she managed to unify them. She promised them war. With *us*."

Ravenna lifted her head and studied the sky, watching the clouds for a moment. There were only a few and those provided little protection from the stinging rays of the sun. It was both hot and familiar, this desert heat that beat down upon her even in the shade. It had been too long since she had felt this. "We came here to fetch Davorin back, to return him to Lenore's custody. If he can be dealt with, then Lenore can regain sovereignty over the Red Desert, and the other kingdoms conquered by Davorin and his predecessor can start the process of regaining autonomy. Surely Seraphina will not have a wing to fly with in the face of that. But even more than political manoeuvrings, would you leave him, mad and broken, to be executed unceremoniously by his sister? Even insane I would not wish that upon anybody. My sister and I have our fair share of problems, but we never wanted each other dead."

"We need to get back to the others and warn them. Autonomy may mean absolutely nothing in the face of this. Seraphina stated clearly that she wants to conquer everything. Your Stormbringers may have no choice but to retreat back to your home and never see the world again. You came as a preventative measure to be sure that your people were free, now and forever. But now you are known throughout the land and people like Seraphina are going to want to lay claim to you. I don't want you to be a slave again."

Water traced down Miska's cheek and his eyes shone. He turned sideways so he would not have to see Ravenna's response, and they had not been communicating with mind to mind magic since he was already weakened. It was a ploy, Ravenna knew, to change the subject to avoid the depth of conversation they needed to have. She reached out and brushed Miska's long hair from his eyes. He looked at her. Shook his head.

"If Seraphina kills Davorin without taking his magic into account, what will happen? Even if his magic is splintered from the death of that creature, it is not gone, surely. What will be the consequences?" Ravenna asked, the last argument she had. Her voice sounded cold even to her, but thankfully Miska could not hear. He could only see. She hoped her eyes were not as dark as she felt.

"I don't know. When you killed the demon he summoned, something…happened. To Davorin, and to me, and to, well, reality. I don't know if it fixed whatever wrong had occurred with the original summons Davorin made or if it made everything worse. But…Why do you have to be right? Why couldn't we just turn back now? Return to Hullgard or Shinalea and live in peace?"

"When this is done, we will have that chance. We are going to fetch Davorin and then will go back and deal with Seraphina as she comes. Having Davorin will not solve everything, but it will help. Then, I promise, then we will live in peace." Ravenna touched her forehead to Miska's, letting that simple connection between them bear them up for a moment. Then, she pulled back and reached for the blades at her back. "If I'm not back by nightfall, go without me."

She turned away so she would not have to see Miska's thoughts written across his face, so that he could not initiate an argument. She could hear him where he could not hear her, but he said nothing.

Ravenna peered around the rock, looking at the oasis through her own eyes instead of her mind's eye. She had been there once already today and she could tell where the soldiers were, where they had been, where they were guarding and where they were lax. It would be enough to get her inside. From there, she would have to hope that she could handle whatever came her way. Given the blood already on her hands, she had little doubt of that. The only doubt came from whether she could do it quietly.

Ravenna reached the oasis and felt the familiar moisture touch her face. She moved soundlessly through the plants that brushed against her, pausing when footsteps came and moving on when they vanished. After half an hour, she reached the palace itself. She entered into the stone building by means of one of the large windows that opened onto the gardens. The chamber she climbed into was almost identical to the one that she had occupied during her residency: a wide bed with light linens, a stool and side table, a small painting on the wall.

It was familiar in a way that even Shinalea was not. This palace in an oasis in the desert was where she had come to terms with her life, where she had understood what she was and what her place was in this world of humans and legends. Now, it was occupied by an enemy she hadn't even known she had. One whose anger was far-reaching and long-lived.

Ravenna poked her head into the hallway and listened carefully, doing her best to anticipate the movement of the patrols. This was a residential part of the palace, not one that contained any treasures or things of interest except places to sleep, so hopefully the Southron people would not be hugely interested in wandering there. The hallway in front of her would take her to the library, the one to her left would take her to the healer's chambers deep below the palace. If the dungeons were anywhere, they would be near there.

She slipped out of the room and crept along the hallway, swords poised for attack and wings ready for combat at a moment's notice. She did not wish to make a ruckus fetching Davorin, but she would if she had to. She would kill easily if it was required of her. She had long since stopped worrying about the blood on her wings.

Ravenna moved down grand hallways carved with bas-relief of legends from histories long past, of wars between humans and their gods, of festivals and the making of constellations. When the carvings stopped, Ravenna knew she was in the right place. The hallway sloped downwards, leading to several chambers that were in the caverns beneath the palace. The air was cooler, more moisture beading on her face.

Footsteps echoed along the hallway, the sound of people who did not care if anyone heard them, came in her direction. Ravenna hissed to herself and ducked into an alcove, shielding herself in the shadows with her wings. She peered out between the feathers and held her breath.

Two soldiers, one male one female, sauntered along the hallways as if they owned it. They carried longbows across their back even though the weapons would be nearly useless inside. The female carried a long shafted two-headed axe like the one Ravenna had seen Sisu wield. The male carried a curved sword which he swung casually through the air. They talked amongst themselves, laughing and waving their weapons about as if they had not a single care in the world. They sauntered past Ravenna's alcove, hardly glancing towards it. She willed her heart to be quieter in case they could hear, no matter that the notion was ridiculous.

They paused a few moments longer then continued on, arguing about some spoils or some such. Ravenna released her breath only when she could hear no more footsteps. Her feathers trembled and her wings shook from being held so still. She slipped out of the alcove and walked down the hallway on soft leather clad feet, the sound a whisper compared to the soldiers that had just passed.

This happened two more times, with Ravenna ducking into small rooms or alcoves just before soldiers passed by, all bearing bows and some other weapon. She passed Warra's healing rooms, the memory of the old healer rising in Ravenna's mind like the scent of freshly baked bread: pleasant, tantalising, and ephemeral. Had Warra survived Davorin's sacking of the Red Desert? Had she been forced to flee? Or was her life one of the ones that Davorin could not be punished for, on account of his mind? Ravenna forced herself to move on.

The dungeons, surprisingly, were not hard to find, being only one level down from Warra's chambers. They were not guarded. Apparently Seraphina trusted the metal bars to keep her brother in place as much as his madness would keep him compliant. After all, he had come to her and had failed to understand what she was doing. Ravenna found him behind the second door, leaning against the wall and tapping his hands on the floor as if a child at play. He paused when she appeared and looked up

"You came to free me," he said. His words made sense, but his voice was strange, that same mad tone he had used before. "You want to shape the world in your image. So you are going to do everything you can. You are thinking you would save me from death, but you don't understand life. It's all going to change."

"That may be so," Ravenna said voice hard, "but at least I shall not sit idly by while someone tries to kill me. Do you wish to be free or not?"

Davorin rubbed a finger along a crack in the stone floor, tracing its lines. "Freedom is an impossibility," he said. Ravenna frowned; she had not considered what she would do if Davorin refused to accompany her. She had assumed that he would be as compliant with her as he had been with Seraphina.

"Then why do we fight for it?" Ravenna asked, desperately hoping she would not have to argue philosophy with a madman in order to affect his escape. Davorin tilted his head, finger poised to start tracing the rock again. He shrugged and rose to his feet, walking to the door and reaching through the bars until Ravenna recoiled, her wings flaring as she avoided his touch.

The door clicked open, swinging back on its hinges though no one had touched it. More magic, though this left a sour taste in Ravenna's mouth the way Miska's never did. She stepped back another step and waited for Davorin to come to her. He giggled like a child and skipped forwards, reaching out his hand and grabbing hers before she had a chance to protest. She flinched. Nothing happened. There was no magic, no pressure into doing his will, just holding her hand.

Even knowing that he was not the man who had captured her, scarred her, threatened her, that simple touch set bile rising in her throat. Ravenna forced herself to remember that the Davorin she hated was gone. Dead, likely with the same stroke that had killed the monstrosity in Nadezdha's body. This man may have the same looks, the same eyes, but he was not the same. Though she repeated the thought several times, she found it difficult to prevent her dislike. Davorin just stood there, gripping her hand tightly.

"You hate me," he said, tilting his head.

"I do," Ravenna agreed. "But my feelings on the matter are irrelevant. We must go if you wish to live to see another dawn."

"Dawn," Davorin mused, tilting his head. His brown eyes gleamed with some unreadable emotion. "A herald of beginnings, a crier to change. And yet no one seems to remember the death in its wake. If you hate me, why save me?"

"Because I must," she said, gritting her teeth. She had lingered here long enough already. Guards would surely be coming for Davorin sooner rather than later, to prepare him for his execution by his sister's vengeful hand. Ravenna could have slipped away easily on her own, but with Davorin in tow she had to be more careful.

"Let's go," Davorin said smiling wide enough to show his teeth. Ravenna inclined her head and they went. Whether it was through some strange phenomenon of magic or because Seraphina had just called all her soldiers to one place, but escaping from the Red Palace was far safer then breaking into it. The ease with which they escaped turned Ravenna's stomach. She suspected Davorin had a hand in the matter, and her suspicions were soon confirmed. They saw one patrol, moving in their direction with eagerness, bows across their back, curved swords in their hands. Davorin waved his hand and the patrol turned on their heel and walked away as though they had something pressing to attend somewhere else.

Ravenna swallowed back bile.

Was she playing right into Davorin's hand by retrieving him from this place? His magic was obviously not as broken or splintered as he had suggested to Seraphina if he could influence people so easily. If he could cause soldiers to turn away from their quarry, then who was to say that he was not exercising that same influence on her?

She forced the thoughts down, trusting in the fact that Miska's magic was stronger than Davorin's. She had to believe such a thing, or she would begin to doubt her own mind. That was the one thing she had yet remaining to herself. Her battle skills were given to her people, freely, but fully. Her blood was Sisu's and her mother's. Her heart was Miska's. Her mind was hers alone, though. She would not believe that Davorin had influenced that part of her.

A glance at Davorin had Ravenna flinching, even if only inwardly. He grinned at her, eyes following her movements with blatant admiration.

Another hour of quietly stepping through the halls and listening for approaching soldiers and they were out to the oasis. From there, it was a simple matter to go find Miska hiding behind the rock. The closer they got, the more Ravenna's fears fell aside. Miska would protect her from whatever malignant influence Davorin exerted, surely. And if he could not, then Ravenna would rather not know.

Her charge clapped gleefully as they approached Beringer. The bear snorted and rose up, looking at the newcomer with distaste. Miska sat on Beringer's back, eyes cold and expression grim, ready to move at a moment's notice.

"This will not end well," he said. He did not look at Ravenna for a response. He just watched as Davorin clambered up Beringer's back and sat behind him. Ravenna followed, her hands tentatively on Davorin's waist to keep them both steady. Beringer snorted and shook his head. Then, with no one stopping them or shouting at them to return and yield, they clambered off into the beginnings of the sunset.

Ravenna left her fears in the sand behind them. Or so she told herself.

CHAPTER TWELVE

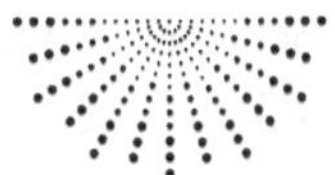

*H*alfway through the journey back through the desert, Miska lost all pretence of patience with Davorin. Ravenna knew it was coming; his shoulders grew more and more tense as they went. The flashes she caught of his face as Beringer lumbered onwards were dark, brooding. Davorin, stuck between Miska and Ravenna was constantly moving about as much as their travelling arrangements would allow, just kicking his heels against Beringer's side and half turning to talk with Ravenna. She supposed it was fortunate that Miska couldn't actually *hear* Davorin, or he would have lost his normally even temper long ago.

Ravenna herself was growing tired of Davorin's movements, having to adjust her own seat on Beringer's back to accommodate his shiftings. Then there was his constant chatter, enough to make her wish that she could borrow Miska's shroud of silence to block him out. He spoke in a stream of commentary on the rocks that they were passing, the colour of the sand, how it was that a bear could have come down from the Iron Mountains, how the reality that they knew was fracturing beneath them, how Ravenna was doing her best to change the world and make it more to her liking, how Miska was doing his best to just protect Ravenna despite the unprecedented power flowing through his veins, how hungry Davorin was, how he had so many plans for his impending godhood, theories about the colour blue...everything and anything under the stars was fair game for him to talk about. A trip that had seemed to take so little time the first time they made it, even though it was some twelve hours' journey on Beringer's back—a speed that Ravenna knew could not be matched by a horse at the same pace—now seemed an eternity. A loud one.

"Stop," Miska said, at last at the end of his tether. Beringer halted accordingly. The bear shook his shoulders as Davorin kicked his heels in, letting out a low growl. Miska sighed, but just slid off his back. Ravenna followed suit, Davorin scrambling after her like an eager child. "I cannot stand this. He is driving me insane, which is saying something since he *is* insane. I cannot even *hear* him and he is driving me out of my mind. Beringer is fed up with his movements and is growing tired. I can feel *your* disapproval like a cloud. This cannot be worth saving him. We have to prepare for *war* and instead we are escorting a deranged madman back to, what, be merely imprisoned?"

Ravenna folded her arms and stretched her wings, slightly cramped from riding all those hours. She took in the empty land around them, the ground made up of dry, cracked dirt, loose gravel and some sand piled up at the base of rocks and the scrub grass and twisted, stunted trees that grew in this desolate place. Desolate and quiet. Peaceful, even. Davorin crouched down and started drawing in the sand, the designs barely illuminated by the stars and moon that had just begun appearing in the sky. They were making decent time, even with the delays.

Ravenna turned her attention from the landscape to where Miska waited for an answer to his demands, green eyes searching her every expression and movement to try and determine what she was thinking. "How is your back? You seem to have an easier time standing and walking than you did before."

Miska gaped at her. He threw up his hands and paced a small circle before turning back to her, wide eyed with astonishment. "That is what you have to say? You ask about my back?"

"I had thought that you would be pleased of my concern. But if you wish to discuss the madman that we are transporting back to our people then feel free. I shall not stop you." Ravenna resisted the urge to fold her arms and spread her wings.

Miska snarled wordlessly and jabbed his finger in Davorin's direction. She looked and saw that the man was drawing a picture of some sort of cataclysmic event, monsters that were unrecognisable in the sand drawing were clashing in violent images. She turned back to Miska, unmoved. He frowned. "We should not be transporting him at all. We could be moving far faster if we left him behind. Or better yet, took care of him ourselves. I understand not leaving him for his sister to execute —for the *magical* repercussions, not the cruelty at being killed by his sister—but he is becoming a hindrance."

Ravenna lifted her chin. "We discussed this. Killing him now that his mind has shattered would do no one any good. Do you not think that I want him to suffer for all that he put me through? Do you not think that I wish to do to him as I did to Jazer, drawing my sword through his stomach? Revenge would be sweet, but it would be pointless. With Jazer, it was useful to free her slaves, to help arm my people and to free those who had done nothing to deserve captivity. Killing Davorin now would serve no purpose at all, not even to exact revenge. The Davorin we knew is gone and this one will remain alive and be dealt with accordingly. Once he returns, Lenore can claim her auton-omy. The situation can be dealt with politically."

"There will be nothing to gain from taking him back with us! I don't care how politics works. He may be insane, but he still has access to his magic, in whatever limited capacity. I can only contain him for so long. Then what? And even if we didn't want to kill him, we face a far greater threat. Who *cares* about revenge? Leaving him behind, killing him, is the most practical thing for us to do. We have to go and prepare for the arrival of Seraphina's army. They will not be far behind us. Davorin's purpose in reclaiming my home is pointless now that his sister rides for our deaths. Or do you honestly think that she cares about a signed document or some declared autonomy."

Ravenna turned and took three deep breaths, wondering why it was she wished she had Crispinus or Desarra there to advise her. Had she grown so used to sharing her thoughts with others? Had she grown so used to acting on mutual counsel rather than individual thought and action? This was her mate; surely she could explain her thoughts to him. She shivered, pulling her wings close.

Returning to Miska's side, being reunited and travelling together on this wayward adventure, it should have been that same easy relationship they had in those few days before Ravenna left the Red Palace to save her people. They should have been able to start where it left off, capable and comfortable and easy. And it had been like that, at first. But as soon as difficulty reared its ugly head, they were arguing over the most fundamental of things.

The truth was that she was no longer the broken sylph that Miska had pieced back together. She had changed during all those moons away. She would never be able to take simple comfort in the shelter of his arms, because her demons were now more internal than external. And, it would appear that he had changed, also. He had grown into his strength, standing up for what he thought and leaping into battle when perhaps before he would have stayed his hand. That was the part she needed, just then. Not another warrior. Ravenna was perfectly glad to hear other opinions, even argue, but she knew when an action needed to be taken that she would do it. And she was *not* going to do this. There was no point.

She turned back to Miska, stepping close enough that even in the soft light of the moon he could see her mouth clearly to understand. "If we wish to face the army of this Seraphina, then we will need more than a few days' head start. The sylphs have lost many. Almost three companies were wiped out entirely. Three *hundred* of my people, dead. That number again and more were wounded gravely. All of my people, no matter how capable, were injured in some manner. There may be a thousand sylphs that can fight still at the same level that they did before. The army that Davorin controlled—the one that Lenore will have control over once we officially return her power—are scattered to the desert and beyond. The *politics* of returning Davorin is all that matters at the moment and you want to set that aside —set aside the life of a person—for a few hours' more warning. No matter what we do, Miska, the war is already lost. There is little point in attempting to salvage it with the life of one man."

He stood frozen. Eyes wide and disbelieving. Mouth gaping like a starving raptor chick begging for food. Beringer growled behind him, shifting his weight on his massive paws and drawing lines on the ground with his claws. Even Davorin had stilled, his inane chatter falling silent as he scribbled in the sand.

"You think our efforts are futile? After all that we went through to get here, we two, all the training and the preparing and the endless nights wondering what was happening when we were not there, you think all that was for nothing now that we face a greater challenge? We have one battle ahead. This is just one more challenge until we are free. And you doubt that." Miska took a step backwards, his hand reaching behind him to rest against Beringer's head. He clenched his other hand into a fist; the tremble was slight, but it was a knife to Ravenna's heart.

"Wings, Miska, you believe I've given up." Ravenna folded her arms and shook her head. She pressed her wings in close.

"Do you believe that I've lost all hope? I *know* what that feels like, that wing-weariness that weighs down your very soul, but *this* is not *that*. This is reality, Miska, this is the truth that we face. Unless Seraphina's army is gloriously incompetent, we stand little chance at winning with an offensive battle, let alone a defensive one, and there will be nowhere to hide. It does not mean I will not fight. I will fight with every feather in my wings and every bone in my body until my blood washes the desert into a green oasis. I will do anything for the future of my people. Except kill a man who does not understand his crimes."

Miska leaned back against Beringer, supporting his weight with the shoulder of his familiar, a being with whom he shared a bond that Ravenna could never match. "So that's it, then. You won't let me kill him."

"Davorin standing before Lenore as she declares sovereignty is the only way, Miska. No matter how much I desired it, razing Davorin and his forces to the ground was never truly going to do anything but reap chaos. Killing him now will save no one. So, yes, that's it. There is nothing else."

Miska said nothing. Ravenna had no more arguments to spare. They faced off, shifting uncomfortably, each waiting for the other to speak and receiving only silence. Finally, Miska lowered his gaze and turned to Beringer. Ravenna sighed, knowing something between the two of them had fractured. She did not know how to fix it except to give in and she could not do that. So she walked over to Davorin and helped him to his feet. Davorin followed behind her as she went to Beringer, skipping stones across his palm with that innocence of a child. Innocence he did not deserve.

Being around him was difficult enough. The scar on Ravenna's back twinged every time he caught her in those brown eyes. She felt the horror of having her wings pinned down, of being treated like property, like a toy. But he did not understand, or even properly remember what he had done, and that was the end of it. They would deal with the repercussions of his existence later. Now, they had to return to their people.

They had to warn them, for all the good it would do.

Ravenna helped Davorin climb onto the bear's back, his fingers pulling at Beringer's fur. Beringer snorted and rumbled in annoyance, curling his lip and showing a great fang to the oblivious Davorin. Once he was situated, Ravenna climbed up behind him, taking care to be gentle. She folded her wings against her back, placed her hands on Davorin's waist, and then they were off again into the desert.

"You have shadows following you," Davorin said, turning his head over his shoulder to look at Ravenna. She swallowed down her anger, locking it firmly behind her empty eyes. She had worked for moons to become the monster her people needed her to be. She had fought against herself, against grief for Tacitus and for her lost friends, against her anger at the hypocrisy of her people listening raptly to her when before they had shunned her. She had done all of this to become the Warlord that would stand against what threatened them, and win. She would not give that up now.

"Shadows?" she asked, the word falling from her tongue before she could consider the consequence. Traveling in silence only gave her time to think, and that was as dangerous as conversation.

"You fight battles of steel with wing, and you fight battles of discourse with thought. But you cannot fight the battles of mind with wing or with thought. You must fight them with soul. And you bear shadows in your mind, in your soul. How can you win if you let them weigh you down?"

"I did not say it was a hopeless battle. I did not say that there was not merit in fighting. I simply said that the consequences would be perhaps too great." Her hands clenched on his waist almost involuntarily. Ravenna quickly loosened her grip, her hands burning where she touched him. Davorin did not even seem to notice. He just kept talking.

"Consequences have actions. And actions have consequences. You must decide which you like the better."

There was no point in talking nonsense with him. Whatever magic he bore was being used to spread sand amongst the desert, nonsense to the wind. His malice seemed to be completely gone. His mind was a maze comprised of entirely dead ends. She would find no help nor solace from him.

Then, he turned farther so that he could gaze at her with both eyes. In that brief moment, Ravenna saw the last vestiges of his sanity, the last piece that made him Davorin. "Do you know," he whispered, "I think I might have been wrong about a lot of things."

"You were," she said definitively. Davorin blinked, and that last piece was gone. In its place was a person she did not recognise. Even his features seemed to become more soft, rounded, innocent. The magic he woke from its slumber had changed him completely. Perhaps it had changed Ravenna, too.

Davorin began humming to himself, tapping out a rhythm with his heels against Beringer's side. Miska's shoulders tightened again. But though the hours passed, they did not stop. None wanted another conversation that left more wounds than solutions.

A water skin was passed from the pack, and food was eaten as they rode. Beringer's tireless energy, fuelled by his bond with Miska, bore them back to the edge of the desert. This time when the dawn arose, the unfamiliar foothills to the Iron Mountains were in sharp relief. She longed for the familiar palace that she had known as home, not this wild landscape that, no matter how beautiful, would be remembered as a place of blood. Miska straightened. Ravenna saw a slip of a smile spread across his features as the weak sun caught his profile. She folded her wings tighter.

They had reunited, yes. It was wonderful to again be with Miska. But there were things now between them that would never be undone. They would have to simply move forwards. Only, death stood in their midst and Ravenna was not sure how to circumvent it. Nor was she sure she should. All of this, every event that happened over the last cycle and more, it was her doing. She had been the one to get captured. She had been the one who set Davorin off on this course. Perhaps not at first—his ambitions were always there—but his later drive had been strengthened by her words, her very existence. She had done her best to remedy this and still everything she touched would be forever changed. Maybe all of this was the price she had to pay for what she had done. Were her actions really worth such death and destruction?

She had one more thing to fix, one more challenge to face before her people would be safe and free to chart whatever future course they chose. Before Miska would be able to choose his future, whether she was there or not. He had a new family, including Ravenna's own human father. He had a heart-daughter. And while she longed to be part of it, while she longed to go back to that connection that they shared all those moons ago and carry it into the future, perhaps it was not to be. Perhaps out of all of this, she was the expendable one.

They approached the encampment, the light canvas of the tents reflecting the early desert sun. Ravenna's wings tightened against her back and then relaxed. She would fight. Just as she said, with every feather and drop of blood in her body. But eventually, there would be nothing left. She would find a way to be all right with that.

CHAPTER THIRTEEN

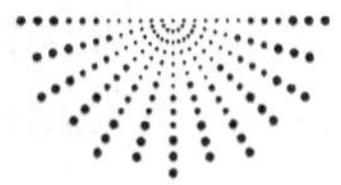

iska put a binding spell on Davorin and walked away. It was a simple binding, one that tied off Davorin's magic and would keep him within the camp. Miska had no idea if he even did it right; Cavaris had not taught him such complexities, instead grudgingly focusing on the more violent aspects of magic. Once Miska had learned the basics, of course. But the threads had complied and Davorin sat docilely in the tent guarded by both sylph and human, playing with stones that he had gathered. It seemed that whether the binding worked or not, Davorin was unlikely to cause much trouble. He hoped never to see Davorin again, or to think of him. He just turned his back on the tent and moved on.

He would never admit as such out loud, but Miska was secretly glad that he did not have to kill the madman. As he was now, Davorin was almost childlike. He reminded Miska of Allora. That comparison wrenched at Miska's mind, though he tried to push the thought aside. He still wished that Davorin—and the stain that man left on the world—was gone, but a magical binding would have to suffice. He would grudgingly acknowledge that Ravenna had been right in that regard; killing the former tyrant would serve no purpose.

His and Ravenna's arrival at the encampment had not gone spectacularly well. Not only had they been arguing—or rather stewing in silence—but Davorin's return coupled with the news of Seraphina's advancement was not well received. Many of the sylphs and humans alike wanted Davorin dead in the face of this new threat. They had wanted him dead before, but acquiesced to keeping him alive because of some ancient law or practise. Now, they all but clamoured for his blood. Ravenna had made her political argument to Lenore, stating that if Lenore could prove Davorin's ineptness in the face of others, such as with a signed document that had Desarra as Chosen Queen of the sylphs and Sisu as representative of Hullgard as witnesses, then the Red Desert would revert to Lenore's power, as would a good portion of the Salusian Empire. Davorin's wrongs could begin to be righted.

This argument was countered by one simple fact stated over and over: Seraphina rode to war.

An impossible stalemate had resulted in Davorin being put under binding and guard, with the promise that his fate would be decided properly once this new threat had been dealt with, whatever that required. Ravenna had acquiesced, and turned silent. Miska wanted nothing more than to comfort her, but he, too, remained silent.

Miska left the tent, debating whether or not he should seek Ravenna out and put this to rights. It felt wrong to be at odds with her. He need not have wondered. She was waiting for him a few paces away, her wings folded around herself to shield from the sun or to keep her warm as the day had barely begun to dissipate the chill of desert night. Miska knew also that this was a sign of her discomfort with the current situation, a way for her to close in on herself. He stepped forward to approach her and was immediately pulled aside.

"I've seen many a woman brooding when their man has done something wrong. I would suggest you leave her be," Sisu said. He jerked his head towards Ravenna. When she turned and watched Sisu and Miska, her icy eyes were unexpressive. He wished that she would rage at him, that she would beat him with her wings or yell or show anything but this icy emptiness. When she had displayed such emptiness before, during her time at the Red Palace, she had been in the midst of despair. Her ice, her lack of feeling came from that. This was something deeper, as if she had cast aside all emotions in favour of emptiness for the purpose of doing what had to be done. She was darker, deeper, stiller.

"Are you telling me this as a friend or as her father?" Miska asked, turning his gaze away from Ravenna. He felt the bite behind the words and almost wished that Sisu would have winced. But the man did nothing more than smirk.

"It doesn't matter. Whatever has happened to cause the argument, it was your doing not mine. She will punish me in her own way, just as she punishes you in her own way, now."

Miska pulled his arm from Sisu's grasp and looked warily to where Ravenna had turned back to studying the array of people before her. The sylphs had begun mingling in with the humans. It was easier to do that than to have to fly back and forth every day from their encampment. Especially now with news of this new impending threat. Training drills had begun again, as had the organising of weapons and supplies. This was now no more a place where the future was to be decided by words and discussion. This was once more a place of war, and no one appeared to be pleased by that.

"I don't think she does that. Punish, I mean. She just takes every blow as if it were deserved."

Sisu rubbed his jaw with his hand, eyes flicking over to where she stood silently. He took in a breath and let it out, possibly whistling as he did, though Miska could not tell by the movement of Sisu's mouth.

"She is a mysterious one, that. And I thought her mother was a mystery. But she loves you. I can tell you that much. So whatever it is that you've done, apologise." Sisu clapped Miska on the shoulder, causing him to stumble forwards. Miska grumbled and rubbed the offending limb. Sisu walked away, seemingly unconcerned by everything.

Miska sighed and shook his head, moving his hand from his arm to his neck and upper back, massaging the aches there. He still felt the ridges on his back. They were improving, no longer impeding his movement, but they were not fading as they had before. Perhaps he was still using too much magic. Perhaps he should stop worrying about things he could not fix and worry about things he could.

Deciding it was probably safer to take Sisu's advice, Miska advanced towards Ravenna, reaching out with his hand and calling out to her. She turned. There was a slight smile on her face, enough to make Miska's heart swell. And then, there was screaming in his mind.

The pressure filled his head, forcing him to his knees. The screaming was overwhelming, dripping with rage. The pressure inside his head seemed to throb in time with the suddenly changing pressure outside. Sand was kicked up and thrown into the air with abandon, swirling around the humans and the sylphs. Miska clapped his hands to his ears, ineffectually keeping out the screams. He tried with his magic to push it away, but it did nothing. He looked to the sky. And he trembled.

Out of the shadows of the mountains, a dragon bore down on them.

Cavaris, scales shining white in the desert sun, red eyes gleaming even from such a distance, his wings beating the air mercilessly, descended upon the encampment. He settled his massive bulk some several tens of meters away from the tents, his long neck twining through the air, his fangs bared and snarling. In the back of Miska's mind, Beringer roared and barrelled towards the dragon. His familiar paused when he recalled Allora still on his back, but the anger remained to amplify Miska's own.

This was the dragon that had ruined Miska's chances of bringing more people with him to fight against Davorin and now Seraphina. It was because of Cavaris that they now faced the impossible decision of whether to flee or die. And here he was, come to scream rage at Miska. He knew that he could not fight the dragon, could not win. He was nothing more than a speck to the dragon, some insignificant creature who would die shortly. That did not stop him from wanting to try.

Only, someone else had gotten there first.

In the time that Miska fell to his knees and regained enough composure to be able to look at what he faced, Ravenna had drawn her swords and was running towards Cavaris. He could see her wings folding in the shape of the Dalketh, that battle form that had seen her through so much. The other sylphs hesitated, though; they were uncertain what to do when faced with a being out of their stories, one dangerous enough to kill them all. Ravenna did not hesitate.

Cavaris' voice rang out in Miska's mind, directed at Ravenna and heard by all. *You think to face me? Insignificant bird.*

The dragon lashed out with his tail, sweeping it towards Ravenna. In a move so fluid that it had to have been pure instinct, muscle memory learned over a lifetime, Ravenna dropped her right wing and slid her body along that line, her left-wing folding behind her and then snapping up as the dragon's tail passed overhead. She knocked it out of the way, following behind with a slice from her sword. Cavaris roared, his maw opening and showing fangs and fire.

Ravenna was unfazed. She dashed forwards, getting close enough to Cavaris that he would have a hard time fighting her off. She was too close for him to use his claws without harming himself. His wings were too large to beat her back. He snapped at her with his jaws, only to find that she had moved too quickly for him.

Ravenna leaped onto his side, climbing up by digging her feet into his scales, beating her wings to move her forwards and upwards. Cavaris twisted and turned, writhing beneath her. He got close enough to nearly take her wing off, for which he received a slice across the nose. He roared again, the sound echoing through Miska's mind, and released a torrent of magical fire. Ravenna was too slow.

Miska screamed, throwing everything he had at the dragon, putting a barrier, a tapestry of glowing threads, between Ravenna and the flames.

His vision blackened, going as dark as his hearing. He fell face first into the sand, feeling the grit dig into his skin. A few moments later and his sight returned, both blurry and sharp simultaneously. Cavaris stood before him, wearing his human guise, the horns rising from his head, splitting his white hair and contrasting his furious red eyes. In front of him stood Ravenna, a burn across her left shoulder, the edges touching the scars that the desert lion had left. She was breathing heavily, her swords still drawn, her wings spread wide as she stood between Cavaris and Miska.

You think to stand in my way? I will kill you and use your wings for decoration. I will drag my claws down your spine. Stand aside sylph. You will never fly again if you do not stand aside!

The words burned in Miska's mind, making him wince further. Ravenna said something in return, which made Cavaris tilt his head and consider. Miska wished he could hear what she said, but she was there and she was well and that was what mattered. He sat up and climbed to his feet as best he could, the pain in his back throbbing but not overwhelming.

The dragon sneered and lifted his chin at whatever Ravenna

had said. *Do you think I care whether you can fly or not? You have attacked me!*

Ravenna shook her head, her black feathers bristling. Miska tried to reach her, tried to get close enough to push her aside and face Cavaris' wrath himself, but she stood firmly between them, too far away for his sluggish movements.

Cavaris turned to Miska, brows drawn. *She says that she was protecting you and her people. She says that she will take any punishment that I thought to mete out on them for herself.*

"No," Miska pleaded. Ravenna stiffened but did not turn to face him. She just kept her wings wide. "Please."

I have no intention of killing those here, little bird...despite my threats. I came only for him. And not to kill him. Cavaris pointed at Miska, the claws on the tip of his fingers touched with red where he must have managed to graze Ravenna. Miska stepped forward, staggering as he put out a hand to touch Ravenna's wing, to calm her. The appendage fluttered away from him and she folded her wings at last. She turned to look at him.

"Ravenna," Miska said. "This is Cavaris. He trained me in my magic. He helped me."

Ravenna nodded, but her expression simply darkened. Miska recalled that he had shown her the images of Cavaris during their journey down to the Red Palace. She knew the price of that help.

A figure ran past the two of them, small and swift. She launched herself at Cavaris, wrapping her arms around his side. The dragon smiled and awkwardly patted Allora's head. His menace seemed to dissipate with Allora's presence, instead becoming the philosophical and infuriating dragon Miska had known.

It is good to see you as well, child.

Allora tilted her head up, her face showing enough for Miska to read her mouth as she spoke, words accusing. "You let us come down here alone. You wouldn't help Miska. Or

Ravenna. And now they say that I have to go away because someone else is coming to fight them. Someone stronger."

You know full well, child, that I had no intention of fighting. Nor had I any intention of propagating war and bloodshed.

Ravenna said something, her mouth moving out of the corner of Miska's eye. He was too slow to catch what she said, but he could guess that it was something along the lines of "why are you here, then." She knew his anger towards Cavaris. She knew how much he wanted the dragon to suffer for what he had done. What he *hadn't* done. Miska felt a presence on his other side and looked up to see Sisu, the large man glowering at the dragon.

I came for you Miska, Cavaris said, still communicating mind to mind so that all could hear and understand. *You have done something. You have broken the fabric of existence. That monster that Davorin summoned, the one that you saw him wield seasons ago, it was the cause. I felt it die and I felt its essence slip into the cracks. Widening them. What have you done?*

Cavaris bared his fangs. They grew longer even in his human form. White scales formed around his eyes which seemed to pulsate with power.

"*I* killed the monster. The dragon-thing," Ravenna said, turning her head to Miska to be sure that he saw her speak. "You came for me."

It was not a dragon. It was the shadow of the demon trying to reassert itself in the world. A nightmare that should have been forgotten and left to rot where we buried its form...You say that you were the one responsible for killing it? Cavaris tilted his head and examined Ravenna, inhaling deeply. Ravenna faced Cavaris as calm and still as ever. Miska knew that the burn across her shoulder must be in agony, but she did not seem to notice it. She just stood between him and danger. Again.

"Yes," Ravenna said simply. "I killed it."

Cavaris considered her, silent for a few moments. He took

a breath and the scales and fangs retreated into something more human. Not that anyone would mistake him for human, even with hands and feet. He blinked, his red eyes flashing with magic. *Do you know what you have done? In killing something born of magic—no matter how corrupted—without taking the proper steps, you have changed things in ways that cannot be predicted.*

"Things of magic have died in the past," Ravenna countered. "Yet we still continue to exist."

The changes that have been wrought cannot be predicted. Cavaris curled a lip, but said nothing more.

"I know nothing of magic. But I know that this thing needed to die. So whatever cracks that it made in the world, whatever reality fracturing events that will unfold from this, it is not my fault. It is Davorin's. Or yours, for not burying your relics better," Ravenna said. At the last words, her eyes shadowed with fury. A moment later and the shadow was gone.

The implications of this are many. But...As you say, it is possible that I moved too swiftly. Nevertheless the ramifications must be dealt with.

"You will stay," Miska said. It was not a question. He could see the resolve in Cavaris' eyes. He was merely one more complication in the upcoming battle that would decide what course the rest of the war took. If the war would end, or if another would begin. Cavaris would witness it all, even when he was wished elsewhere. Miska knew the answer to Ravenna's next question before she even asked it.

"Will you help us fight? Will you defend us, fight on our side against Seraphina?" Ravenna clenched her fist at her side and her wings rustled, but that was all the emotion she showed. For Miska it was like shouting, a desperate plea into the void. The void shook his head.

I swore generations ago that I would never fight in battle again. I will not be responsible for more death. I will not be charged with answering to crimes that are the making of you and yours. I will stay. But I will not fight.

"Miska was right," Ravenna said. She shook her head and sheathed her swords. She turned and Miska saw the words, felt their whisper in his mind. "You are a coward. By your inaction, you may doom us all…And yet, I understand."

CHAPTER FOURTEEN

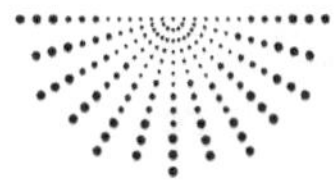

"If they are travelling through the desert to come attack us, then they will not be prepared for an offensive attack in the meanwhile," Lenore said, leaning back in her chair at the table in the council tent with a slight wince as she shifted her weight to accommodate her pregnancy. Miska shook his head, trying to bite back the disbelief at such a comment. Had he not conveyed the danger that they faced well enough? Had he not described the size of the army to sufficient specifications? All he knew was that he was now sitting in a counsel with Lenore, Desarra, Sisu, Ravenna and her two generals and that it was not going well.

Tensions had already been high, and now they were close to splintering. Ravenna had argued against this new battle to Miska, and then remained silent when he disagreed. Now, she was alone in her opinion and he was on the other side. Things had not improved from there.

"We don't have the forces for an initial strike," Ravenna said. She sat in one of the chairs around the table with her arms folded and her feathers fluttering in annoyance. Her expression was calm but she was obviously worked up about this, something that Miska had seen only rarely. Her sister spoke, the words somewhat familiar and yet still foreign. He could only grasp about a third of what she was saying, which was why Ravenna was translating.

"She wishes to know why a surprise attack like before would not work again. These people would not be expecting attack from the skies."

"Did you explain the nature of the army we face?" Miska asked. Beside him, Cavaris sat, listening to every word that was said and offering no insight or support or critique. He just watched. His presence seemed to unsettle many on this war council, though they talked and argued all the same. Miska was still unsure as to why the dragon was there. Why he chose to listen to this discussion of blood and death and war.

I find all of this translation tedious. You will never decide anything if you are continuously translating and interpreting. Would anyone mind if I wove a spell so that we could all communicate well with each other for this particular meeting? Cavaris spread his claws to encompass the entire table. No one made any objection, though the sylphs' wings shuffled slightly. Cavaris took in a breath and breathed out, blowing air over all who were at the table. Miska felt the pressure of the spell on his mind and then it faded, a far more elegant solution than anything he could ever have come up with. Just another example of how much power the dragon held in his apathetic claws.

"The reason that we cannot attack from the skies is because our forces are diminished. Seraphina's army is triple that of Davorin's. We are down three whole companies, not to mention the others that have been seriously injured and sent back to Shinalea, or who are recuperating here until they can fly. We could send at most half of those we came with." Ravenna traced a finger on the table, drawing out numbers as she spoke. Her general Crispinus shook his head.

He paced behind Desarra, wings opening and folding as he walked, like a shadow eager to strike. "Even with our forces diminished the advantage would be ours. An aerial force against people trapped on an open landscape would be difficult to fight."

"The people of Southron are expert archers," Lenore replied, frowning. "They hunt and fight from a distance before finishing their kills up close. Each one of them is trained with the bow and the arrow. You would have to eliminate a goodly number of them before you even came into range of their bows or you would all be cut down."

Brianna snorted. Miska could understand why it was that Ravenna had chosen the large-winged sylph for her general; she was obviously capable and well-liked amongst her people, as well as powerful and intelligent. But she was also prone to arguing and she did not care for humans at all, despite knowing Ravenna's connection. Miska did not like her overmuch. "We have trained archers of our own. And I doubt that they could hit a target that moves as fast as we do with Dalketh on our side."

Ravenna curled her lip and shook her head. "Dalketh is not a perfect form. It is an effective one, but we can still be killed. Easily."

Brianna shuffled her wings, flaring them upwards in a display of dominance. They were large enough that the tips brushed the edges of the tent, making it feel smaller for all of them. The two queens in the Council straightened and looked at Brianna with fire flashing in their eyes. Neither said anything. "You trained us, Warlord, to fight a battle against impossible odds. We always knew that the humans would outnumber us, perhaps ten to one. That did not stop us from training or from following you into battle. Yet you would rather have us do what? Hide away? Flee back to Shinalea with our wings clipped? Or would you rather have us abandon the island entirely and vanish into the unknown?"

"I do not know what all the options would be as an alternative to facing this Seraphina. A battle with Davorin was the only option when he led. I do not know her. Miska says that she will fight. I believe him. But we do not have the ability to fight back on her terms. Or even ours. Not without heavy casualties. Yet you seem unwilling to even *discuss* an alternative. Are you so changed—are we all so changed—from what we were to this? Have you grown so fond of the taste of blood?" Ravenna locked eyes with her general, icy blue staring down the fiery amber. After a few heartbeats, Brianna looked away.

"Cavaris?" Lenore asked, interrupting the argument to between the sylphs before it could escalate further. "I'm told that you will not help us in our endeavours to win freedom and to stand independent from those who would oppress us. With your power on our side, we could easily be free from the tyrants that seek to silence us."

Miska saw the dragon's head shake, perhaps with a silent chuckle evidenced by the faint smile that stretched across his mouth. Outrage flared across Lenore's features as Cavaris smiled wide enough to expose a fang, his gaze focused on the table beneath his fingers. Miska felt that familiar anger flare in his stomach, crawling up his throat. He wanted to bind Cavaris as he had Davorin. He wanted to throttle the dragon. All this death could have been prevented if he hadn't done *nothing*.

Instead, Cavaris spoke, his mouth moving smoothly, almost gracefully. "Pretty speeches will not sway my mind. Do you not think that your servant did his best to persuade me of that all those moons in the Iron Mountains? I am firm in my resolve. You humans and sylphs may choose to do battle and invoke bloodshed however you like. I see no need to be involved in incurring death."

"Do you not incur death by doing nothing?" Desarra asked tilting her head. Miska hadn't had a chance to converse with Ravenna's sister, but he had seen enough to know that she held great power in her wings. Little of it had to do with the diadem that she wore on her brow. It was more to do with her bearing and the way that she commanded respect. Even Ravenna, who held a power of her own, seemed to respect her.

Cavaris just scoffed.

"Your lives are insignificant compared to the countless cycles that I hold within my wings. I have been alive for numerous generations. I was there at the beginning of the Fire Wars, and I remained awake when my kin slept. I have seen nations rise and I have seen nations fall. I have watched the decline of humankind and the disappearance of the elves and the sylphs. I have seen the shadren and the nusox vanish to far off corners, becoming less than legends, mere whispers on the wind. I have seen a landscape change as it was watered with blood. Death will come to you no matter what I do. I refuse to have blood on my claws. So you may say that I incur more death by doing nothing, but I know that if I were to fight, there would be nothing left to die at all. *That's* the power I withhold from you." Cavaris' mouth moved with a sharp twist, a sneer hidden by fangs. Contempt.

"It is no use asking for help from him," Miska growled, unable to remain quiet any longer. "Any assistance that he does offer will be met with conditions and will be revoked or adjusted at any time that he chooses. He basks in his superiority, his magical power grown so strong while the other dragons sleep. He cares nothing for any of us. And he never will."

Cavaris turned to Miska with a frown, his slitted eyes narrowed. He opened his mouth to speak, but Ravenna cut him off, her expression sharper and more dangerous than the dragon's. She had faced him down once and Miska could see that she would happily do it again. "We are, as always, on our own. Are you content with throwing away all that we have worked for, all that we have built, on some pitched battle with human forces? Fighting Davorin was one thing, but you seem to take that victory as a sign that we can battle anyone, win anything."

"We are Stormbringers," Crispin said. He lifted his dark chin, brows drawn. "Our ancestors brought the Storm to end wars. We were the demise of battles, the forces that could halt slaughter or cause it. Our numbers were always few, and yet our ancestors prevailed. They always prevailed."

Ravenna surged upwards, her black wings spread wide, light shining through the feathers. "Then why did they die out?"

Silence.

The sylphs, Desarra included, looked away. The humans studied Ravenna for a moment before they too looked away. Even Sisu lowered his gaze. Cavaris merely sighed, his shoulders moving with the effort. Ravenna sank back into her chair. Miska wanted to reach across the table and draw her into his arms, to provide that quiet comfort that had supported her before. But now was not the time. Now they were deciding their fate. And no matter what faced them, Miska did not want to flee.

Lenore swallowed, her throat tightening as she did so. Miska focused his attention on her mouth, catching the hesitant twist. "If we gather support from the resistance, then perhaps we have more resources than previously thought. Many of my armies, my people that remained under Davorin's rule, have returned. They are perhaps weak and injured from the battle, but—"

Ravenna sat back and scoffed silently. She said nothing, just leaned back and watched. Miska wondered what she watched for, but he did not dare ask. Crispin turned to Ravenna and inclined his head. She waved a wing for him to speak as he would.

He turned to Lenore. "What resistance is this?"

"In the last several cycles, Davorin and his brother Dagan managed to conquer many small fiefdoms and kingdoms and city states and independent nations. They all folded relatively easily and without much fighting, meaning that many of the warriors and soldiers were still alive. A good number of those banded together to form a resistance, preparing to destabilise the Salusian Empire so that they could regain their independence. I have offered them any assistance that I could in hopes that we could return the Red Desert to its rightful place."

Lenore tightened her mouth, blinking uncertainly at Ravenna, before continuing. "My former training master Vareis is one of their key leaders. She and another have been gathering resources and doing what they can to help."

Ravenna spoke with emotionless expression, neither accusing nor encouraging. "They were there when they we attacked Davorin's army?"

Lenore shifted. She did not have to speak for Miska to know the answer she would give. He had fought exclusively on the side of the sylphs, facing down their enemies. He and Sisu were the only humans that had stood against Davorin's forces. The resistance had not been there.

"Your people moved swiftly. The resistance were not yet ready to mobilise. But now that we have sufficient warning, it is possible that they will move with us, fight against Seraphina." Lenore's hands shook as she rested against her stomach.

"If this is true, then it could be a great boon," Desarra said, folding her fingers together and leaning forwards. "Any help to even the odds…"

"I will ask," Lenore whispered, lips barely moving. Miska swallowed, seeing the uncertainty in her eyes. He had never seen her uncertain until recently. She had always been strong and proud and now she did not even know whether she could help her people. He wanted to look away, but he had to keep watching to know what was being said.

Brianna turned to Miska. "And what of you? You are a sorcerer to match Davorin. I saw you. You used magic to fight against his people, shaped like wolves and bears to tear them apart. Could you not do great damage against this new human's assault?"

Ravenna stiffened, her eyes widening a fraction. Was this concern, and more, for him? Miska hoped it would be so, but he knew that he could not give in to her concern. He could not hide in her arms with her wings wrapped around him. The ridges on his back were fading, but he felt them twinge at that moment. A shiver ran down his spine. He had to be here to help his people, his queen. Even if it went against Ravenna's concern.

Miska licked his lips against the dryness of the desert, his body not yet acclimated. Or so he hoped; he did not want his own doubts to rule him. He took a moment more before answering. "I have magic, I suppose. I have used much in the last few days, but I believe that I should been recovered enough to do some damage. I do not know if it will be enough."

Cavaris spoke, interrupting the plans for war. *If you do this, then your price may be higher than you can imagine.* The thought brushed Miska's mind, a whisper. The dragon's mouth had not moved, so the warning statement was for him alone. He looked away from Cavaris and chose not to respond.

"So it is decided then," Crispin said, a glint in his amber eyes. "We will fight a war, prepare a preemptive strike. Whatever ground forces we can assemble with the sylphs above."

Ravenna turned her head away from him.

"We would like you at our side, Warlord. We want to fight with you leading us. You taught us to fight, after all. To be fierce in the face of danger. To not fear the potential overwhelming odds that stood in our way. You taught us to be strong, to channel the spirit of the Stormbringers that came before. And we won. The cost might be high in this new fight, but we are prepared to pay it. We would greatly appreciate having you fight on our side. You need not be afraid for us. You were the one who told us we could be warriors. That we *were* warriors. And you are the greatest amongst us."

Ravenna's icy calm shattered. She rose to her feet and beat her wings twice, drawing sand up from the ground and causing it to streak through the air. She slammed her hands to the table and bared her teeth, feral. And she screamed. "*I was wrong!*"

The other sylphs in the tent drew their wings in close, eyes wide. Lenore cradled her belly. Even Miska drew back. Cavaris was the only one who made no movement, eyes watching Ravenna with interest.

"I should have remained here, no matter how much pain it would cause me. I should have destroyed that tome that spoke of the others on Shinalea. I should have fought Davorin myself before he could become this monster that you all seem so terrified of, no matter his current, helpless state. I should have never returned to Shinalea, even if it meant my demise." Ravenna's chest heaved as she sucked in breath to continue speaking. Miska's heart cracked in that moment, seeing the pain in her eyes and knowing the inevitable outcome of this council. "I should have left you all in peace. The cost is always high. Too high. We have already lost so many. And now we face another entity, another enemy. And if you win this battle, there will be another one after that and another and another until there is *nothing left*. And even if we win, what will we have bought? Our society of philosophy, of art and music and fetes, it will no longer exist. We will be warmongers, blood drinkers. There will be no going back. I was wrong to ever think that this was the right path. War might be what *I* was made for, but I should have spared you. I cannot take all of this back, though. So if you choose to go and die, then the consequences lie with you. I will not watch it unfold."

Without another glance at anyone in the tent, she left. In her place was a void that pulled at Miska, like part of him had shattered with her and vanished, also.

Cavaris was the one that broke the silence. He seemed unaffected, the only one without wounds from Ravenna's words.

"So what will you do now that your Warlord has spoken?"

All eyes turned to Desarra. She turned her eyes to Crispin. To Miska. To Lenore. To Brianna. To Sisu. And then she spoke, her mouth moving slowly as though an echo after Ravenna's outburst. "We fly to war."

CHAPTER FIFTEEN

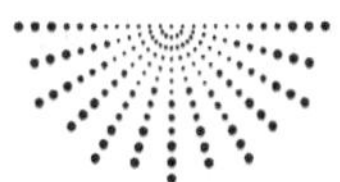

*L*enore was not certain what it was that brought her to this place. She should have been glad to have nothing more to do with Davorin. But the remains of her army —people still loyal to her—had moved on and prepared to go fight an enemy in the desert, and she could not follow. Her heart pounded in fear every moment she waited and did nothing. So instead she stood outside Davorin's tent, the sylphs and one of the human guards gone, leaving only one human in their place. The guard watched Lenore, sympathy in his eyes, but said nothing as she stood before the tent.

She wrung her hands and paced, her footprints smoothing out the sand. Davorin was bound. His magic was no danger to her. He could not fight. He had no power anymore. Not over her, not over her people.

Why, then, was she afraid?

Lenore took a deep breath, the calming effect negated by the kicks that the child she carried placed to her side. She shook her head. Took another breath to soothe her and ignore the pain from her child. Then, she pushed her way inside the tent, the canvas flaps falling into place behind her and muffling the sound of an empty camp.

She had expected to see Davorin, bound in chains, eyes wild and raging. She had expected to be confronted with his hate, his ranting fury and a violent madness that would explain his actions these last moons. She did not expect to see Beringer laying placidly off to one side, eyes watching as Allora drew pictures in the sand with Davorin as her playmate, completely docile.

Lenore's breath caught.

"Lenore!" Allora leapt up and ran to Lenore, wrapping her arms around the Queen's leg. She looked up and smiled. Lenore had spent little time with Miska's foundling, instead watching her from a distance while she dealt with any number of more important things that her position required. But the child was endearing from even that far. "I came to teach draw. Miska gone, Beringer stayed, so come to play."

"You have picked up our tongue well." Lenore ran her hand over Allora's pale blonde hair and wondered if the child she carried was a daughter or a son. If her child would grow up and play with Allora as friend. She had never wanted children, but this was her lot now and she would do her best to be a good mother. As Miska had become a father to this child, so would Lenore work to become a mother. But a mother was not a queen. Could she truly raise a child and still lead her people?

"Miska teach me some. I learn other." Lenore nodded and smiled more praise at the child, though her thoughts were elsewhere, in a place of shadows. Allora gave her one more squeeze and then turned back to go play with Davorin in the sand. They chattered at each other, a mix of languages that moved too quickly for Lenore to follow, but which they both seemed to understand with ease. Davorin obeyed Allora's every order, drawing out pictures. And when Allora rubbed them out, he did not even bite back. He played. He laughed. He sounded more like a child then the heir apparent to the Salusian Empire.

Whatever reason Lenore had for coming here, one she did not even know herself, it fell away.

Something else in her broke.

She could not ask Davorin why he had done all those things, to her, to Ravenna, to her people. She could not get the answers to questions she hadn't even known existed until then. She could not even gloat. That man—that *monster*—was gone. In his place was a child, a person with an entirely different soul. One Lenore did not recognise. With this realisation came the understanding that Ravenna had been right, at least about Davorin. His mind was so far gone that there would be little point in punishing him for his crimes. He did not even know what those crimes were. Nor could he understand their consequences. For all intents and purposes, Davorin was dead. In his place was someone more suited to telling stories and playing games with Allora, watched over by Beringer.

And yet, proof of Davorin's wrongs resided in Lenore. The child she carried was his as well. She had never worried that the child would be a reminder of what had happened to her, not when she had the presence of its father to do that job. Now Davorin was gone and Lenore's world was—no matter the outcome of the next few days—irrevocably changed. Her world was shattered, more than she had thought. Picking up the pieces would require more from her than her defiant strutting around, playing resistance with fools who were too coward to fight, pretending that all of this was just a setback, that things would return to the way they were.

She was going to have a *child*. Would it remind her of what she had lost or would it help her to move forwards? Her throat tightened, fearful of the answer.

She closed her eyes and turned to go.

"Things are not the same," Davorin said. Lenore turned to

look at him. He was looking at her, not at Allora or the pictures in the sand. His eyes were unexpectedly solemn. "You want things to be the same. But they aren't. This stream of time does not bend back upon itself. It only moves forwards, carrying its currents left or right into a river or out to sea. But the shadows…Our shadows. They remain."

Allora turned to look at Lenore as well, her face and her expression no longer belonging to the cheerful child that she had been. She said nothing, only studied Lenore for a moment before turning back to her play. Davorin joined her. And an emptiness yawned inside Lenore, wrapping its fingers around her heart.

She fled.

LENORE RAN straight into another figure. She stumbled backwards and the figure reached out a hand to steady her. It was Desarra, the Chosen Queen of the sylphs and Ravenna's sister. Lenore had dealt with her during the council sessions and found her to be remarkably capable. She was perhaps not fully aware of all of the situations, but that was more a lack of knowledge than a lack of understanding. Obviously Desarra had changed just as much as everyone else since Ravenna had described her sister to Lenore all those seasons ago. Desarra was not what she had expected.

Now she stood before Lenore, her expression troubled, but calm. Lenore would have thought that the sylph, burnished gold hair and fiery eyes with wings that were like sun on shadow, would be off leading her people into battle since Ravenna had remained behind. Instead, she wore no armour and no weapons, her clothing the simple desert style, the only indication of her station the gold diadem she wore.

"Careful," Desarra said. Lenore wondered if it was a growing understanding or whether Cavaris's translation spell lingered and made the word clear. "You must be cautious for your child."

Lenore spread her fingers on her stomach, her throat suddenly tight. She choked back a sob.

Before she could take a breath and regain the dignity expected of a queen, especially one who had recently regained her kingdom, Desarra had whisked her away into the privacy of a small tent. It was a storage tent, holding supplies for healers and for food preparation. With the bulk of their forces off to battle, they would not need this right away. They were safe to talk for a while.

"I'm surprised that you were…that you remained behind," Lenore said before she could choke up again. Desarra gave a wing-shrug, the motion so like Ravenna that Lenore was struck by its movement.

"I… I made a promise to Ravenna and to my mate. I could accompany them to battle, but I would have to remain on the sidelines with the healers. Ravenna asked me not to follow in her wing beats. She wanted me to be safe, to be sure that I could lead our people into whatever future remains to us. That request seems so pointless now that she has stepped aside. And yet, the others still flew off without me. I feel a little useless." Desarra did not look at Lenore as she spoke, instead inspecting the various supplies in the tent. A mound of bedrolls, a crate of dried fruits, her fingers now ran over a selection of bandages and poultices encased in wax covered clay.

Lenore nodded. She rubbed her eye with her hand, brushing away the remains of her unfathomable emotions. "I have felt useless for moons now."

"How could you feel useless? You are carrying a child. You are a great queen and you will be a mother. I know that you were suppressed under Davorin, that you sacrificed much for your people, but that is far from uselessness."

Desarra stepped forward, her wings shuffling against her

back. Her hand reached out almost as if to touch Lenore's stom-ach, but she pulled back. Lenore took Desarra's hand and pressed it to where the child was kicking, pressure building against her organs. Desarra's eyes widened. She smiled.

"It *felt* useless. This child is mine, yes, but it is also the offspring of the madman that resides in that tent. The madman your sister wanted to hunt and to kill. He stole my *people* from me. He made it so that my sacrifice to protect them meant that I had to sit in my room and weave when I should have been governing, ruling. And all I have to show for it is his child. My child, too. I can't even hate him anymore. I just..." Lenore rubbed her eyes again, somehow still surprised when they came away streaked with moisture. She scoffed and lifted her eyes to the roof of the tent, blinking away the tears. "I am not a warrior queen. I was never trained in the fine art of battle, though I knew enough to protect myself. But...I feel as though I have done nothing for moons but watch Davorin pour sand into the foundation of my kingdom. It is crumbling beneath me and I don't know how to stop it. And now my forces are gone off to war with a new threat. Ravenna is broken. Miska, my friend, is changed beyond recognition. What do I have left?"

Desarra picked up a strand of Lenore's auburn hair. She ran it through her fingers, her touch light and soothing. The sylph queen stepped around behind Lenore and gathered up her hair, carefully unknotting it with her fingers, manipulating it. Lenore closed her eyes, the feeling exotic and sublime. Blodwen often did Lenore's hair, brushing it or helping to wash it, but this was different. Blodwen had the respect of his servant, a friend yes, but someone who believed that Lenore's status was higher. There would always be a barrier there. But this was respect between equals. They did not need to explain their actions, only did what was right and necessary for their people.

Desarra's fingers flowed rhythmically through Lenore's hair.

It was friendly. It was soothing. And it pushed Lenore's eyes to water openly.

"I was going to have a child," Desarra said, her voice barely above a whisper. Lenore straightened her shoulders at that, but said nothing. "Sylphs do not bear young easily. The Intellecti have studied it for generations, but no matter what concoctions they come up with, or understanding of our anatomy or biology, they cannot improve the chances of childbirth. Only one in three pregnancies results in a child. And it takes a great deal to become pregnant. I was *so* close. I *so* wanted it. Almost more than being the Chosen Queen. I thought I was being punished for being so selfish, for wanting that child above anything."

"It is not selfish to want a child." Lenore resisted the urge to press her hand against her stomach again. Instead, she relaxed into Desarra's ministrations of her hair.

"My people had Ravenna to lead them. She was—is—their Warlord. She was doing more to lead them into the new era than I ever could. So I thought that having a child would be my contribution, my legacy. My proof of my love for Crispin." Desarra paused, her fingers stilling long enough for Lenore to look over her shoulder. The sylphs queen's eyes were wide, shining gently in the dim light in the tent. She took a breath and shook her head. "Ravenna found me after…after I lost him, my child. I hated her for being there and witnessing my failure. Everything was being taken from me. But it was not her fault. And it was not my fault. It was no one's fault. It was just the way things were. You sacrificed your freedom to keep your people from being destroyed. You were given the opportunity to have a child with a human that you despised, to save your people. You took it. And you will bear this child until it sees the light of day. And I would imagine that you will not once think of all that you have lost when you hold it in your arms."

"How can you be sure?" Lenore asked. She turned around to face Desarra, one hand resting on either side of her stomach.

"How can you be sure that I won't blame this child for everything? That I will love it?"

Desarra nodded her head, eyes flashing to Lenore's hands. "Because you are gentle. You hold it gently, and you speak gently. I need no more fact that."

Oh, to be sure that it would be true.

Desarra dropped Lenore's fingers and turned away, pacing around the small tent again, her fingers brushing over the items she had already touched. She lingered over one of the jars of poultice. "I wish I were not just standing here and doing nothing. Ravenna will not let me talk with her. And I know nothing of the healing arts to help prepare."

A thought occurred in Lenore's mind, widening and blooming into fruition. "I was told by Miska that the child I bear is not Davorin's only offspring. That Seraphina was going to use another child of his—his firstborn—against him, to solidify her control over the region. Over the Empire. She will not have taken the child to war, for fear that it would be lost. That means that it still remains at the Red Palace. Were someone able to go fetch the child, to claim it, then perhaps some of her leverage would be taken. Perhaps further options could be presented. For all our peoples."

Desarra stiffened, as though Lenore's words had offended her or struck some cord of anger within her. Her wings trembled slightly, the feathers barely moving under her ironclad control. "A human child. You suggest...A human child."

"I cannot raise it. The lines of succession would be blurred and we might have the same situation in twenty cycles. But...I am not the only possibility." Lenore stepped forward, feeling a strength and purpose rise in her. "Ravenna could not fly, and she still managed to make an imprint on your society. To be something great. Would a human child really be any different?"

Desarra lowered her chin, the gold on her brow winking in the low light. "Is it a male or female?"

"Female. A girl."

Desarra swallowed, casting her eyes to the sands beneath their feet. She turned her back on Lenore and went to the entrance to the small tent, pulling back the canvas flap far enough to see out into the dwindling daylight.

"Do you think they will return?" Lenore asked, the words falling out of her mouth before she could stop them. She had not wanted to voice her concerns out loud. She had quietly prayed to The Watcher that she would do almost anything to see her people and the sylphs return. But she was afraid that they would not. That the nightmare of Seraphina—one that she had not even imagined in all of her time—would come to fruition. Seraphina had been cunning and sharp and clever when Lenore had met her at her wedding. But she had not sensed any ambition to ruin that which her brothers held. Only the desire to encourage a small amount of trouble. Lenore had assumed it was from boredom. She had underestimated Seraphina, even Davorin had underestimated Seraphina, and the price was on all their heads. This was so much more than boredom. And Lenore had sent her people—the last fighting forces that she commanded—to face her.

Desarra gave another wing shrug. She took a deep breath and wrapped her arms around her middle, her wings folding in close. "I hope so. Ravenna was a great teacher. She inspired us to become something so much greater than what we were. But I don't know if that will be enough. Her disagreement, her belief that we should find an alternative, it shook Crispin more than I've seen in him for some time. Even when he learned of my loss, he was not quite as uncertain as I saw him today."

Lenore nodded. Ravenna's outburst had disturbed her, too. But perhaps not for the same reasons. "I am told that they should meet Seraphina's army by midmorning. It will not be too much longer after that when we know the truth."

Desarra reached out and took Lenore's hand, squeezing it.

She licked her lips, her eyes wide. The colouring was distinct, the wings larger, but Desarra was so much like Ravenna that it was hard not to see her sister standing there. "Can we be stronger than the history that made us?"

"By The Watcher, so I pray."

Desarra nodded. Smiled. And without another word, she left the tent. Lenore knew that if she were to leave also, she would see Desarra's winged form flying off into the early evening. To go find her purpose while her people flew to war. To go take a human child and make it her own.

CHAPTER SIXTEEN

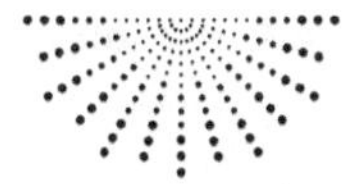

I have never known sylphs to be so angry as you are. It is curious.

Ravenna looked up from where she was studying the encampment laid out on the sands below. She had fled to the hills so that she would not have to explain herself or deal with the unintended consequences of rescinding her decision to accompany her people to war. To face this new demon. To abandon them in their time of need. She had watched them fly off many hours ago as they accompanied the remainder of Lenore's forces and had not yet returned from the hills, choosing to wait vigil alone, so that she could fully feel the pain at what she had done without interference. She wanted to be alone with her decision.

Now, Cavaris was striding serenely towards her, his movements fluid with immortal grace. He acted as though she was not angry at him. As though he had the right to talk with her after all he had done to Miska. It was as though he could understand.

Perhaps he could.

She inhaled deeply; the dragon brought with him the scent

of mountain air, of pine trees and crispness. Miska had borne that scent when he first came. It had soon faded to the familiar scent of dryness and sand. Ravenna had a feeling that Cavaris' scent would not so soon fade; he was slightly more permanent in his nature. He settled beside her, his fingers folded together and relaxed.

"It is not anger," Ravenna said, voice steady and quiet.

Isn't it? He tilted his head, the obsidian horns glinting in the evening light.

Ravenna took another deep breath. "No. It's not anger. It is mostly…pain."

For abandoning your people? Had he not asked the question to her mind with such sincerity, had he not seemed genuinely interested, Ravenna would have ignored him and moved away. As it was, conversation was better than wondering if her people were alive or dead, if Miska would ever return. Suddenly her solitude felt like being back in chains in the Slave Pits.

"Some, I suppose. But then, the fault is mine for bringing this war to them to begin with. I was the one captured. I was the one who reminded the humans that legends have a basis in fact. It was my doing that led Davorin and Nadezhda to discover that I was not alone. After that, I went back to Shinalea. I taught my people the art and the necessity of war. I meant to save them. Now I have led them to their doom."

Cavaris was quiet for a moment. He studied the encampment below, watching the few people who remained moving about. To Ravenna, they seemed so small, so impossibly fragile. She wondered what Cavaris saw when he looked down on them.

His voice was deep, quiet, still. Precisely what she would have expected. She wished it to be different. "Dragons were meant to be guides to the younger races. We were meant to show them what it is to live, how to improve their minds and raise themselves up to be something great. Instead, we went to war for a reason even I have forgotten, and condemned them to death. My brethren sleep, but I remained awake and I have seen the consequences of our actions all those generations ago. I have seen everything we thought we were building fall to pieces, to die. What should have been a great and beautiful world is worse off now than a thousand cycles past. I know what it is to regret. And I know what it is change my mind, to decide to never again be the cause of such pain. I am not well loved for the decision, but I stand by it. It is possible that all of this is your fault, but I find that things are rarely so simple. You are a mortal being, one whose wings, though strong, do not stretch wide. This land would be embroiled in war whether you were here or not. Your capture was chance, or perhaps one of the interference of some of the human gods. Even a Walker, one of the Old Ones, could have exerted their influence on the world. Even if it was pure chance, then it was still not your fault."

Ravenna's eyes rose from studying the people on the flat desert plains below her. She leaned back against a rock, her wings flat and relaxed despite the turmoil she bore inside. The burns on her left shoulder twinged slightly; she pushed that pain away. She had not been healed by Miska or Cavaris, though both had offered. No, she preferred to keep the injury. It would serve as another reminder of her folly. "I have heard your arguments before, though perhaps without the references to beings whose names have long been forgotten. The fact of the matter is that I taught my people battle. I reminded them of the heritage that we had left behind in crumbling tomes. And we won our battle. *My* battle. Now they think they are invincible, more powerful than ever before, no matter what we lost, who we lost. That is my doing. And I would give my wings to have it undone. But they had flown to war without me. The path is set."

Cavaris nodded. He opened one hand and a small ball of red light appeared, lifting into the air and illuminating their position. As the light floated, the sun sank below the horizon and darkness spread. Ravenna almost wished that he would put the light out, but she said nothing.

"I trained Miska, knowing full well that his only goal was to gather forces to return, to fight a war and free his people. He wanted at first to find you to get your assistance. I instead directed him to Sisu, to a man who could help him understand himself. That was what he needed more than running to find help. Every decision he has made since has been his doing, but he has now the knowledge to make his decisions well. I, you could argue, have perpetuated war and death by training the only sorcerer in generations to fight. If you choose to see it that way, then there will be nothing to persuade you otherwise."

Ravenna scoffed and leaned her head back, studying the wisps of clouds against the darkening sky. "Sisu claims to be my father."

Cavaris blinked and tilted his head again. He studied her for a moment, then nodded. "Indeed. I had not seen it before, but it is true. Does this bother you?"

"Not as much as I would have thought," Ravenna admitted. She only reeled at the truth when she had time to think, time to understand what she was. It paled in comparison to what she had done. It was easier to accept it and move on. It was not as though she required a relationship with Sisu; having Tacitus as a heart-father had been strange enough in sylph society, had been enough to ostracise Ravenna further from her people. Yet, she missed Tacitus. She had loved him. She did not need to know or to love Sisu to know who she was. To know her place as the one who had caused so much death. "I think it surprised Sisu more than it did me. He seemed...shocked that his memories were actually real, rather than a figment of his imagination."

"Sisu is, in some ways, a simple man. His thoughts are not varied, but they are deep. He has a firm sense of right and wrong. You could do worse to have his blood running through yours. I am surprised, though you retained your wings. Most human-sylph scions do not." If that was all that Cavaris found significant, then Ravenna would accept it. She did not need to bear her soul to the dragon. Somehow it happened, regardless.

"Flightless wings." She spread her wings, scratching the feathers against the rough rock behind her. "They have weighed me down my whole life. And yet, without them, I would be nothing but an ordinary human. I cannot decide which fate—the one I suffered or the one I avoided—would be worse."

"Yet, you learned to use them. To bend them to your will and to become something new, something greater. That is all that you were offering to your people. And they took it with an eagerness that does not surprise me. Sylphs have always been curious, capable. When your ancestors, the last of the Storm-bringers, failed to return from their final battle, your people fell into great despair. They withdrew from the world, like so many others before them. Like I did." Cavaris studied his claws, shining in the faint red light that he had produced. In the growing darkness, the red became like blood, highlighting the shadow and turning it to gore.

He turned back to watching Ravenna. She wondered if she had that same bloody look in the light. "You have resurrected something powerful and noble. A people whose goal it was to prevent bloodshed, to end war. They did not care if the war was not theirs to fight, if the people had not asked it of them. They knew only that it was their duty, and they did it. They faded from existence not because they could not fight, but because the wars were fought despite the fear of Stormbringers bearing down on the participants. They became a certainty, not a means to prevent what should never have been…With their return, you were a catalyst, but only for familiar patterns. And yet, I am not unsympathetic to your desire not to perpetuate the killing. You have blood in your feathers and on your hands, and you know exactly the price. They do not. Because you hide it behind your mask of stone, behind a heart of ice. You have been trying to protect them this whole time. And in doing so, you have crippled them. They know only the surge of wonder at their newfound skills. They don't know the true cost except mild grief from their losses in a glorious cause."

Ravenna said nothing for a moment, eyes focusing on the red light bobbing gently in front of her. Maybe it wasn't blood that it represented, but was simply a light in the darkness. She reached out a hand to touch it and felt nothing. It was as if it did not even exist. It was not like the touch of Miska's magic, with threads that bound her inevitably to him. It was just there and yet not.

"Hiding your pain does no one any good."

"Odd," Ravenna said, pulling back her hand. "I had thought that it was displaying my pain that called my people to war."

Cavaris inclined his head, a grudging acknowledgment. The two let the conversation fall off, just watching the world as it went by, waiting for whomever would return. Whenever they would return. Ravenna hoped against impossible odds that she was wrong, that her people would prevail. That they were more than she thought. She did not want to do them the disservice of shrouding them in doubt, but nor would she shrink from reality.

She wished she had gone with them. To fight with them and lend her protection for as long as she could. It would change anything, except perhaps her guilty conscience.

"Miska hates you, you know," Ravenna said. She did not know what made her say those words, and she already knew the dragon's pain. He just nodded and accepted the words as fact, leaning back to rest against the rock. Ravenna moved her wings so he would have more space.

"He believes that I purposely and intentionally wronged him, forcing the choice out of him. The choice of whether to push on and possibly injure those that he loved, or to care for them and perhaps lose his chance of bringing an army with him. An impossible decision. And yet I forced him to make it." Cavaris held out a hand and the ball of light hovered above his palm. He smiled and released it so that it floated gently before them once more. "I will admit that I did not wish for another army to be gathered beneath my very claws. That I did not wish to bear witness to another group of people marching off to war. But the choice was not to spare my feelings. I have seen enough death in my many cycles to know precisely how far people will go when they feel their cause is just. I had to know which cause Miska cared about."

Ravenna turned to look at the dragon, his red eyes glowing almost grey in the light. He flicked them to her and waited. She gave in and asked, "If he cared about rescuing his people or protecting Allora and Beringer?"

"If he sought glory of bringing down the Salusian Empire, no matter the cost to people who owed him no allegiance but the association of his having lived there a short time and had influence from me, or if he truly cared about those he loved. Whether he would fight for an individual life just as hard as he fought for his people." Cavaris stretched out his hand and the light floated down into it, taking on the shape of Miska, his expression injured and furious and terrified. It was what he must have looked like after Cavaris's ordeal.

Water slipped down Ravenna's cheeks. She brushed it away before the dryness of the desert could steal it. "As you said. An impossible choice. But he made it. And he hates you for it."

"Magic has been absent from this land for a long time. It faded after the dragons slept, and even those races that were awash in magic—elves, shadren, sabrine, a few spirits of nature, such like that—they lost some of their ability to wield it. I had thought it gone completely from the hands of humans, and yet Miska falls into my claws. Innocent, untrained, untried..." Cavaris lowered his hand and the light formed back into a sphere, Miska's wrath erased as if it were nothing. "You have to understand, magic is a force that can bend and warp reality to make truth. It creates and it destroys. It is a fundamental force of this world and it is dangerous. I have seen what magic unchecked can do. I know what it is to use magic not for the love of people, but for fury and fire and revenge."

Ravenna said nothing for a moment, only continued to watch Cavaris. He stared down at the encampment, watching the ever-darkening collection of tents transform into an island of torchlight, a single place of refuge amongst the darkness. "The Fire Wars," she whispered. "The dragons…you…"

"My brethren sleep partly because of the energy they expelled, but also because it was easier to sleep than to remember. To face the consequences."

"Why do you not explain this to Miska?" she asked quietly. "Surely if he knew the truth, the real reason why you did what you did, then he wouldn't…he wouldn't wish you dead and gone."

This time it was Cavaris who drew in a deep breath, his nostrils flaring and white scales forming around his eyes. "Dragons were not chosen to be the guides to the younger races because we were long-lived or powerful. We were chosen because we feel pain. Deeper than any mortals could possibly imagine."

"Arrogant," Ravenna whispered, the sound barely a chuckle. Cavaris snorted and shook his head, but he smiled. It, too, was slight.

"Perhaps. We are entitled to some, after all."

Ravenna reached out and slipped her hand into Cavaris', tightening her fingers around his so that they wove together. Her skin was almost as pale as his, and in the red witch-light, they looked like spirits brought back from the beyond.

"Will you keep vigil with me?" Ravenna asked.

"Until the last star dies and the sun shall nevermore rise. Yes."

CHAPTER SEVENTEEN

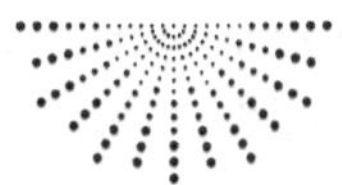

Miska had known that fighting Seraphina would be disastrous, that she was far more dangerous than Davorin, even with his magic, and that her army outnumbered them greatly. He didn't know why that surprised him, that the terror he had worked so hard to fight against was small compared to the one he faced, but he was surprised all the same. Those who rode and flew to fight Seraphina were even more surprised than he was.

Perhaps it was because Davorin fell relatively easily. A surprise aerial attack by the sylphs, Miska's arrival and magic, and Davorin had fallen. Seraphina had no magic, and was as unaware of their impending attack as Davorin had been. Then, they arrived. Miska had known the battle would be pitched and that many would die. He had known all of this, and yet the reality was so much worse.

The forces that Lenore had promised to supplement the sylphs were still weary and wounded from their previous battle. Their numbers were small. Any fighters from the resistance were mostly drawn from the local village, those who had witnessed the sylphs flying in to save them. Their armour was mismatched and their weapons were dull. The professional soldiers were skilled but greatly outnumbered. Miska had left Beringer behind to facilitate speed. The bear moved very swiftly for a creature of his size, even outstripping some horses, but Miska had still left him behind. Part of him wondered if he left the bear behind to protect those that remained. Ravenna. Allora. Lenore.

As it was, Miska went into battle on the back of a borrowed horse, his legs already saddle sore and his vision ready for casting and weaving threads. The sylphs flew slowly overhead, their wings like rumbling and rolling thunder, their bows at the ready and their other weapons prepared. When this ragtag force, determined to fight for everything they believed, caught up with Seraphina's army, the sylphs flew on ahead to fight with bow and arrow, to cut down as many of their enemies as they could. They had been armed with every spare arrow and quiver that they could carry.

It would not be enough.

Miska was not close enough to see the volleys of missiles that flew back to the sylphs, their aim true. He was close enough, however, to see a number of sylphs drop from the sky like stones. Some beat their wings in an attempt to regain altitude. Some just fell, unmoving. Before they had even landed, their numbers were cut down. And then Miska and the ground troops arrived. There were enough shields to form a small barrier that could deflect some of the remaining arrows that the Southron warriors fired upon them. It was almost as ineffectual as doing nothing. There were not enough shields, and the enemy's aim was too straight. Horses fell, screaming. Those that marched on foot were riddled with shafts of wood, the points embedded deeply. Many of the Southron archers were still busy fighting off the sylphs from above, but the damage had already been done.

Miska and the army of the Red Desert waded into battle over the bodies of their allies and friends.

Sword hit sword. Staff with spearhead beat against shield. The remaining horses lashed out with their hooves, but their enemy was mounted as well. Miska soon lost track of who was near, who was doing what. It was chaos all around him and he was barely able to keep holding his own. He drew upon the smallest threads that he could in an effort to conserve his magic, but the enemy was very talented and fast. They were made up of warrior tribes who thrived on war and battle. To them, this was perhaps an afternoon's sport, not a desperate fight for their lives.

One thread sharpened into the point of a knife, plunging into an enemy breast. Another thread became a falcon that plucked out an enemy's eyes. A wolf sank his fangs into a soldier's legs. A desert lion mauled a warhorse. Miska drew on as much energy from the dying around him that he could, but it was ephemeral and gone too swiftly. His concentration was too shattered.

A man easily the size of Sisu bore down on Miska with a single-headed war axe, a fierce grin splitting his face, which was already painted red with spilled blood. Miska raised an arm, shrouding it in threads to form a shield. He drew his hunting knife and attempted to thrust it into his enemy's groin or his stomach, but the man was prepared for that and easily dodged. He swung towards Miska's arm, the axe barely meeting the skin. It caused enough pain for Miska's concentration to fall to pieces. The threads that he commanded pulsated, flashing out of existence. He lost control of the wolf and the falcon. A moment later they were back, but the strain was pulling at Miska's mind, forcing him to fight through a fog.

Sisu came out of Miska's peripheral vision, wielding his own battle axe. He clashed with the other man, lips moving, though the angle was off for Miska to catch the words. The man snarled something in return, laughing, and then he and Sisu surged together, doing their best to cut each other to ribbons, and when that did not work, to hit each other with fist and foot. Miska did not have time to worry about his friend, though the knowledge of Sisu's strength in battle kept him strong.

Before he could lend assistance, magical or otherwise, another warrior barrelled towards him, this time wielding the curved swords favoured by many in the Salusian Empire and some of the more northern tribes in Southron. The blade cut past Miska's ear, so close that Miska could have sworn he almost heard it. He pulled on threads flashing in his vision and wrapped them around the other man, tearing him to pieces with barbed hooks.

Another soldier, another warrior, another push, another shove, another slice, another cut, another bruise, the battle kept coming. The enemies that Miska faced seemed endless. He could not even take a moment to catch his breath. No matter how many men and women Miska killed, maimed, or knocked unconscious, more kept coming. He could not feel the shock and horror of his actions, of what he was doing through the fear that kept him doing it. They seemed especially focused on him, perhaps because he had magic. Some of his allies managed to get close enough to help him for a minute or two before they were swept away. Miska saw ten sylphs mowed down by a score of warriors. He saw two villagers that had accompanied them fall with their heads gone from their shoulders.

Exhaustion seemed to be moving in with every breath that he took.

Miska pulled the energy from the dead around him, already feeling the strain of using so much magic. His back was beginning to ache, not from the sharp pain that came when he had already overdone himself, but the beginnings of the end. Every piece of energy that he drew in from the dead and the dying pushed it off for a moment longer, but he had never learned from Cavaris how to take energy from the world around him. He was simply pulling and forcing it to do his bidding. And then he would turn around and form a pack of hunting hounds that fought the warhorse bearing down on him. Or he would weave a thread around three warriors throats, pulling until they stopped breathing.

He did not know how long he had been fighting when he became aware of someone fighting beside him. It was one of the villagers, one of the men that had come with only a dull sword to defend himself. The man was scrawny and yet seemed to keep up with those fighting against him. He was covered in blood from hacking at his enemy, using the flat edge of the blade to deliver blows as often as he used the edge. He would step in when a warrior got too close to Miska, pushing them back until they could be killed.

How long had this man been protecting him?

Miska twirled his fingers, weaving threads together to form a low barrier that tripped up several warriors running his direction. The man took the opportunity and hacked into their necks, severing them as best he could. Some, he stabbed in the chest where their armour did not cover, saving the effort of swinging his arms. When he moved to kick at one to dislodge his blade, Miska nearly staggered back.

Qilas. This was the one who had beaten Miska as a child, and here he was fighting to defend him and protect him.

Miska's moment of hesitation cost him, though. Where he should have been weaving a desert lion to attack and defend, he paused. It was nothing more than a few seconds, barely long enough for anything to happen. But it was long enough for one fighter to get too close, a woman dressed in garish copper clothes completely unsuited for battle, a wild look in her eyes, her brown hair streaming even as it clumped with blood. She did not fight with sword or shield, but had metal claws as long as Miska's thumb tipping each finger. She cut and sliced at all in her way, their swords deflecting off her copper garb, leaving the scratches and dents in their wake. When they managed to get close at all.

The woman came up behind Qilas. He turned, lifting his sword swiftly, those hunters instincts honed over a lifetime. He was too slow. The woman pulled her claws across Qilas' neck, cutting into it as though it were sand. He fell.

She turned to face Miska. He turned to face her.

Her features were familiar somehow, even covered in blood and grit. Perhaps it was the gleam in her eye, or the wicked smile that she bestowed. Perhaps it was the way the warriors of Southron fell back so that she could fight however she saw fit. Whatever it was, it was only a heartbeat later that Miska knew who he faced and trembled. Seraphina.

Her mouth moved. He did not want to know what it was the she said, but he had seen the movements and his mind automatically converted them into words. "A true sorcerer. Poorly trained, if any of the stories are an indication. But to see such *power*. Do you not feel it running through your blood? Is it not glorious?"

They had a word for things like this, for people who took such pleasure in power and in death. Bloodlust. It was in the way her tongue darted out to catch a drop of blood falling down her face. It was in the gleam in her eyes as she took in Miska and the carnage he wore. It was in the way her warriors allowed her to find the battle without their assistance. This was one of the reasons why she was fighting this war. Not only for control over the Salusian Empire, not only to get back at her brothers for whatever slights they had dealt her. This was not simply for her glory or for conquest. All of those pieces fit together, yes, but this moment, right then, was more. Her fighting, her clawing people to shreds in the midst of an unplanned battle, facing down people who might easily kill her—facing down

Miska with all his powers—was because she loved the battle and she craved the blood.

Couple that with her ambition and his estimation of her shuddered, horrified. They were all going to die.

Miska surged into action, waving his hands to grab what threads remained to him, some of them seeming impossibly out of reach. She moved just as quickly, surging forwards with practiced gracefulness. Miska constructed a wolf to tear her to pieces and a shield to keep him safe. He had already done too much, though. He had already pulled as much energy as he could from the battlefield. He could not grasp the energy that supported him, his concentration slipping, his power almost beyond his grasp. He just had to defeat her, and this would all be over. The head of the snake, gone.

He failed.

Pain, stronger than anything he had felt up to this point, worse even than when he had lost his hearing as a child at the hands of the dead man resting at his feet, burst through him. His back exploded into agony, turning his vision black and sending fire up his spine. His legs collapsed beneath him, Seraphina's claws passing overhead in a whisper of air as he fell to the ground. He could not move his legs, nor escape the pain that was immobilising him. He screamed. At least, he thought he screamed. He could not see and he could not hear. He could only feel the pain.

A few moments later, his vision cleared, as it had done in the last battle. What he saw was almost worse than the pain.

Crispin stood before him, wings spread wide, his charcoal-dark skin smeared with gore. A snarl twisted his features so that he looked like something out of a nightmare. If nightmares could be afraid, that is. He held his blade out to fight Seraphina, to defend Miska as he had done before. She just laughed, her smile wide, mirth in every pore of her features. Crispin swung.

Seraphina dodged. She feinted right and lunged left, the claws on her hand spread wide to cut and to tear. Crispin moved to counter, but he was too slow, even with the Dalketh movements on his side.

Seraphina's claws tore into his right wing. It crumpled, some of the feathers falling away, the tendons cut. Crispin threw back his head, face in anguish. Miska wanted to do anything to help him, but he could not. He could not do anything but move his arms hopelessly, trying to claw at the ground to pull himself closer. The threads upon which he relied for so much power and strength were gone, leaving his vision dull. So he could do nothing but watch as Seraphina cut across Crispin's chest with her other hand, claws digging deep into the leather to reach the flesh beneath. Crispin staggered backwards, one arm across his chest, the other holding his sword loosely.

Another sylph, Brianna, landed with enough force to shake the ground. Miska blinked, still struggling to move. He tried to pull the threads, the ones he knew were there but not seen. He tried to pull energy from the dying around him, but it was slipping through his fingers. He tried to scream. His vision darkened again.

When next it cleared, Miska was being scooped into the arms of a sylph, one he did not recognise, her amber eyes wide and terrified, her golden skin smeared dirty, cut and raw. She beat her wings twice and lifted into the air, fleeing the battlefield with him in her arms. He looked around as much as he could and saw that other sylphs were carrying the wounded away, retreating in the face of death.

Miska turned his head, searching for any familiar face. For Crispin, for Brianna, for Sisu. His vision blurred once again. This time he welcomed unconsciousness. The pain followed him into the blackness.

—

. . .

THE ONLY WARNING that heralded the return of the sylphs and the army were specks, black against the sky. At first, Ravenna thought they were nothing more than the large desert carrion birds that often circled during the day, looking for something that had died in the heat. But they grew closer, and they grew more numerous. Then they were there, landing.

Without a word, Ravenna released Cavaris' hand and leaped to her feet. She beat her wings twice to gather momentum and launched herself down the hill, to be the one to reach them first. To see who remained. Afraid the ones she wanted would not be there. She did not hesitate, pushing through other soldiers and villagers and healers running to the arrivals. No one seemed to begrudge her, getting out of her way to let her move as swiftly as possible. Her wings were tilted to split the air, to gather more speed. She reached the edge of the encampment, vision focused on only the sight in front of her, everything else lost.

Sylphs landed. Perhaps a hundred, maybe two. Many of them carried wounded in their arms, some of them with wings, some of them without. Ravenna saw Crispin fall from the arms of a male who had borne him back. Her sister's mate was alive, his breathing laboured and heavy, his eyes wide with horror. His mouth moved, but no words came out. Ravenna saw his right wing had been cut down to the bone, many of the feathers missing, muscles split and the tendons severed. He had smaller cuts and abrasions all over his body, but Ravenna knew without having to examine the wound or say anything, without having to have been trained as a healer or be knowledgeable in the reconstruction of wings, that he would never fly again. Judging by the horrified emptiness in his eyes, he knew it too.

Ravenna stumbled back from his body, unable to help him, even to provide comfort. She turned, looking around, desperate for signs of Miska. She saw Sisu moving towards her, carrying something in his arms. Miska.

"He is not dead," Sisu said in her tongue.

No, Cavaris' voice cut into her mind. *He is not dead, but he has done what I feared he would. He has used too much magic, tried to do too much to save those around him. He did not know how to use what energy that was offered him and so he took it from himself. The damage will be substantial and it is likely permanent. Sisu, can you carry him to his tent? I will see to him. I will do all I can.*

Sisu nodded and walked off after Cavaris, seemingly oblivious to his own wounds. No one bothered to turn back to Ravenna, to spare her a word of comfort or hope. She stood, rooted to the spot, unable to follow after. Her breath hitched in her throat.

"Warlord."

Ravenna spun, found a female sylph, belonging to the Harrower company, her armour in tatters, her weapon lost, her wings drooping. She sank to her knees before Ravenna, wings dragging on the ground as if she were too weary to even keep them from getting dirty, to keep the feathers from caking together with gore and sand.

Ravenna sank to her knees as well, drawing as close to the sylph as she could. Tears streamed down her face, her pain impossible to hide behind stoicism and ice.

"You were right, Warlord. We should have never gone." The female sobbed, burying her face in her hands, her shoulders shaking. Ravenna moved forward even more, wrapping her arms around the sylph, her wings enveloping them together.

"I'm sorry," Ravenna said, voice breaking. She did not bother to wipe away her tears this time. She just lifted her head to the sky and cried. "I'm so sorry."

The remains of the tattered army fell around her, some of them moving off of their own volition to get their wounds seen to, others, like the sylph Ravenna held in her arms, too shattered or weary to move. Of sylphs that remained, Ravenna saw only a handful of the original force. Two thousand of her people had come to the desert to fight, and perhaps one tenth of that remained. It was all her fault. No matter what Cavaris said. No matter what Desarra thought, what Crispin argued, what Miska whispered to her in the night.

This was her doing.

And to finish it would be her undoing. She would fight anyways.

CHAPTER EIGHTEEN

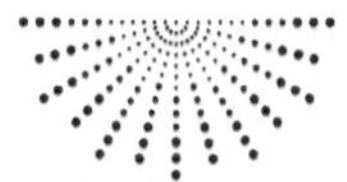

$\mathcal{I}$t had been two days since everyone had returned from the devastation that was the battle with Seraphina. The healers were still tending to the wounded and desperately scrounging for supplies since their routes to other villages and resources within the desert were either too far or cut off by the advancing army. Everyone who had remained back from the battle were busy helping the healers. Those who had returned were too busy being healed themselves to offer much more than cursory assistance.

One healer, a master wing reconstructor amongst the sylphs, had been tending to Crispin since he returned broken in wing and spirit. Two days and still they fought to return what mobility they could to the ruined wing. Desarra had been distraught, pacing outside the tent where the reconstruction was being attempted. Ravenna had attempted to comfort her once, but her sister wanted none of what Ravenna could offer. She did not want to be told that being flightless was not the death sentence that it used to be. That a sylph could live a fulfilled life without once tasting the wind.

Ravenna remembered vividly the sheer pleasure on Crispin's

face as he would fly with her in his arms, his wings tasting air in a way that was somewhat more profound for him than from any other sylphs. He had loved flying above everything. Above even, Ravenna suspected, Desarra. And now he lay drugged in a tent while healers tried to knit tendons back together and repair muscles that had been severed. His feathers would grow back eventually, but the damage had already been done. It was not a simple break. It was so much worse. So Ravenna had turned away and left to go tend to her own problems.

Cavaris and Sisu had spent nearly as much time with Miska as the healers had done with Crispin. Cavaris applied what magical remedies he could, and Sisu did what he could for the physical wounds. But the ridges on Miska's back, the ones that told of the price that he was to pay for the use of his magic, they were now a labyrinth of lines and small dots, some extending down to the base of his spine where they gathered in more concrete patterns. They nearly blackened his reddish skin. Cavaris could offer no comfort, no idea of what the true extent of the damage would be. He said only that they would have to wait for Miska to wake and discover the true price on his own. So far, he had been asleep since he returned. Ravenna had remained by his side.

The sun was setting. She could tell by the way that the light in the tent changed from dimly yellow blocking out the harsh sun, to slightly red, fire lighting up the sky as it did every evening. In another hour or so, someone would come and bring a lamp for her to see by. For now, she was alone, dabbing a damp cloth over Miska's brow.

He looked so peaceful. Calm. Unburdened. If it were not for the slight rise and fall of his chest, the way his breath hitched from some unknown pain every fourth or fifth breath, she would have thought him dead. He bore several deep scratches across his face, some of which might scar. There were other abrasions and cuts on his body, but they would be healed within another week or so. No, the real battle lay within Miska's mind.

Ravenna could not help him there.

"I should have been there," Ravenna said, sitting back on the stool she was using while she tended to Miska. Her wings lay limply at her sides, more out of weariness than true relaxation. She brushed a strand of Miska's hair away from his face and straightened the braids that lay across his shoulders, fingering one of the beads tied in the strands. "I should never have let you go into battle without me. I should never let any of you, any of them, go without me. I should have been there, risking my wings and my life right alongside you, no matter my feelings on the matter. Instead, my people are almost wiped out. Those that remain on Shinalea, and nearly two hundred souls here, that is all that is left of my people. Perhaps we will fall into legend once again, only this time it will be permanent."

She waited for him to open his eyes, to smile at her, to assuage their fears and regrets. He slept on.

"I suppose we are even now. I left you behind to return to my people and train them in the art of war. To save them. And you left me behind to save yours. I'm not sure either decision has done any of us much good."

Ravenna closed her eyes and took a breath, trying to conceal the tremble in her lips, though she did not know why. No one would care. Not any more.

"Why you talk to him if he not hear?"

Ravenna turned and saw Miska's heart daughter, Allora, standing in the entrance of the tent. The dying sunlight framed her hair with a golden halo, shadowed only by the creature behind her. Miska's massive familiar, Beringer stood beside her, both their eyes sheepish and worried. Beringer even shuffled his claws against the sands, as if a child caught at stealing food from the kitchens. Ravenna gestured them both to come inside the tent and they did, stepping close enough to see Miska as he lay on the cot, but not close enough to get in the way of Ravenna.

"Maybe wherever he is he can hear me," Ravenna said. "We do not know how the realms of dreams and magic work." She brushed her hair away from her eyes and slumped her shoulders. "I'm mostly talking for myself. Trying to figure out if any of this could have been prevented."

Allora inched forward, reaching out her hand tentatively, as if afraid that Ravenna would shun her and turn her way. Ravenna reached out and took the girl child's hand, squeezing it tightly. "He returned to us. He would never leave you," she said, trying to reassure the child.

"He would leave me for you."

Ravenna raised her brows and examined the small human. She had white blonde hair streaked with sand and dirt, as if she had been running around trying to help the healers. She was a little too skinny, as if she hadn't eaten properly recently, or as if she were just growing too quickly for food to keep up. But there was something in her stormy eyes that told Ravenna this child had seen more than most of her age. And little of that had to do with war. Though the aftermath certainly did not help.

Ravenna had been afraid when Miska first introduced her to the child. She had been afraid that he had found someone to replace her, someone to love and to make into his family, that he would no longer need her. She had been afraid that his affection would not be great enough for both. She had been wrong.

"Then *I* would leave *him* for you. But it will never happen. You are his heart daughter. And as his mate, that makes you mine as well." Ravenna reached out with a wing and pulled Allora close, wrapping her with the feathers in an attempt to soothe her. The child's trembling increased for a moment before relaxing. "I know that we have not gotten to know each other very well, but in the future we shall have all the time in the world for talking and for playing and for teaching."

Allora looked up at her solemnly as if she did not quite believe all that Ravenna was offering. Ravenna held her gaze. After a few moments, the child nodded. Beringer shuffled forward and nuzzled Ravenna's hair, apparently accepting Allora's nod as indication of a truce, or acceptance or whatever it was that had just happened. Ravenna's heart swelled, closing her throat painfully. She squeezed Allora tighter and the girl leaned her head into Ravenna's chest.

"What happens if we lose? If the bad lady that Miska went to fight wins?"

Did the child know that this was Ravenna's greatest fear? That she worried that in giving up on battle so soon that she had doomed her people to extinction, or worse?

"I promise you, with every feather in my wing and every bone in my body, with every drop of blood I possess and with all of the love in my heart, that I will do everything in my power to ensure that does not happen. To ensure that you and Miska and Beringer all have a future."

Allora nodded. Ravenna almost expected the girl to ask more questions, to demand specific answers and a solution that Ravenna did not have. Instead, she just took the damp cloth from Ravenna's hand, dipped it in the basin of water and dabbed it over Miska's brow. He continued to sleep, but he seemed to relax, the harshness of his breath reducing and a slight smile appearing on his features.

"Allora," Ravenna said, pulling her wings back and standing. "I have some things to see to. Would you watch over him?"

She nodded and took Ravenna's stool. Beringer shuffled closer to the child, his eyes watching Miska. Ravenna took a deep breath, that feeling of loneliness and of being slightly outside returning. She turned and left the tent, certain that Miska would be perfectly all right without her. Allora would be there if he woke up, as would his familiar. He would not be alone. Ravenna might not be there, but he would not be alone. That was what mattered.

The activity in the encampment was as fervid as always, people running from tent to tent, some healers with their hands up to their elbows in gore, others wounded who had already seen their injuries tended going off to rest. A few guards who remained strong were keeping watch, bandages peeking out beneath armour. None acknowledged Ravenna as she passed.

She slipped into Lenore's tent, not bothering to announce herself. Lenore sat on a cot, her hands protectively rubbing against her belly, her servant cradling a child in her arms. Ravenna had learned that this was Davorin's first child, the one that Seraphina had tried to dangle before her mad sibling as leverage, the one she would used to control the future of this land. Apparently, Desarra had flown off to fetch her from the Red Palace, deciding to adopt the child. It was not something Ravenna would have done, but she understood the impulse. Politically, it made perfect sense. Ravenna doubted that politics had much to do with Desarra's decision.

The servant of Lenore was watching the child while Desarra tended to Crispin. Ravenna wondered if Desarra had told Crispin about the new addition to her family. Or if she'd even had the opportunity.

Sylphs and humans seemed inextricably linked. Ravenna's mother had lain with one to bear her. Ravenna had taken Miska as a mate. Desarra adopted a human child.

The barriers of the past were being broken. Perhaps this was like before, when the Stormbringers roamed the lands. Or perhaps this was something new.

Whatever it was, it was threatened.

"Ravenna," Lenore said, her breath like a whisper, her eyes red rimmed from grief. She struggled to stand, her ungainly figure finding such a simple task difficult the closer she neared her birthing. Ravenna held up a hand, indicating that Lenore should remain seated. "What is the news?"

"Miska still sleeps. My sister is distraught with grief for Crispin, distracted by her child. She has not performed any of her duties as Chosen Queen since what's left of our army is returned. The final death count is in, though. Unless more die from their injuries, which the healers assure me is unlikely, then my people have only two hundred and three of our original force of two thousand. Your army is similarly decimated. They had a more difficult time escaping given that Seraphina's forces were happy to pursue. We believe that no more than four hundred remain there. I estimate we have two days before she can get the bulk of her army here. The reports say that she is moving slowly given that she has so many people...Is there anything that you have been holding back? The resistance? Anything that might help us rally against Seraphina?"

Desperation. Ravenna could not hold it in any longer.

Lenore's eyes watered. She shook her head, pressing her lips together. Blodwen cradled the child closer, patting its back to calm its rising wails. She glared at Ravenna. "How dare you accuse her of–"

"It is not an accusation. It is a question." Ravenna had little time for argument and little patience for it.

Blodwen glared further but silenced, turning her back to Ravenna and bouncing gently with the child.

Lenore shook her head and did her best to lift her chin in a semblance of that queenly pride she had once held. "The resistance has failed me. Vareis, who I thought I could trust, has promised me again and again that forces would be brought, that everyone who wanted to stand against the Salusian Empire would fight with us so that we might all win our independence. Again and again I have asked for this to happen. I have seen ten, maybe twenty soldiers arrive at a time. And no matter how much I plead, no more than that ever comes. A hundred total perhaps is all that has been offered me. I do not know if it is because they have lied about their reach, about the people that they have working for them, or if it is because they are afraid. Davorin's acquisition of magic changed many minds. And now that Seraphina marches against us, I fear that...It is far easier to accept submission than to fight for freedom. I have not seen Vareis in three days."

Ravenna took in a breath and closed her eyes. She had not expected much but she had expected more than this. Ever since her people flew off to battle without her, she had been thinking, desperate for a solution to the problem. And she had two options. Three, if she decided to surrender: flee and do their best to regroup, or to fight. To regroup would now require many generations, their numbers were so slim. They had not enough force for even a mild skirmish. And the humans were badly beaten as well. The Red Desert as a kingdom had fallen. Unless there was some miracle and Seraphina decided to just give up because of boredom, then Lenore would fall, the sylphs would fall, and the world would be forever changed. They could not fight and if they fled it would be forever. If they surrendered, then everything they knew would die. They would be used as tools, slaves to whatever brutal purpose Seraphina held. Ravenna's people, a free people, would fall and their memory would be forgotten.

"We found her." The new voice was deep, male, familiar. Ravenna turned as Lenore stiffened. Almost immediately though, Ravenna's feathers relaxed, relief filling her breast.

"Radim. Tekko." The two men, the former slaves that had helped Ravenna build her army stood in the tent, bearing the wear and dirt of having traveled far. They were armed, their weapons looking more the worse for wear. But they had come. They had promised to come and here they were.

"Hello Ravenna." Tekko stepped forward, his arms spread. Ravenna stepped into them and took comfort from his embrace.

"I see you gathered some new scars since last we saw you." He nodded to the still raw burns that graced Ravenna's left shoulder, covering the top of the scratches she had received from the desert lion. She shrugged.

"Radim, Tekko, may I present to you Queen Lenore of the Red Desert. Of what remains of it. Lenore, these two helped me when I first came here, making me into what I am." The three exchanged nods, their expressions all solemn, more than Ravenna would have liked for a meeting of friends.

"It is a pleasure to meet you, even in these dark times. We had heard that a gathering of forces was here at the edge of the desert in the mountains, but it took too long for us to find you. We had hoped to come and help, to be there at your side when you would fight Davorin or whatever found you. But as we took our people from the desert, we encountered..." Radim lowered his head, swallowing down whatever emotion he could. Ravenna saw a flash of pain across his face. The relief that she had felt with his coming was gone.

"Seraphina. She decided that she would march against Davorin as well. Only we got there first, now we are her target. She had already decimated our forces," Ravenna said. Tekko closed his eyes and took a deep breath, letting it out slowly as though it pained him to do so. Ravenna saw beneath the dirt of travel that he was bruised, beaten. Radim was in little better shape.

"We had hoped to come to you for help. She killed everyone. A band from Southron, larger than any single tribe, came and razed the former slave markets, stealing what little we had in the way of resources. We had brought our people to go and fight with you and left little defence, thinking that no one would wish to attack it. They came after us, bearing the weapons of those who were dead. Maybe twenty of our force survived, all fled into the northern parts of the desert. Radim and I are the only ones who made it this far." Tekko licked his dry lips.

"Blodwen, fetch some water. And see if there is a place for our guests to stay. We may be facing death ourselves, but there is no need for rudeness. We will offer them hospitality for as long as we can." Lenore smiled weakly. Blodwen nodded and left the tent, putting the child into her temporary crib and looking at the warriors with hopelessness in her eyes.

"There will be a solution," Ravenna said, unable to keep the fear in her voice down.

"I believed that *you* could do anything, that you could face any enemy and win. Then this happened. Would it have been different if you were there?" Lenore squeezed her fists at her side, looking at Ravenna desperately.

"Maybe. I doubt it."

Lenore turned away, a ripple of pain spreading across her features. "We'll never know, now will we?"

Ravenna felt the sting of her words deeper than any wound she had ever received. She had lost her mask of ice when she saw how few of her people remained. She was not able to find it again and instead felt emotion shine openly across her features, tears rising her eyes. Before anyone could say anything, do anything, offer false hope, she turned and fled the tent. And found Desarra waiting for her, eyes narrowed, golden wings spread wide.

"He wishes to see you," Desarra spat. Had she slapped Ravenna it could not have hurt more. Ravenna nodded, swallowing down her anguish and following her sister to the tent where Crispin was being healed. Her eyes remained fixed on the darkening sand, glad for the falling of night so that her pain might at least not be seen by all.

Was this all her fault? Had she truly brought her people to this? Yes. It was the only answer that made sense. It was the one that explained why everyone looked at her with loathing and anger and disappointment now instead of the hope that they had carried before.

Ravenna had grown used to people looking up to her, treating her as though she had all the answers, as though she could take on the world and win. They saw her now for what she really was: a fraud. She had brought her people nothing but death, and now they saw it. Maybe if she had died on the battle-field it would be different. She shook her head, pushing the thought away. She has lived her whole life reviled and ignored by her people. Had a cycle and a half really made that much difference? Had it really made her that arrogant and that proud that she had hoped her people would look up to her with admiration and awe forever? Folly. Lunacy.

No, they finally saw her for who she was. They saw that all of this was her fault. As she followed her sister across the encampment to go and speak with Crispin, Ravenna knew only one thing. This was truly all her fault. And she would have to fix it. Alone.

CHAPTER NINETEEN

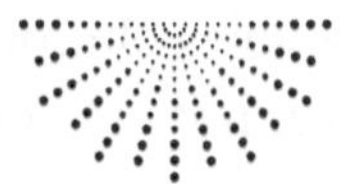

The tent where Crispin was being healed was dark, lit only by a single lantern. The healer was cleaning up, his hands shaking and covered in blood. Ravenna saw Crispin lying on his stomach, his good left-wing folded naturally against his side, the other stretched out as far as it would go, wrapped in bandages and smeared with poultices. A slight sheen of sweat shown on his face, making the darkness of his skin shimmer. His eyes were open, glazed and in pain.

Desarra lifted her chin towards her mate and indicated Ravenna with a sweep of her wing. "I have brought her. Though it will do you no good."

With that, Desarra strode over to the corner of the tent where she could watch and still be out of the way. Ravenna sank gratefully onto a stool offered her by the healer and then he, too, got out of the way, leaving to go rest or see to another self.

Ravenna shuffled her wings behind her, careful not to block out the only light that was in the tent. Crispin looked up at her, brows furrowed as he tried to push away the pain with nothing but sheer force of will. Ravenna wanted to reach out and grab his hand, to offer whatever comfort she could, but with Desarra glaring daggers into her back, she did not feel this was a good option. So she just sat there and watched as Crispin tried to control the uncontrollable.

"Tell me you have a plan," Crispin said, the words hoarse. He looked up at her, eyes wide. Moisture gathered there. "Please, tell me you have a plan."

Ravenna took a breath and let it out slowly. She closed her eyes. "I have…I have a possible solution, but I cannot guarantee that it will be effective. I cannot guarantee that it will not make things worse."

"How could you make things any worse than they already are?" So much for removing herself from the situation. Desarra had already strode from the corner of the tent, her hands clenched into fists, her wings bristling with fury. "Crispin cannot fly. The healer says that he may gain full mobility of his wings, but the muscles will never again hold him in flight. And what of the rest of our people? Your other general, Brianna, lies dead on the battlefield. Of the forces that you trained, of the Stormbringers that you brought back from the dead, only two hundred remain. The humans we were to ally ourselves with are just as weak. And another army marches towards us. We could go back to Shinalea." Desarra's eyes blinked furiously and she seized upon the idea with fervour. "If we go back and never return, never go anywhere near the mainland, make the penalty far worse than ever before, then we have a chance. We could defend our borders. We could leave for another thousand generations."

"And one of those that we would leave behind? Seraphina knows full well that we exist. She is not one to give up simply because we ran away. That was the whole reason why I came back in the first place," Ravenna said. She turned to look her sister fully in the face, taking in the fire in her eyes, the unkempt nature of her hair, the way her wings seemed to be bushed up to twice their size. Ravenna just sat, too weary to posture. "I came back to Shinalea because Davorin was going to find us no matter what. I wanted us to strike at him before he had a chance to destroy us. Then we would have a fighting chance. We have done that. We have won that battle. But now, because of that, we face a greater threat. I do not think that fleeing back to Shinalea will do us any good. Seraphina will come for us either way."

"You should never have come back. You should have stayed here in this horrible place and died with these horrible people."

Ravenna wanted to feel the sting of Desarra's words, wanted to feel the hate and the anger raking over her soul, but she could not feel hurt because it was true. This was not an opinion, it was a fact. Beside her, Crispin stirred on the cot, his outstretched wing twitching against its bindings.

"That is not fair, Des. You know full well that she did what she had to. That we would not have survived without her." He tried to lift his head, but he could not. Desarra stepped forward and put her hand on his back, golden skin meeting the flesh between the wings. He tensed and then relaxed, staying still under his mate's touch.

"She's not wrong Crispin," Ravenna said, her voice quiet, barely above a whisper. She took another deep breath and let it out just as slowly, keeping her eyes narrowed, her gaze unfocused. "My interactions with the human people led us to this point. Perhaps it was inevitable. Perhaps the slavers that captured me on the shores of Shinalea would have returned and sought out the others. Perhaps if I had stayed, then Davorin would have sought you out anyways and you would have had no defence. Perhaps perhaps perhaps. The fact is that the events of the last cycle can be drawn back to me. I was the one who started this and I shall be the one to finish it."

"What do you mean?" Desarra demanded. She folded her arms and stared down at Ravenna, challenging her. "Do you mean to lead to the rest of our people to their deaths? Do you mean to lead us into exile, to flee everything that we have known and never return, not even to Shinalea? What would the great warlord Ravenna Wingsword have us do."

"You? I would have you do nothing. I would have none of you do anything. I told you, this is my battle to fight. And I shall fight it. Alone."

Crispin made a strangled sound in his throat, his eyes alarmed. Desarra just tossed back her head and laughed, the sound harsh and mocking. She wiped an imaginary tear from her eye. "I always knew you were arrogant, but I never expected you to go to this level of absurdity. Are you just going to slay every human on the battlefield? Are you going to do what *companies* of Stormbringers could not? Is the mighty Ravenna Wingsword going to unleash some sort of magical power?"

Ravenna curled her lip. "If I could have done something that fantastical, don't you think I would have by now? Do you think I would have abandoned our people when they went off to fight? I didn't go with them because I thought that course of action was the wrong one. I thought that facing this new threat as we had done before, without knowing its size or its strength or anything, was wrong. I thought that flying into battle with the high of having just won would have been foolish. I did not wish to see anyone else die. I had wished to come up with a potential solution. To even the odds perhaps, to make the battle more able to be fought. Instead, I let them all fly off without me and they came back broken or they didn't come back at all. Do you think if I could have stopped this that I would have? No, I cannot face down Seraphina's army alone. But I can face down Seraphina alone."

"Single combat," Crispin wheezed. He coughed slightly, groaning as the movement jostled his injured wing.

"You are as insane as Davorin." Desarra shook her head, sneering. "Have you even considered the consequences if you lose? If you demand that Seraphina hold her progress to face you in single combat, to declare that the winner takes all. I know you are a good fighter Ravenna, but if you lose then the deaths that you caused will have been for nothing."

Ravenna shook her head and closed her eyes. Whatever emotion she had shared with her people, crying and raging alongside them, whatever pain she had seen in Lenore and mirrored, whatever sorrow she had shown Tekko and Radim, she had nothing left. She had felt wing-weariness before. She knew exactly what it was when it weighed down your soul. In that moment, she felt not even that.

"I told you that it was not a perfect solution. Yes, it could make things worse. But as you said, we have not the forces to fight when she arrives, nor do we have the recourse to flee unless you wish to flee forever. No one else is coming to help us. Sisu has said that the elders of Hullgard will remain precisely where they are. The Salusian Empire is ruled by an old man whose mind fails him; his grief for his dead son blinds him. The dragon will not fight. Southron rides against us. I can only offer that which I have left. And I will fight with everything I have. I will fight if she shears my wings off, if she opens my scars. I will fight until there is nothing left of me but spirit and wind. I will give everything. It may not be enough, but it is all that I have. If it is not good enough for you, then say so. You are Chosen Queen."

Desarra's hands clenched into fists and she turned her back on Ravenna. "Before we left, Tytira told me that you had been offered the crown. When you first came back to Shinalea, and you first told the Council of the threat, convinced them that we needed to fight or we would all die, they offered you the crown. Don't mock me and pretend that I don't know that you turned them down. You said you did not love us well enough for that."

Ravenna stood, reaching her wing out to her sister. Desarra drew away, stumbling in the sand until her back pressed against the canvas tent. Ravenna followed her wings neatly behind her.

"It is true. I refused the crown. My reasoning was valid. All my life, I have been shunned by the sylph society. I was pushed into gullies, I was kicked down the stairs, I was mocked and derided and ignored and forgotten. Do you know how many sylphs that I trained told me that they didn't even know I had existed except in whispers and rumours? I was Queen Marialla's granddaughter and I never once attended a fete. I had Tacitus, I had the Intellecti, but even among them I was an oddity.

"What sylph cannot fly? What place is there for one of us amongst beings who taste the wind. I hated my people. I hated you. And Crispin and everyone there. So no, I did not love you well enough to take the crown. But I *came back*. I came back to offer my life and my wings and even my soul if that was what was required of me. I gained much. My relationship with you. Friendship with Crispin. People who would talk with me and dance with me at a fete. People who valued my opinion. So if I were offered the crown today, would I take it? Have I grown to love you all that much more? I don't know. But the fact is Desarra, the crown will never again be offered to me. You wear it now. And I swore at your crowning that I would serve *you*. Not the Council. Not my own ideas of right and wrong, not my own desires to run away. I would serve you. *You*. And now I am offering the only thing I have left to you. My life. I will go and I will fight in single combat against Seraphina in the hopes that it might save our people. I might die. But it does not matter. So my Queen, will you accept my offering?"

Desarra did not meet Ravenna's gaze. She did not move forward to touch her wings to Ravenna, nor did she offer her hand. She just straightened in the corner of the tent and spoke, her voice commanding and her gaze fixed on the ground. "Very well. Go and fight. Die if you must. But if you do, do not expect your name to live on in history. You will be forgotten, not even worthy of a curse, of moderate fury in the night. You will not be reviled or feared, you will be nothing."

"And if I win?" She should not have asked the question. She

should have just taken Desarra's answer, bowed her head, and moved on. She should not have wanted to know what would happen if she did manage to succeed and save her people. But the words came.

"Then we will feel free to return to Shinalea. And you shall remain amongst your beloved humans. Never once remembered by us." With that, Desarra strode from the tent, her wings thrusting back the canvas flaps with serious effect. The tent rattled around them, shaking from the abrupt movement. Ravenna sank back down onto the stool and turned to Crispin. His dark charcoal skin had turned more ash than shadow. The small pillow under his head was damp with moisture. His hands were clenched into fists at his side and both his wings trembled, though Ravenna doubted it was solely from pain.

"Not being able to fly is far from the end of the world," Ravenna said, trying to offer what comfort she could. She knew that was only part of what troubled him, that there were words now between them that could not have been unsaid nor unheard. "The Dalketh will serve you just as well on the ground as it did in the air. You will be able to run through the forest to leap through the trees, to move faster than you can imagine, to leap from rock to rock, to move with grace and ease. You might not be able to fly, but you shall be far from incapable."

Crispin reached out a hand to Ravenna. "Please…"

Ravenna blinked back tears in her own eyes and took Crispin's hand. "You should have no troubles getting around the Aerial City. You can create rope ladders or jump off of balconies. If you don't want to do that, then the Intellecti will happily take you. You can write tomes on the aerodynamics of flight. You can raise falcons."

"Ravenna…*Don't.*"

"Desarra has adopted a human child. Davorin's first child by a servant girl. Seraphina was going to use her to control the region, to rule not only the Red Desert but the Salusian Empire.

Desarra saved her from that fate. Do not let Desarra abandon the child. Take her with you. Teach her the Dalketh, modify it for a wingless being. Teach her what it means to be Intellecti, what it means to be strong and capable. Do not let them mock her for what she is not, but rather praise her for what she is. And remind Desarra of her promise. No matter what it takes." She squeezed Crispin's hand, barely able to keep her wings from crumbling. She drew in a breath, shuddering as it fell through her lungs.

"You remind her." Crispin offered a watery smile, but it faded a moment later. "*You* do it."

"Promise me," Ravenna breathed. Crispin nodded, his face brushing against the pillows and smearing his tears. Ravenna squeezed his hand once more and then stood, turning to go into the night.

Crispin's words followed her. "I'm sorry."

Ravenna realised that she was not as empty of emotion as she had thought. The weariness was not as soul deep as it appeared. She realised that she could still feel the pain and the fear of what awaited her. She would not let herself think about what was to come after. She did not offer herself hope of the future or worry at its downfall. She felt enough pain for the present. She did not think she could handle more.

Ravenna went to her own tent at the edge of the encampment, a small affair that was big enough for her small cot and her gear, but no more. She had been fortunate to find a tent for herself, and had used it for solitude and for meditation. Now, she wished she was again with Miska, with Lenore. She wished she had not spent so much time alone in her thoughts, letting silence speak for her. She put on the armour that Tekko had made for her so very many moons ago. It was worn and scratched and needed a good oiling, but it fit snug and sure. The sheaths on her back for her swords were a familiar weight to that she found almost as comforting as the people she had grown to love. She braided her hair, weaving a spiked strip into it and tying it tightly at the end. She put on her heaviest boots, still splattered with blood from the battle between her forces and Davorin's. Then, sniffling and wiping away tears, she took ten meditative breaths to settle herself.

One. Tacitus.

Two. Kratos.

Three. Radim.

Four. Tekko.

Five. Crispinus.

Six. Itonus.

Seven. Brianna.

Eight. Lenore.

Nine. Desarra.

Ten. Miska.

Calm slipped over her mind like a familiar shroud, relaxing her muscles and slowing her heartbeat. There was fire in her veins instead of ice, determination stronger than any fear she had felt before. Ravenna stepped out from the tent into the cool desert night, ready for whatever might stand in her way. She lingered long enough to gather two water skins, enough to take her far into the desert so she could meet Seraphina's army away from her people. She did not linger long enough to say her goodbyes, knowing that if she saw Miska's sleeping face again, or if she saw the terror in Lenore's eyes, the anger that Desarra bore, that she might second-guess herself.

"I will come with you," a voice said, causing Ravenna to turn over her shoulder and look at the approaching figure. His robes shown as white as his hair, his horns black against the purple sky. His hands were calmly folded into the sleeves of his robes, his eyes half-lidded and relaxed. "I may not fight, but I can be sure that whatever bargain is struck is kept."

"Does not Miska need you?" Ravenna asked, though she turned away and allowed Cavaris to walk by her side.

"I think you need me more."

She nodded. It was probably true. Dragon and sylph walked off into the desert. No one noticed their departure. But as they walked to the horizon, leaving the encampment behind, a woman's scream split the air, carrying far enough in the empty land to reach even Ravenna's ears. She closed her eyes and paused, inhaling the harsh breath. "Lenore's birthing."

"Then we must see this done."

Ravenna nodded. She adjusted her wings and put her hand on the water skins at her belt. Then she left her people behind.

CHAPTER TWENTY

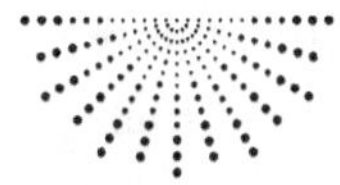

There were shadows in Miska's mind. He was in a place that seemed to stretch on forever, full of grey mist and shapes that were impossible to make out. He could not see threads of magic and he could not feel the pain that he thought had followed him into the darkness. He could hear whispers, passing overhead and quickly muted by the fog. Was that Cavaris' voice he heard? Allora's?

Part of him knew that this was impossible, that he hadn't been able to hear since he was a child. He would never be able to hear, let alone recognise a voice that he had never heard. Yet he also knew that this was perfectly normal. That whatever this place was, the whispers were an inherent part of it.

Some of the whispers belong to Ravenna. Her voice was smooth and quiet, the words lilting ever so slightly as she spoke with her accent the language of humans. He knew it was Ravenna because he could feel the pain in her voice crying almost as loud as his own. And he could feel her affection and love too. Love for *him*. He wanted to call out, but the whispers were indistinct, vague. No matter how hard he tried, his voice could never reach out loud enough for her to hear him.

Some of the whispers belonged to Sisu. The man's pride and cheer filtered through his voice, making it booming and deep, even when the words were indistinct. He could speak with a certain amount of tenderness when he chose, but he was never halting or quiet. Always sure, always strong, even when it meant that he would get himself into trouble, or when his actions caused the opinion of others to turn against him. Miska was sure that he could reach Sisu, that he could yell loud enough for his friend to hear, but he failed there, too.

Some of the whispers belonged to Allora, young and capable if a little afraid. She would grow to be sure and strong, of that Miska had no doubt. Why did he wonder, then, if he would see that come to be? She was always accompanied by the grumblings of Beringer, his snorts of laughter or his shuffling sniffs as an attempt to suss out information. The two were inseparable and neither of them heard him, either.

The whispers grew and swelled around him, causing Miska to turn and run through this shadowy place, desperate to find the source or to get to the edge so that he could call out to reach those who called for him. But this place went on endlessly, each step the same as the last. He felt neither weariness nor hunger nor thirst, only desperation. His steps slowed and he fell to his knees, hands trembling. Was this a prison of his own making? Was this the price that he paid for using magic beyond his means? Would he never see those he loved again?

"Hello."

Miska turned on his knees, looking up at the figure who stood above him. It was a sylph, charcoal-ash skin three shades deeper than the fog, amber eyes shining like beacons. His golden brown wings were calmly arched above his head, relaxed and unmoving as if he had no need to hurry and no fears to pester him. His eyes looked careworn but there was a smile on his face. He seemed young and yet ageless.

"Can you hear me?" Miska breathed, afraid that even this person would find him as insubstantial as the whispers.

"Oh yes. And I even know why you are here. You are Miklos, known as Miska, human servant to the Red Queen Lenore of the Red Desert, mate to Ravenna a sylph of Shinalea, sorcerer of Hullgard, familiar to the great bear, heart-father to the child Allora."

The sylph fixed him with a smile while Miska gaped. "Am I dead?" Was it even worth asking when this sylph, whom he had never met, knew all of this? Knew, perhaps, so much more.

The sylph held out a hand, which Miska took tentatively, afraid that his flesh would just fall right through. But the sylph was as solid as anything else, as real as any person Miska had ever known. He pulled Miska to his feet and waited until Miska was steady before pulling back and folding his hand calmly again behind his back. "You are not dead. But I am."

Miska took a step backward, mist swirling around his legs. He could not feel that, but he could still feel where he had touched this person's hand. He was *real*. And he claimed to be dead.

The sylph chuckled, the sound light, a beacon in the shadows that had been Miska's life for so many moons. "I am Tacitus." He tilted his head and nodded. "Ah, I see you know me. That would be Ravenna's doing?"

Miska nodded wordlessly, his jaw dropping open. By the Watcher, he was talking with Ravenna's dead heart-father. How was this possible? He did not think that the sylphs believed in an afterlife. He did not know that he did. But, he was here in this between land. And Tacitus was there. Was real.

"I see you have many questions. But we do not have the time to delve into the metaphysical, nor the philosophical, though that would please me greatly. I cannot tell you that which you wish to know about the spirit world or about the afterlife or even why it is I that I'm here to talk with you and not someone from your past. Not the dead Qilas, perhaps. Unfortunately, it is not my purview to be able to explain. Ironic, given that I was dedicated to facts and to history and things that you could touch and sense and prove, for most of my life. It just goes to show that one never stops learning." Tacitus paced a little while he spoke, a small circle that reminded Miska of tutors that he had seen come for Lenore when they were both growing in the Red Palace. He hadn't thought about those times for cycles.

Tacitus paused, raising a skeptical eyebrow, stretching his wings. The feathers fluttered as if there were a wind in this place instead of mist and shadow. "I apologise. It seems that even when I am not explaining something, my words tend to run long. I have come here for a specific purpose. This was the only place that I could reach out. And you were the only messenger available."

"Messenger?" Miska asked. Tacitus wanted him to send a message to Ravenna. A solution? A way out of all of this. Miska licked his lips and nodded eagerly, waiting for Tacitus to reveal what it was that the gods had to say. The sylph just chuckled again.

"The message is not for Ravenna. She has chosen her path and must see it through to the end. Neither you nor I nor anyone else can stop her. No, Ravenna knows precisely where she walks, though her reasoning as to why is perhaps flawed. This message is for her sister. The Chosen Queen of the sylphs, Desarra."

Miska frowned. He shook his head. "Desarra is…"

"You have been asleep for too long. Things are not as stable as they were. The foundations of this place are cracking and the ripples of that event are stretching across time. The past is going to rise up to meet the future. Not now, and you may never need to be involved, but it is happening. The conse-quences are felt even now. All of this will come, perhaps now, perhaps later, but it is not why I am here. No my message for

Desarra is something more immediate. She has become afraid. Her whole life, she has been afraid. Of sylphs not accepting her, of being judged by connections that she could not prevent, of being found wanting in a society where she held no real power but her beauty. She has been afraid of being alone, even when she had Crispinus as a mate. And now, she has power and the ability to lead her people into a golden era, but she is afraid of doing wrong. She is afraid that Ravenna was the one meant for the crown, even when she refused." Tacitus tilted his head and his amber eyes seemed to intensify, boring into Miska. His voice took on a double timbre, echoing inside Miska's head as well as without. Miska put his hands over his ears and ground his teeth, trying to still the vibrations in his mind.

He took several breaths, seeming to suck in the moisture in the mists. Or was that cool moisture on his brow and not his tongue? He forced himself to focus.

"Ravenna refused the crown?" Miska asked when the strangeness subsided. Tacitus inclined his head.

"She is wiser than many give her credit for. The crown would have done her no good. Nor the people of Shinalea. Desarra though, has a chance. She is afraid enough to be humble and proud enough to be strong. If she will only listen."

Miska could feel the ground beneath his feet softening, as if becoming less solid. Was he leaving this place or was Tacitus leaving him? "Why have you come here?"

"I told you I would not answer that question. I can tell you this: Desarra is as stubborn as her sister. She would not listen to anyone unless they had an objective voice. I could not approach directly. But if you do not tell her, if she does not choose to listen, then it is possible that Shinalea will fall to ruin and be forgotten."

"I will tell her," Miska said. He was sinking into the fog, his knees already encumbered by the strange liquid, unable to move forward or to move back. Tacitus seemed to remain there on the solid ground, his wings unmoving and his expression a little sad. "I promise."

"Tell her this. She is *wrong*. She must stand where ancestors have stood and offer up to the people everything that they did. Peace. War. Thought. She must not be afraid to ask questions for fear of their answers. And if the Storm that rages around her keeps her from flying, tell her to find the eye. Then, she can soar above it."

Miska did not understand. He did not know what any of this meant except that there were vague references to a storm or the Storm or Stormbringers. But, then, the message was not meant for him. He only hoped that Desarra would be able to understand, because the world of fog and whispers and shadow was fading away, replaced by silence and pain. Familiar silence, comforting pain. When Miska opened his eyes again, Tacitus was gone. In his place, Sisu sat over him, head bowed and face grim.

Miska tried to speak, but he found that he could not get any sound past his throat. Instead, he reached out with his hand, weak and difficult to move. He tapped Sisu on the knee. The warrior and hunter of Hullgard looked up in surprise, straightening on the stool.

"You live. You woke." He seemed to want to say more, but like Miska the words got stopped in his throat. A myriad of emotions flashed over his face, half hidden by his beard, but also more expressive because of it. Sisu patted Miska's hand and cracked a relieved smile.

"Water," Miska mouthed. Sisu nodded. He reached over and grabbed a cloth from a basin, holding the dripping rag to Miska's mouth, a few drops of water slipping past his lips and soothing his throat impossibly. Miska took all that he could before it was too much and then turned his head away. Sisu removed the rag and Miska turned his head back. "How long?"

"Three days. Cavaris says that your magic has done something to you, that you overburdened yourself past the point that you should have done. He says the price will be severe, but I don't know what that means." Sisu looked like he wanted to turn his head away, but he flashed his eyes to Miska's and grimaced. If he wanted to keep talking and have Miska understand, then he had to look at him, to show every ounce of grief that he held. "I have been to war before. I have fought many battles, before losing my hand and after. But I have never...I've never experienced something quite so horrible. It was as if the very world turned against us. In some ways, it did. The sylphs are all but eliminated, their force about one tenth of what it was. The humans are less than five hundred. Lenore is in the middle of birthing her child and it is not going well. Crispinus will never fly again. Brianna is dead. The sylphs' queen is furious. Ravenna and Cavaris have gone. And Seraphina—"

Miska sat up as best he could, the motion causing his head to split open in pain. He tried to bend his knees and sink his head into them, to change the blood flow maybe, but his legs would not move. His spine flared in agony and Miska could almost feel the ridges there writhing. He gasped in a breath and choked it back out. He was still recovering from using his magic. Of course. He would be immobilised for a while, if the pain was any indication. But there were more important things.

"What do you mean Ravenna and Cavaris are gone?" Miska coughed, looking up at Sisu with wide eyes.

"You should not move so swiftly. We do not know what the damage is." Sisu reached out to push Miska back down into a lying position, but Miska swatted his hand away. He turned at the waist, trying to swing his legs over the side. They remained immobile. He reached out and touch them, but he could feel nothing. Not the brush of fabric on his skin, nor the pressure of his hands around his thigh. Nor could he feel his legs experience any pain at all. "Miska?"

Miska was staring at Sisu's mouth, unsure he had comprehended anything the man had said.

Mouth suddenly dry again, he croaked, "I cannot move my legs. I cannot feel them."

Sisu straightened, nostrils flaring as he took in a shocked breath. "Maybe you just need time to recover, like before."

"I don't know. I would be immobile before, but I could always feel...I don't... it doesn't matter. Not right now. Whatever it is I'll deal with it. Tell me about Ravenna. Tell me why she is gone. She and Cavaris were not at the battle. They should be..." Desperate thoughts flitted through Miska's mind like the whispers of that shadowland. Had Ravenna abandoned him again? Had she gone off with Cavaris after deciding that she couldn't handle more bloodshed? The dragon would have happily transported her away, Miska knew. Anything to avoid war. Or had Seraphina managed to send some advance scout and kill her?

"She is alive," Sisu said. He shook his head, pressing his mouth together in a thin line. "She was alive last anyone knew. The rumours are all over the camp. She has gone with Cavaris to go and fight Seraphina in single combat. To end this the only way that she can."

Miska swallowed, sure that he had sand in his mouth. *No.* Was this what Tacitus had meant? Was this what he knew when he said Ravenna was set on her path, that she knew the way she had to walk, that she was doing what she must? No. It could not be. She would not... She could not...She had left him *again*. Oh, it might be the right thing for her to do. She might be the only one to have a chance of saving them from Seraphina's wrath, but Miska could not believe that she would do this to him again. That she would leave him behind and go to fight her own battle without even consulting him. He wanted to rage at her, to shake her and make her seek sense, but it was too late. Did she even love him at all?

He must've said that last question out loud, because Sisu reached out and lifted Miska's chin so that he was staring him in the face. Sisu's mouth was curled in anger, his eyes blazing. "Do not *ever* doubt her. From what I understand, she has been doubted her whole life. She does not need it from you. She has gone because she loves you, and that is the simple truth."

Miska nodded, and only then did Sisu release his hand. He wiped his hands over his eyes, pulling black strands away from his face and rubbing his beard. Miska wanted to comfort him, but he did not know how. Was Sisu feeling concern for his daughter? Was he worried that all of this effort had been for nothing?

"She will prevail," Miska said. "Ravenna is the most capable woman I have ever known. She fought and killed a desert lion to save me. She did not let her spirit break when she was in chains as a slave, or when she was bound by Davorin. She has fought to make her people into warriors. She killed the demon that Davorin summoned. She has done everything for her people and for me and for Desarra and Lenore. Seraphina might be vicious and bloodthirsty, ambitious and dangerous, but she has not the heart that Ravenna has."

Sisu nodded. Smiled. "I know. It doesn't stop me from being afraid. I've never actually had family before. Yes, I hunted with Asgeir and Cai and Ib, but is not the same. And now I have family, and she goes off to fight a war on her own."

Miska laughed, trying not to feel the fear that still constricted his chest. "She takes after you that way. Now help me get out of this tent. I have to go deliver a message to Desarra. And then I wish to know what has become of my Queen. Just because Ravenna has gone off does not mean that we should wallow in fear while she is gone. If she wins—when she wins—we will be here waiting for her."

Sisu nodded. He stood, almost too tall for the tent. He put one arm under Miska's shoulders and the other under his knees.

Again, there was the strange sensation of not being able to feel. Miska saw Sisu's arm beneath his legs, yet could not feel it. He shoved the feeling down. He could not deal with the thought of maybe never being able to walk again just then. He had other matters to attend to. He had a message to deliver from Tacitus. And then, whether Ravenna needed it or not, he was going to rally the people to go after her, to stand by her side and show her that she was not alone. She was never alone. And never would be again.

CHAPTER TWENTY-ONE

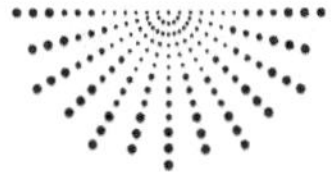

"It's not quite time yet," the healer said, leaning over to examine Lenore from beneath the sheets. She stood up and smiled at Lenore, the motion anything but endearing at that particular moment. "Just keep breathing through the pain."

Two hours into the start of her birthing, and Lenore was ready to kill somebody. Especially if they kept telling her to breathe. The pain was excruciating, growing worse with each contraction, her hands digging like claws into the bedding, her mouth spouting every foul curse she had ever learned and been forced to never repeat. She wanted this child out of her *now*, and the healers were all being extremely un-obliging.

Another spasm of pain rippled through her and Lenore threw back her head, letting out a low scream. She kicked at the sheets and tried not to think of all the things happening to her just then. When she could manage it, she sucked in a breath and did her best to keep breathing, as she had been told over and over and over again. The contractions were still many minutes apart, so she could relax for a small time, her eyes leaking water involuntarily and her hands finding it difficult to extract themselves from the bed clothes.

"Drink this," Blodwen said, holding a damp rag to Lenore's mouth. Lenore laughed at the few droplets of water like an eager dog before leaning back against the pillows, exhausted. Even her hands trembled, and she was barely into her birthing. Her friend squeezed the excess moisture over Lenore's brow, the water feeling graciously cool amidst the cloying heat attend. It was still dark, the morning being some hours off, but the coolness of the desert seemed to have ignored the tent entirely, seeing as it was full of healers and attendants, wanting to see that the Red Queen's birthing went well. Lenore had tried to throw them out and had failed miserably, being scolded by Blodwen that they were all necessary.

"You must do something to distract me or I am like to go mad. Tell me that things are going well out there. Tell me that we stand a chance with Ravenna off to fight the battle. Tell me something," Lenore said hoarsely, looking up at Blodwen with pleading eyes, desperate for any news, good or bad. Anything to distract her from what she was going through. What fears lurked in her mind, about whether or not she would love the child as Desarra had said, or whether she would prove to be a difficult mother in light of what Davorin had done to her. She feared she would not be able to give the child what it needed. She feared that the world was too harsh a place to bring it into being. And yet through all of this, she wished she held her child in her arms, safe and warm. And not currently causing her pain.

"Her absence has barely been noted. The sylphs all seem exhausted, broken. I don't know if they do not know that she has gone to fight or if they just do not care. Perhaps they think she betrayed them when she did not accompany them to war," Blodwen said. She wiped again at Lenore's brow, water already evaporated. Lenore pushed through the haze of her thoughts and nodded, licking her dry lips. Blodwen quickly gave her more water, glaring at the healers in attendance who simply stood there, waiting for Lenore's next contraction instead of fetching more water or getting out of the way. At least they were talking amongst themselves, pacing or making herbal parcels, leaving Lenore to her own conversation.

"I doubt that. They seem to revere her. No, Ravenna's only guilt is in her mind alone." Lenore sucked in a breath, then let it out again. This birthing was taking too long and it hurt too much. "Is there nothing else that we can do to help her odds? I would not send my friend off to such a fate alone, no matter how these last few days have played out. Nnnnggg..."

Immediately, healers were there, checking her, putting hands on her belly and telling her that once again, it was not yet time and she needed to breathe. If they told her that once more, Lenore would have Blodwen throw something at them. Instead, Lenore glared, sweat dripping down the back of her neck, her lips curled as she trying to get her breathing under control.

"Glaring like that, you look like a warrior queen of legend," a new voice said, stepping into the tent and earning the verbalised ire of several of the healers. Lenore lifted her head and tried to focus her eyes on the newcomer. Vareis. As much as Lenore did not really wish to deal with the former training master, the de facto leader of the nonexistent resistance, there was really no other time to do so. Ravenna had gone to fight Seraphina and if she lost, then it would not matter whether Vareis could finally deliver on her promises. Still, Lenore would like to send whatever assistance she could, just in case. She had to do *something*.

"If I were a warrior queen of legend," Lenore said between deep breathing exercises, "I would have a spear in my hand and a sword at your throat. Unless you have come here to tell me that the resistance has finally mustered its forces and is prepared to ride into battle, then I suggest you leave."

Instead of leaving, Vareis strode forward and knelt at Lenore's left side, out of the way of the furious Blodwen and the preening healers as they patted Lenore down with cloths, preparing more water. "You have to understand," Vareis said, grabbing Lenore's hand. Lenore bore down on Vareis' hand with all the strength of her pain in her grip. Vareis gasped, but did not pull away. Good, Lenore thought. She had more strength in her than she thought. Maybe she would be of some use, after all. Then again, maybe not. "Gathering together such ragtag forces has been incredibly difficult. The people are afraid. Of Davorin. Of the sylphs. Of—"

"Of what? Of losing their lives? Instead, they are happy to stand on the sidelines while we who are left risk everything for them." Lenore managed the words between gritted teeth, letting out a slow hiss of air. The healer pressed some herbal tea on her, the hot liquid unwelcome in this cloying heat. Lenore drank it anyways.

"You know that the people are grateful for—" Vareis said, trying to smile though she failed.

"Grateful for every drop of blood shed so that they might have a nice quiet existence, so that they might never risk their own hides or their own properties or their own names? Oh yes, I know exactly how grateful they are. Your great resistance is a sham. And you, of all my friends from the Red Palace, of all the people that I trusted to help me as I tried to lead this kingdom, I never expected that you would be the one to fall for such false hope." Lenore leaned up as much as she could and bared her teeth feraly at Vareis. The woman pulled back, eyes wide. Lenore had never seen such shame and fear on the former training master's face, so foreign to her that it seemed a completely different person. Then, Vareis had never tasted war before this time. She had only trained to those who would defend the Red Desert.

How could she have trained Ravenna, no matter how short the time was, and be so different? How could Vareis, whose skills were legendary amongst the Red Desert, be so much more afraid to fight with an army at her back than Ravenna, who fought alone?

"I haven't fallen for it." Vareis had the gall to look hurt. "I truly believe that the resistance is working towards a goal that can be achieved. They are doing their best to organise, to win back the independence of all of those city states and kingdoms and nations that have fallen to the Salusian Empire. This *situation* just came before they were ready."

"They will never be ready, these cowards who hide in the shadows and pretend that they are fighting for altruistic purposes." Lenore ground her teeth and tossed her head back again, squeezing Vareis's hand to the point where she could feel bones grinding on one another. She let out another scream, the pain shadowing her mind. The healers checked her again, exchanging worried glances between them.

"No," Vareis said, removing her hand from Lenore's grasp and shaking it to restore circulation. She did not offer it again. "I can't believe that. These people have risked so much, working under the shadow of the Empire."

"They have not fought even one skirmish. They have not stopped one food or supply transport. They have not sold everything they have so that their people might live. Everything I had. Everything that I was, it is all changed now. I gave myself to the Empire so that my people would be safe. I have sacrificed *everything*. Do you have the nerve to tell me that these people believe they are risking more? Go back to your cowards, Vareis. When Ravenna returns—and she will return, and she will return victorious—I wish to never see you again. You have dashed my hopes for the last time. You have wasted my good will, absconded with my resources, and sold me lies. Your resistance may have avoided fighting now, but when I can stand and take my kingdom back, by whatever means necessary, I will be sure to hunt down everyone who took part in demand to know why they did not fight. Why they stood by and did nothing while good men and women and sylphs died in agony."

"Lenore—"

"Your *Majesty*," Lenore spat. "I am still Queen, whether you like it or not. Soon, I shall have all the control and power of the Red Desert behind me once more. And unless you plan to have your resistance fight *me*, kill *me*, then I suggest you leave."

By the end of this, Lenore was panting, the pain growing impossibly worse. Vareis started to say something. Lenore shook her off with another scream, the contractions seeming stronger than ever. She barely noticed through the haze of her mind Blodwen moistening her brow and the healers murmuring to one another or Vareis leaving. She did not spare the woman another thought, instead too focused with fears about her people and her own pain.

"The child is turned around in the womb," the head healer said, her eyes wide with terror. "We must turn it."

Lenore nodded, focusing all her attention on taking one breath in and letting it out. They squeezed her belly, turning the child with enough force to have Lenore screaming again. By this time, she was sobbing, tears leaking freely and pain radiating up her back and into her shoulders. She heard something about blood, about the fluids, and then she was seized again by spasms.

"We must get the child out now. If we do not, then both shall be lost." Was that Blodwen or the healer who spoke? Lenore's vision was going hazy, her mind too occupied by pain and fear to pay attention to such measly things as sights and sounds. Someone whispered something into her ear, and Lenore turned her head dully away from the buzz, unable to face another discomfort. She licked her dry lips, wondering why she hadn't had water in so long. It was so hot. More pain spasmed through her, but she had not the energy to fight or to brace herself against it. She just let it come as it would, relaxing into the fire that burned through her body. She had no more fight left in her.

All the things she had done were to protect her people. She wanted nothing more than for her people to thrive, to live well and free. She had not worked so hard as Queen to be reduced to nothing but a puppet wielded by Davorin for pretty dances and bragging. And yet that was what she had become. Paraded about like a doll, like a prized horse. The pretty clothes, the pointless frippery and delicate ornaments, all that she had accepted without question just as she had accepted the fact that Davorin would not let her do anything. She had hardly fought to keep control over her kingdom. A few looks, a glare, a threat, a slap, and she was as cowed as ever. For what? Her people died just as easily under the swords of Seraphina's warriors. The people had given all they had to support Davorin's grand progress. They starved. Fought. Died. And what did she have to show for it now? Pain.

She didn't know why there was pain. It was important. It was more important than she could say.

"The father had magic," a voice said in the shadows at the edge of this strange scene with people rushing about, holding bloody fabric. None of them seemed to notice the voice, nor Lenore's disappointment in herself. Some Queen she was.

"Stolen magic." Another voice, matching the other in terms of quiet power that flowed through it, ancient and magnificent. Something in Lenore seemed to recognise that those voices should not exist, should be lost to myth and legend. But wasn't that the way with things? Legend seemed to want to do everything to become reality. And reality was becoming more legendary every day. These voices were old, and Lenore had no name for them. She was not sure she had a name for herself. The world seemed so hazy, so disjointed. Wasn't there meant to be something she was doing just then?

"Stolen magic is still magic. The child will be marked. Important."

"Only if it lives. If its mother lives." the second voice said, seeming louder than before. It drew closer to Lenore, and she could've sworn she felt the presence, something in the same in between space she was occupying without knowing how or why. Something breathed on her, the touch of its magic so much more potent than Miska's or Davorin's. "Fight, human. Your battle is not lost yet. Your future still stands before you, bright on the horizon."

Lenore sucked in a sharp breath, the haze surrounding her falling away. She heard Blodwen at her head, desperately pleading with her to stay with them, to fight, to bear down. She felt Blodwen's hand in hers, the touch familiar, comforting. Lenore squeezed the fingers with his much strength she had, and nodded. This time, when the healers told her to bear down, to push, she did. She tossed back her head, screamed, the sound louder than ever before, reverberating through the encampment. The vision or the memory of those ancient voices faded with the pain, completely gone by the time it fell quiet.

Something loosened, and suddenly Lenore's body felt as if a great weight had been lifted, and simultaneously as if a thread in her soul had been pulled to extend somewhere close by, forever connecting her to this new mysterious object. One weight gone, another in its place. This one was far easier to bear.

She heard silence for a moment, then the impossibly beautiful cry of a wailing child.

"Congratulations, my Queen. You have a son." The healer wiped away the last of the birthing fluid that covered the child with a cloth, then handed the swaddled bundle to Lenore. She took the child and suddenly the world was righted. The thread in her soul connected to *him*. There was no longer any question of her loving the child for fear of his father's demons haunting her. There was no fear of her not being able to mother him as he needed. She just looked down at the bundle in her arms, brushed a trembling finger over his beautiful brownish gold skin, his shock of dark brown hair, matted flat with moisture. She touched his face, afraid that if she touched too hard that he would shatter beneath her. He wiggled in her arms and snuggled in closer.

"He's beautiful," Blodwen said. Lenore nodded, mindless of the healers still moving about and doing their best to see to things, to make her well and whole again. "He looks like that statue of the sylph in your garden. Your ancestor."

"He has a noble heritage," Lenore said, pressing the tip of her finger to his nose delighting as he squirmed, his eyes still shut. "And even if he did not, I would not love him any less. My son."

Her *son*. She swore, by The One Who Watches, by the god Materior in whose name she was married, by any being of power old and forgotten and strong, that she would watch over him. She would care for this child as she cared for her kingdom. And for that, she had given—and would give again—everything. She would build it up from the ground, if necessary, making the Red Desert once again a place where the people were strong and proud and free.

She would do it for *him*.

"Do you have a name for him?" Blodwen asked, putting a hand on Lenore's head and smoothing some of her hair. Lenore smiled and looked up at Blodwen. She seemed hazy again, the image distorting, though this time for no more reason than tears.

"Erowain," Lenore said. "Erowain, the Red Prince, heir to everything I hold. My beautiful son."

As she settled back in the bed, weak and sore and absurdly delirious with joy, Lenore did not even want to question whether or not she would have anything for her son to inherit before too very long. She just closed her eyes and trusted that Ravenna would, as she had promised, swoop in on flightless wings and save them all.

And if she did not, then Lenore would. For Erowain's sake.

CHAPTER TWENTY-TWO

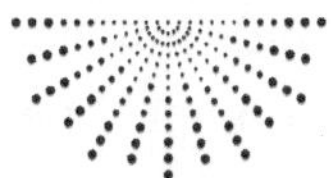

After a day of walking in the desert with Cavaris, Ravenna spotted the seemingly endless army of Seraphina on the horizon. She had not seen the forces of Southron before except in scattered groups at the Red Palace. Seeing them marching together, out for bloodshed, was something else entirely. The silence that had lain between Cavaris and Ravenna this past day seemed to grow thicker, not for fear, but for the weight of what Ravenna was about to do. The dragon had not once tried to talk her out of it, nor had he offered her his support except to say that he would perform the oath binding so that if Ravenna could convince Seraphina to do this, the outcome would be insured.

The winner of this duel would take control of everything. Nothing else would suffice.

With such an overwhelming force though, Ravenna was not entirely sure that Seraphina would agree to her proposal. Why would she, when she was already guaranteed everything she wanted?

False dawn was beginning to light the dark sky, the stars still vibrant and the moon still glowing. Ravenna paused, long enough to gather her energy and her breath for what was to come. She half expected her hands to tremble and her wings to shake as she pulled them in closer. But now that she knew what lay before her, now that she had seen precisely what it was that had torn her people and Lenore's to shreds, she felt oddly calm.

One way or another, all this death would be over.

Of course she was afraid. But her path was set. She knew precisely what she had to do, and she would see it through, no matter the cost. Fear had no place in her actions.

"Am I doing the right thing?" Ravenna asked, the first time she had done so with Cavaris at her side.

"Are you doubting yourself? Or are you seeking assurance?" Cavaris's voice was as calm as Ravenna's, though she sensed that he was uncomfortable being so close to a marauding army. Or perhaps it was just her projecting her own thoughts onto him. After all, he had seen generations of war. Nothing here could harm him. No matter the outcome today, he would survive. Ravenna might not.

"I am just wondering if leaving everyone behind was really the best way to do this. I wonder if marching off to go fight this battle single-handedly was nothing but arrogance on my part. After all, I let my people go off to fight without me. And now here I am, claiming that I can fix this mess alone." Ravenna drank from the water skin at her belt so that she would not have to see the deliberations across Cavaris's face. She did not want to see what the dragon thought of her. It would be too much like looking in a mirror.

"This is a desperate solution brought about not by arrogance but by confidence. Notice that it was not the first solution you sought out. You were not foolish enough to believe that you could start this and end this before it began, that you could take the fate of the world in your wings and bend it to your will. You had to follow the logical course of action, the one that made sense. Fighting against Davorin was that course. And your people went off to fight their logical course before they consider to be ramifications of a battle against the Southron warriors. No, I would not say that this is arrogance. The risks are too high for it to appear that way."

Somehow, that didn't actually help Ravenna at all. He had not said it was the right thing to do, only that it was not borne from arrogance. Then again, she had not asked his opinion on whether she was right. She lifted her head and examined the stars that were fading as the light grew stronger. Already, the almost crisp and cold air of the desert night was warming, becoming something fierce. How many people had watered this desert with blood over the cycles? It was not a fertile land as far as Ravenna knew, though there might be hidden wonders. But it seemed to be the centre of so much conflict. Why?

She did not know. She was doing anything at this point to forestall the inevitable. She drank another mouthful of water, stretched her wings experimentally, watched the false dawn fade into true dawn and measured the army then marched towards her.

"If this goes badly today, will you do something for me?" Ravenna asked. Cavaris inclined his head, folding his hands into his robes.

"If I can then I will." His red eyes seemed to grow brighter the longer Ravenna waited. Eventually, she looked away.

"If I fail, take a message back to the sylphs on Shinalea. Tell them what happened. Help them flee. Surely there must be somewhere in this world that is safe for them." It was not what Ravenna had wanted to ask. She had wanted to ask Cavaris to provide a dagger for each sylph that would be affected by their bargain, so that they might choose to die free instead of being enslaved. She had wanted to ask him to say her farewells to

Miska, to tell Desarra that she was sorry, to teach Crispin how to be strong without flight. She'd wanted to ask him a hundred things, but none of it would actually help. So she asked for the one thing she knew Cavaris could give.

Beside her, the dragon drew in a deep, seemingly endless breath. Perhaps he was feeding that legendary fire that dragons were said to bear in their chests. He held it for several heartbeats before he let it out slowly, the moisture from his lungs evaporating quickly in the air. "Do you really believe you will fail?"

"As you said, it is a desperate solution to an impossible problem. And yet, I would not have offered nor struck out on this path unless I was confident that I could do it. It seems that after all, flightless Intellecti that I am, I was best made for one thing. Battle. It helped me stand tall when my wing-weariness weighed down my soul. It helped me to find balance in a life that seemed to want to tear me to pieces. It is one of the few places where I am thoroughly alive. No, I do not believe that I will fail. The possibility still remains."

Cavaris quirked a brow, struggling to keep a smile from his mouth. He turned to face the oncoming army, back straight eyes relaxed. "You are an unusual sylph."

Ravenna snorted and shook her head. She took one last mouthful of water, stoppered the water skin, and waited until the tip of the sun spread its light over the horizon. Then, she lifted her chin, flared her wings wide, and strode to meet the forces of Southron head on.

"Speak, they will hear," Cavaris breathed at her side. Ravenna nodded and spread her arms, curling her lip in a triumphant smile.

"I am Ravenna Wingsword, Warlord of the Stormbringers, the Oncoming Storm, she who revived the ancient art of Dalketh, Bane of Jazer, killer of Dagan the demon, the angel of death. You have threatened my people and called for the execution of those I hold dear. I have come for *vengeance*. I challenge Seraphina, leader of this army, sister to the madman Davorin, daughter of the Salusian Empire, to single combat. The winner shall take all."

Ravenna's voice echoed over the open desert, impossibly amplified and thrumming with power. She halted twenty paces before the head of the army, her wings outstretched teeth bared, ready. She saw the warriors at the edge draw their bows and knock an arrow, pointing it in her direction. She held her ground.

A horse, decked in gilded tack, bearing a rider whose attire gleamed in the morning sun, emerged from behind the leader of the group. Horse and rider drew closer to Ravenna until she could see past the glare from the sun. It was a woman, wearing what looked to be clothing woven from gold and silver, her hair gilded with it, gold leaf painted across her cheeks, eyes surrounded by silver, headdress of ridiculous proportions jingling as she moved. This rider dismounted and Ravenna saw that the gold and silver clothing was done in the style of the desert, as if it already belonged to her. Her fingers were tipped with claws of metal, though this looked to be hardened steel instead of gold or silver or some other combination. She strode across the desert until she was five paces from Ravenna.

"I am Seraphina. You would challenge me, angel, sylph, whatever you are?" She seemed amused. As though Ravenna were nothing more than a game, a sport. Yet, her brown eyes gleamed with interest, shining almost brighter than her ridiculous clothing.

"For the future of my people, for the freedom of the Red Desert, for control over our future and the future of humans and all who roam this continent, yes. I challenge you," Ravenna said. Seraphina sniffed and looked Ravenna over, taking in her dirty clothes and her scratched armour, the hilts of the sword strapped to her back, her wings, the fury in her eyes. She shifted her gaze to Cavaris, taking in his pale skin, his white hair, his horns that rose above his head.

"Is your companion going to fight as well? Or are you too cowardly for a fair fight?" Seraphina smiled and widened her eyes, feigning innocence. If she sought to anger Ravenna, it wasn't working. Ravenna just stood there, as calm as ever. The emotional turmoil she had felt earlier was gone. All that remained in its place was the knowledge that this was what she needed to do. She hid no more behind ice or behind stone, behind a mask that sheltered her pain. She simply had no reason for it to linger. It no longer mattered.

"This is Cavaris, the dragon of the ages. He will not be fighting. He is simply here to make sure that whatever bargain we strike is upheld, no matter who wins." Ravenna swept a wing towards Cavaris, and he bowed. The movement was not meant to be mocking, but it had an edge. Seraphina's back straightened.

"A dragon. A true dragon. My goodness. I knew my brother had come across legends when he told me about the winged being he bought as a pet, but I did not know that she kept company with true myths. A dragon. Indeed. You know that my brother stole the tooth of a dragon." Seraphina flashed her teeth, a winning smile.

"That was no dragon's tooth. That was something far less powerful, something that should have remained buried. Its death was as wrong as its life. But, one does not expect humans and mortals to understand the ramifications of digging up the past," Cavaris said. Ravenna thought she heard the echo of a hiss in his voice, the flesh of a fang. Yet he sounded as gentle as always, the façade that hid a rage that had injured Ravenna and broken Miska.

Seraphina made a noise in the back of her throat but she kept the smile. "Why should I agree to fight? You would not come to do this unless you had no other recourse. Or are you the magical weapon that your people failed to use the last time? I don't remember seeing you at the battle, though I was fairly busy." Ravenna blinked slowly; she did not look away from Seraphina's gaze, ignoring the smirk there.

"I was not there. My people wished to test their mettle, and they are now aware of their limitations. I, however, am not. I challenge you to single combat, to end this before you spend the next hundred moons trying to subdue a people that should never be subdued. If there is only one sylph remaining, you can be sure that they will fight you. Whereas, if you agreed to battle me now, then I can assure you my people will not fight. The Red Desert will not fight. You will have everything that you came here for." There was a tightness in Ravenna's chest as she spoke those words, but she ignored it. She had to continue to believe that she would prevail. The alternative was unthinkable.

"An intriguing offer. And if you win? Am I expected to simply retreat back to Southron?" Seraphina tilted her head, the metal pieces in her headdress like tiny bells. It struck Ravenna as she watched Seraphina move what the woman was trying to achieve. It was not simply a show of wealth, nor a means to gather attention. It was her way of wearing the armour of dragons, of becoming a legend herself. The pieces were all pieced together, the seams between the scales most invisible. The claws, headdress to imitate horns, the gild and the paint, it was all to become something that she was not. And faced with the reality, with two legends to her people, she must have felt inadequate. The scales around Cavaris' eyes were real, faint white. The scales around hers were gaudy and silver, nowhere near as elegant. Seraphina wanted power. She wanted to see immortality of being a dragon, of being remembered forever. And, by the way her eyes gleamed, she wanted to fight Ravenna.

Ravenna inclined her head. "Yes. You would return to Southron and be content with your lands there, never again venturing forth to conquer those that do not belong to you."

Seraphina clicked her claws together, flashing her teeth and another smile. "I will tell you what. If you win, you may have Southron. You may have the Salusian Empire, as I am its only remaining heir. You may have everything that belongs to me."

Ravenna blinked, this time in surprise. "If that is your wish, then I accept."

Seraphina nodded, her gilded hair clinking together as she moved. "This should be fun. The bargain is struck."

Cavaris lifted a hand, his claws smaller than Seraphina's, but all the more real. He seemed amused by her imitation, or perhaps it was the deal that amused him. But he lifted his hand, moved it through the air to hover over Seraphina and Ravenna, and then pulled his fist together. "So it is spoken, so will it be. You are bound."

A tightness settled over Ravenna's shoulders, not of her own making. This was the dragon's magic, sealing the bargain struck between herself and Seraphina. Ravenna knew it was happening, knew it was meant to be, and yet she still felt a great weight. Seraphina sucked in a breath, obviously feeling it too. She hissed at Ravenna, showing her teeth.

"Very well, sylph. You and I shall fight to the death in an hour. I suggest you prepare yourself, for when I march upon your people, I will wear your wings as a cloak." Seraphina turned and marched back to her horse, swinging up into the saddle and charging off into the midst of her army. Ravenna remained where she was, though she let her wings relax at her side. She turned to Cavaris, who nodded and said nothing.

Ravenna took a seat on the ground, folding her feet beneath her and resting her hands on her knees. She wished for a moment that Miska were there beside her, to offer her comfort and support. She wished that she had not let Desarra leave as she had, furious and doubting herself. She wished that she could be there when Crispin learned to use his crippled wing again, even if it would not bear him in flight. She wanted to see

Lenore's child born. She wanted to consult with Davorin one more time, to see if there were an answer to why all of this had happened.

"In times of turmoil," Cavaris said, looking down at her as he waited patiently for whatever came next, "it is common amongst the humans to pray to whatever gods they worship."

"The sylphs do not worship a god or gods. At least, I have not found any reference to such in any of the tomes in the Stone Tower. The only ritual that I could find was the candlelight vigil that was kept while the Stormbringers were off to fight. I wonder if Kratos stopped his vigil once we sent the wounded back, or if he still waits." Ravenna had not considered that she would never see Kratos again. Somehow the thought of the old healer, standing in the hall of bones where she had left him, struck her more than anything else she had considered in these last days. She had come to grips with losing Miska, with Lenore's forgetting about her, with Desarra and Crispin leading the sylphs, with everything, but Kratos? She would miss him more than she had thought.

"It is striking how much is forgotten as time marches onwards," Cavaris said. "The sylphs were as faithful as many humans, many many generations ago. They had three of them they called upon. Malchis, the warrior. Elyria, the healer. And…" Cavaris smiled down at her. "And Ravenna, the wind in the storm."

Ravenna nodded, smiling. "Tacitus never did explain where he found my name. I have not heard it used amongst the sylphs before, but he assured me that it was an old and ancient and venerable name. That it would keep me strong."

"It is a good name. And you are very worthy of it. No matter what happens today." Cavaris lay hand on Ravenna's head, the gesture somehow more comforting than a hug or a wing touch.

"Tell them I love them. If I don't go back. Tell them all that I did this for them. All of them." Suddenly, it was harder to breathe, like her throat was tight and her eyes blurry.

"Tell them yourself."

Ravenna let out a single, breathy laugh. "Very well, dragon. I will."

CHAPTER TWENTY-THREE

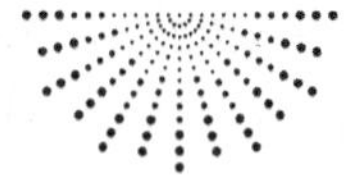

Seraphina stood across from Ravenna, her back to the sylph. The woman had changed, Ravenna noted. She had discarded the gaudy gold and silver clothes in favour of a pair of desert trousers, loose and free moving, made out of some simple brown fabric. From the way they were belted at Seraphina's hips, Ravenna imagined that they were borrowed. It seemed incongruous for the vain queen, but it would be difficult to battle in a dress, even one of the loose desert style. She wore similar boiled leather armour to Ravenna's, with metal plating done in copper, rather than the simple armour that Ravenna wore. The copper would be relatively soft, if Ravenna's knowledge of metal weapons was also true of armour. It would not take blows well, but it would be enough protection if Seraphina was skilled. She had also disposed of the gaudy headdress and tied her hair back in a simple tail. She still had the gilded ends, and she still bore the claws on her fingers.

Around the two fighters, Seraphina's soldiers gathered. One of them, a large man, spoke to the Southron queen as she tightened the belt at her waist and tugged at the bracers on her arms. She sneered at him and snapped something in response. The man quieted and took a step back so that he was within the perimeter of witnesses.

Cavaris stood in the centre of the circle, waiting. Many of the humans eyed him with wariness, or smirked and jangled their weapons at him. This seemed only to amuse the dragon. Were he in his true form, then no one would be doing any such foolish thing as to taunt him. He just stood there calmly, waiting as though he had an infinite well of patience.

Ravenna had given up her water skins, had made sure that the straps on her armour were secure and that the blades were easily accessible on her back. She had no more waiting to do. Her patience was running out. She wanted to get this over with. Her wings opened and closed ever so slightly, stretching and folding, her impatience showing through. She wished she could remain as calm as Cavaris, but with her opponent right there, their battle so close, it was more than difficult.

Finally, Seraphina flexed her hands and the claws attached there one last time, then turned to face Ravenna, a fierce grin on her face. She took three steps forward until she was beside Cavaris. Ravenna did the same, measuring her steps so that she did not appear overeager. She needed to pace herself. In this battle, there was more than fighting happening.

"I think that she should not be allowed to wield two swords," Seraphina said with a sniff. No greeting, no official welcome to the challenge, no acknowledgment of Cavaris, just a declaration.

"You were allowed to choose your armour and your weapons, just as she was. You chose those claws rather than a sword and a shield. If you feel that is unfair, then you are welcome to choose again," Cavaris said. Seraphina barely spared him a glance, instead curling her lip and giving Ravenna the once over.

"She did not choose to have wings. Those are just as capable as any weapon, I'm sure. After all, I've seen her people fight. She has two more weapons than she ought to have. One, if you choose to count them as a pair. Therefore, it is only fair that she should dispose of one of the swords." Seraphina clicked her metal tip fingers together. Cavaris raised his brow.

"Your argument holds many flaws. It does not seem right to cripple someone because they have been born in a certain way. However, it is up to you, Ravenna, whether you choose to allow this or argue." Cavaris tilted his head in her direction. Ravenna swallowed. To lose one of the swords would be unhelpful, to say the least. She could still fight without, but she had grown used to the weight of both in a fight. She wanted to get this over with as quickly as possible, though. Ravenna reached up with her right hand and pulled one of the swords from her back. Seraphina stiffened, eyes flashing, as if she expected some sort of treachery. Ravenna turned and handed the weapon to Cavaris.

"If she feels that it would be a better match with me wielding only the one sword, then I shall accommodate. I would wish there to be no question of who is truly the victor here." Ravenna inclined her head to Cavaris, who responded with a knowing smile. He turned to Seraphina and quirked a brow, waiting for her inevitable response.

"There shall be absolutely no question who the victor is. She shall be the only one still alive." The soldiers around them stomped their feet and cheered at Seraphina's words, already eager for the bloodshed. Seraphina held out her arms and the cheering increased. If Seraphina meant to intimidate Ravenna with the rowdiness of the audience, then she would be sorely disappointed. This was familiar to Ravenna. The cheering of the audience, the cries for blood. It was all just as it had been when she first fell into the Slave Pits in the bloody arena. This was how it had been when she first learned the truth about Dalketh and its use in battle, the feeling of fighting running through her blood, the reality of the Stormbringers. This was so very like the situation in which Ravenna had become what she was. It did not intimidate her. Not in the slightest.

"If there are no more deliberations to be done, then I declare that the binding is intact. The victor of this battle shall bear the spoils. Do not think to engage in poor combat etiquette. I shall be standing by to make certain that no one gathers help from the outside, that proper boundaries are kept. You may not take another weapon offered to you. The only protection is that what you bring with you now. We shall not stop for rest, nor shall we stop until one person can claim victory, either through the death of the other, or the inability to continue fighting no matter the odds. Are you both in agreement?" Cavaris spread his hands, placing a clawed appendage in the air above each woman's shoulder.

"I am agreed," Ravenna said. Seraphina narrowed her eyes.

"Agreed."

Cavaris nodded. He set his clawed hand down, touching the skin. Ravenna felt his magic burn through her, sealing the binding into place and being certain that she would not cheat. Seraphina's breath hitched, so the same must have happened to her.

The dragon stepped back, movements steady until he was at the edge of the circle, the perimeter of witnesses standing just behind him. Silence fell. "You may begin."

Cavaris hadn't finished his sentence before Seraphina flew at Ravenna, right hand held above her face, left hand outstretched to scratch and gouge. Ravenna simply stepped aside, sweeping her wing open and watching as Seraphina stumbled forward. Ravenna slid into the Dalketh stance and drew her remaining sword with her left hand. She held it outstretched, wings half flared at her side. Seraphina did not hesitate again, this time lunging forward with a bit more finesse. Ravenna swept the sword underneath Seraphina's cutting claws, her reach extended beyond that of the Southron queen. The steel of her sword skittered across steel of Seraphina's claws and both were pushed back.

Ravenna could have easily stood there all day, dodging Seraphina's attacks and blocking her claws with her sword, but that would do none of them any good. So she surged into an attack, thrusting her wings downwards and forcing herself into a jump, twisting midair so that her sword should scrape across Seraphina's back and neck. The other woman ducked low and turned, her movements catlike and fluid. This was a woman who had fought before. This was a woman who had faced Crispin and nearly severed his wing. So when Ravenna landed, wings before her to balance her fall, she had to stagger backwards and pull her wings out of the way so that Seraphina could not do the same to her. Even so, some of the feathers caught on the claws, pulling from ligaments holding them in place. They fluttered to the ground.

"Are you not going to fly little bird? Are you not going to try to come at me from the sky?" Seraphina taunted, barely seeming to have broken a sweat despite the heat of the day. The sun glared down into both of their eyes, reflecting off the sand and making heat shimmers where they moved.

Ravenna did not answer her taunt, she just tilted her wings to break through the air and surged forward with as much speed as she could muster, pushing her sword passed Seraphina's guard and getting in as close as possible. Claw and steel struggled against each other, their faces inches apart. Ravenna beat her wings once, twice, the extra momentum and power propelling her ever so slightly forward, her sword drawing closer to Seraphina's face. The human female moved one clawed hand to strike at Ravenna, and Ravenna's sword fell towards her. Both staggered back a moment later, each bleeding. The strap over Ravenna's right shoulder had been severed, two mild slashes in her shoulder bleeding. There was a deeper gash across

Seraphina's face, cutting from one cheekbone to the bridge of the nose.

"Well, well," Seraphina said, touching her face and dipping the tip of one claw into the blood. She looked at the liquid. "Seems like you can fight after all. Amazing. I thought Davorin's little pet was domiciled."

"I was never Davorin's little pet, no matter his wishes. And fighting is in my blood. I am a Stormbringer," Ravenna said. She stretched her wings experimentally, testing the range of motion in her shoulder. "And the Storm is meant to end the wars, by any means."

"Then, why do you not end it already?" Seraphina slid a foot back and lifted her hands before her, ready to fight and defend. Ravenna lifted the blade in her left hand, holding the right wing close to her so that she could bat away Seraphina's claws. Somewhere in her mind, Ravenna heard the cheers of the people around them, the conversations and the noise of the army shifting to get a better view. Ravenna blinked once. Then they both pushed off with their back foot and came together.

Ravenna twisted her wings and her body would follow, the Dalketh movements instinctual and like dancing. Her wings beat at her opponent, claws catching on feathers as she managed to push the woman back. Her sword met metal. The blows were rapid, bringing them together and then forcing them to spring apart. They would bear a new scratch or part of them would throb as the other had gained a forceful blow. Ravenna would probably have been the superior fighter if Seraphina had been fighting with a blade, but against these strange curved claws, she felt disadvantaged. Her blade gave her the longer reach, but if Seraphina could get past Ravenna's guard then she could do more damage.

The two sprang apart again, Ravenna with a long cut across her forehead, Seraphina with her armour dented in at her left ribs. Seraphina was actually struggling to breathe at this point, her panting matching that of Ravenna's. The heat shimmer of the desert made things harder to see properly, made the sweat building up underneath Ravenna's armour prohibitively sticky. Blood dripped down into Ravenna's eye. Seraphina pushed on her armour to see if she could bend it outwards again.

Ravenna reached up to wipe away the blood. That moment of defencelessness, that belief that she had a second to clear her vision, would be her undoing. Before Ravenna could lower her arm, Seraphina was there, inside her guard, past the point where Ravenna could strike out with her blade. She tried to buffet the other woman with her wings, but Seraphina had come in close enough to wrap her arms around her and was holding on tight. Her claws scrabbled at Ravenna's leathers until they cut through, slicing into her back where wings met skin. Ravenna screamed, the fire in her back flaring as though someone had poured molten sand onto it. Her wings spasmed as Seraphina cut into muscle. Ravenna scratched at the other woman, pulling her hair and raking her nails down her face, but Seraphina persisted. It wasn't until Ravenna managed to get hand around Seraphina's unprotected throat that the other woman pulled back, coughing.

Ravenna staggered and fell to one knee, then both, her right hand hitting the ground to stabilise her. She felt blood dripping openly from her back, smearing into the feathers there and slipping beneath the armour, what remained of it. She did not know if she could move her wings. She did not know if she should try. She did know that this battle was not yet done.

Air movement behind her, picked up by the sensitive feathers in her wings, alerted her to an attack from behind. Ravenna dropped her left shoulder and rolled onto her back, sweeping out with her sword to cut at Seraphina. Pain raged in Ravenna's back; she ignored it as best she could The unexpected movement caught the Southron queen by surprise and Ravenna's blade dug deep into her thigh. It also caused sand heated by the sun to grind itself into Ravenna's wounds. Whatever damage had been done was now trebled. Ravenna knew that getting dirt into a wing wound was extremely dangerous, given how sensitive and precise the musculature was. But sand and blood, over a wound that was already potentially massive in its damage, that could cripple her.

She did not care.

This woman had cut down Crispin so that he would never taste the air again. She had taken the Red Desert from Lenore. She had declared her intent to conquer what the Salusian Empire now held and had taunted her insane brother to stop her. She had hurt Miska. And now she had probably crippled Ravenna.

But she was not yet dead.

Ravenna rolled onto her stomach again and pushed herself to her feet, her wings screaming in agony as she did so. Her left hand trembled so badly that she dropped the sword that she had been given by Lenore all those moons ago.

Seraphina slid into her fighting stance again, though she rested her injured leg on her toes. She lifted her claws, her face drawn into a furious snarl. "Go on then, come and finish it. Come and seek your death. You cannot fly anymore now, little bird. I have ruined that for you. Why don't you do yourself a favour and let me end it now, so you do not have to witness a flightless life at my feet."

Ravenna closed her eyes and swallowed, pushing down the pain as much as she could. She inhaled, drawing a peace into herself. When that did not work, she took the fire burning in her back and used it to stoke her rage. She set her icy eyes to meet Seraphina's gaze, righteous anger burning there. Then, she lifted her wings, first the right than the left. Her back surged into pain that brought blackness to the edge of her vision. She still persisted.

Blood pounded in her ears, pulsing in time with the

stomping and the cheers that surrounded her. She did not know if they were cheering for her or for her opponent, only that they cheered. This lust for blood, this need to see someone cower before you because you were mightier than they, it was ridiculous. The Dalketh had been used by the Stormbringers to end fights, never to start them. Well, Ravenna had started this and she was going to end it. She lifted her wings higher, stretching them slowly until they were unfurled wide at her side, impossibly still able to move despite the injuries on her back. They trembled, and she knew she would never have a full range of motion again, but for now, the sight was enough.

"I am Ravenna Wingsword, Warlord of Shinalea, leader of the Stormbringers. And I could never fly."

Seraphina took a step back, the movement minuscule, more a shifting of her weight than a true step. It was enough.

Ravenna saw the fear in her opponent's eyes. And then she lunged, wings folding behind her with trained movement and with the natural instinct to reduce the pain. She did not bother with the forgotten sword on the ground, nor did she consider the fact that her armour was shredded. She simply moved, the Dalketh surging through her limbs as though it was the only thing she had ever known. Seraphina raised her claws and skipped forward, ready to face off against Ravenna. And then, Ravenna jinked.

She moved left so swiftly that she had to overcompensate with her wings to time her turn properly. Even so, she had to reach with her fingers to grab on to Seraphina's right wrist, pulling the limb as she moved by. Seraphina was forced to put weight on her injured leg and she stumbled, one wrist caught in Ravenna's grasp, the other reaching out to break her fall. Ravenna held on until Seraphina was on the ground and her wrist snapped.

This time, it was Seraphina who screamed. She pushed

herself upwards with her left hand, cradling her right wrist against her chest.

"Finish her," Seraphina snarled, eyes flashing to the large man she had spoken with earlier. "Baldur, finish her!"

"The rules of single combat preclude the involvement of outside forces," Cavaris said his voice ringing over the arena and laced with power. Baldur, the large man who had spoken with her at the beginning of the fight, shifted his weight and took a step back. He shook his head. Seraphina roared, the sound of sort of combination of fury and pain. She turned to Ravenna, staggering unsteadily on her feet.

"I am going to tear you and your people to shreds. I am going to flay your skin and wear your wings as a cloak. You will never win against me. I have beaten both Dagan and Davorin, pitting them against each other. I'm the only heir of the Salusian Empire left. This is all mine by right!" By the last word, Seraphina's voice was shrill and cracked. Ravenna took a deep breath in through the nose and smelled blood made tacky by the desert heat. Her own wings were shaking uncontrollably, folded at her side. She doubted she could move them right now if she tried. Seraphina was equally shaking, curved inwards to cradle her wrist and to deal with the dented impressions in her armour for Ravenna's fists. Her leg trembled, bleeding freely onto the sand.

"Then I shall take it from you." Ravenna took four steps forward, moving slowly as she tried to keep steady. She lifted her arms and batted away Seraphina's weak attempt to use her remaining left arm to claw her. Ravenna's own right shoulder did not move quite as freely as she would like, but it was enough to block the blow. Ravenna moved in closer, grabbing Seraphina's shoulders and spinning her around until she had her back pressed against Ravenna's chest. Her left arm scrabbled uselessly at Ravenna's wrist, her claws making tiny scratches but no more. Ravenna wrapped her left arm around Seraphina's throat, squeezing.

"Why are you doing this? You have lost. Concede," Ravenna breathed, panting as she held her grip.

"Please," Seraphina pleaded, though for freedom or death Ravenna did not know. "I cannot lose."

"You have lost already," Ravenna replied. She tightened her grip, hearing the other woman's gasp. "Give in."

"No! I can't. I can't be forgotten! I can't be…please…don't let the darkness take me." She clawed weakly at Ravenna's arm, holding her in place. If Ravenna did not finish this soon, she would be too exhausted to finish it. She couldn't let Seraphina go, either. She had to kill this woman, helpless and afraid. Her heart cracked.

She held on, trembling and squeezing until she no longer felt the pulse in Seraphina's neck against her arm. The woman she held was quiet, her struggles ceased. Ravenna lowered her head and took a deep breath, her mouth beside Seraphina's unhearing ear. "I'm sorry. I'm so sorry."

She released her opponent's body, watching as it fell limply to the desert. The blood stopped flowing from Seraphina's wounds. Her eyes stared vacantly into the distance. The soldiers around them, the warriors of Southron, were silent and still.

Seraphina was dead. Ravenna had won.

She fell to her knees, adrenaline leeching from her body and making the pain that much worse. She lowered her head and did not care that her wings were laying in the sand and that her blood was pooling there too. She simply wept.

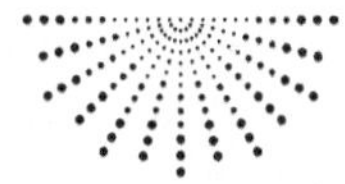

iska found Ravenna some few hours before sunset. He had been strapped to Beringer's back, still unable to move his legs. He tried not to think about that, though he knew the truth. He had felt this way after losing his hearing, after being told by various healers, their mouths exaggerated and slow so he might understand, that he would get it back. He never did. This was like that. Still, he said nothing, since there were other things to think about just then. Bigger things. After all, he had overcome deafness. Right?

Sisu rode at his side, the pair of them silent in their deliberations. Neither seemed to want to talk about what they were riding towards, nor what they had left behind. Miska had seen to Lenore, checking only that she was well and healthy before being thrown out of the tent by Blodwen and the midwives. She had looked extremely uncomfortable and hot, her face contorted by pain. The healers assured him that it would be quite some time before the child was to come. They had told him, pointedly, to wait elsewhere, do something else. He had then attempted to go see Desarra, only to find her in a heated discussion with Crispinus, a human child of her own in her arms. It took Miska a moment to recognise the child as the one Seraphina had lorded over Davorin.

"You have adopted the child?" Miska asked. Miska was seated in a chair that someone had found, his legs strapped in so that they would not fall. Sisu had borne him from his own tent to that of Lenore's, to here. Miska felt the magic fluttering at the edge of his vision, but it was nowhere within reach. Still, he had things he had to do. He had to inform Desarra of Tacitus' message. Then, he had to find Ravenna.

Desarra turned to face him, eyes flashing, wings spreading wide to hide Crispinus behind her back. Miska could not have known what it was that they were discussing, but the way that she held the child closer seemed indication enough. "Last I saw, it was at the Red Palace, caught up in Seraphina's games."

"She is *mine*. Davorin has no claim on her. Nor does this fiend Seraphina. Your queen has given her up to me." From the way that Desarra talked, the way that her mouth tightened as Miska watched, and the way that Sisu's arms tightened around him, he imagined that the tone was accusing.

"If you choose to adopt her, that is your choice. I only ask that you treat her better than you treated Ravenna, who was similarly flightless. This child will grow up without wings in a society where flight is all that matters. It will be...difficult," Miska said. Desarra straightened her shoulders and lifted her chin. Behind her, Miska could see Crispinus stirring, perhaps even saying something. Desarra turned and said something back to him, cradling the child still.

"Maybe that was what we were," Desarra said, turning back to Miska, "but we have moved beyond that. Ravenna taught us a different way. And yet, *I* am the Chosen Queen. I shall do my best to put into effect her visions for the future."

Miska inclined his head, sensing something else there. Some fracture between Desarra and Ravenna. Something that made Tacitus' words all the more important. Miska took a deep breath and rubbed a hand along his jaw, noting the sharpness he felt there. His magical dreams, the aftereffect of doing too much, they had taken more out of them than he could have imagined. For the first time but not the last, he wondered if he would ever be able to move his feet again, if he would ever be able to walk. He shoved the thought down, even as bile rose in his throat.

"I have been asleep for some time. While I was asleep, I met memory, or a spirit or something. He called himself Tacitus," Miska said, feeling how rough his voice was, though he could not hear it. He could see shock settle over Desarra, her wings turning still. The babe in her arms started fussing, waiving its tiny hands about. Desarra blinked and then shifted, bouncing gently. Her eyes never left Miska.

"Tacitus is dead. He died of a wasting disease shortly after Ravenna returned to Shinalea," Desarra said. She drew a hand over the child's brow and it quieted. "It was a dream, nothing more."

"Why would I dream of a sylph that I have never met? Why would he tell me things that are happening in the future? Why would he tell me to tell you to be the calm in the centre of the storm? I hardly know you. I have heard only stories of you from what Ravenna has told me, and while she holds more affection for you now than she did before, shadows still haunt her. She has always been on the periphery of your society, and she will remain that way. Ravenna does not want adoration or attention or leadership. For as long as I have known her, all she wants is a quiet life to practice her Dalketh and to read books...tomes. Tomes. I love Ravenna, and I mean to give her a quiet life. If that means being away from you, then so be it. So why, then, would *my* dream have a message for *you*?"

Miska brushed at the fabric of his trousers, feeling the fine weave of the material on his fingers, but not the pressure on his legs. He clenched his hands into fists and wrapped them around his waist, unwilling to touch his legs. Tiny threads flickered at the edge of his vision, but no more than that. He forced his gaze upwards so that he could see Desarra's response, even as she battled through the emotions of his statement.

"Sylphs do not believe in spirits or memories visiting after death. Whatever it was that you think you saw, you were wrong. Now, please, leave us in peace. Crispin has much healing to do, and I must feed little Elyria." Desarra nodded firmly and turned from Miska so that he could no longer see her face, no longer understand anything more than she said.

"Well, so be it. But you are Ravenna's sister. She cares for you, no matter the past. So I have delivered my message. And I wish you all the very best. With rebuilding your people, with creating something out of the rubble that has been left behind, with Elyria. I don't know what stands between you two, but is it really worth all of this?" Miska didn't wait for Desarra to turn around and respond, he just tapped Sisu's hand on his shoulder and braced himself as his friend lifted him and the chair bodily into the air and carried him from the tent.

Now, Miska rode on Beringer, his legs just as unfeeling, his hands twined into the bear's fur. He had fielded the anxiety from Beringer at his paralysed state and happily rode in silence, unwilling to converse with Sisu on what he would find. Worrying about Lenore, delivering the message to Desarra, it was all so much easier to focus on those tasks than to think about what was going to come. He had to believe that Ravenna would prevail. He did believe it. But that did not stop part of him from fearing the reality of what might come. What would happen if Ravenna had failed? If Seraphina now controlled their fate?

Even worrying about his legs, his magic, the ridges on his back that twinged as he moved with Beringer's gait, it was all nothing compared to the rising anxiety in his mind. Would he find her alive or would he find her dead?

Miska closed his eyes, forcing the thoughts down in his mind. A flash of wariness from Beringer, and an image appeared in his mind showed him the edge of Seraphina's army, warriors milling about on the foot, riding on horses, staying generally stationary but still full of activity. Miska opened his eyes and confirmed the bear's vision. The soldiers were moving about, their activity more to do with setting up camp for the evening than with pressing onwards. They had come far closer to the edge of the Red Desert than Miska had anticipated, their press from the Red Palace and towards the encampment faster than his prediction. But who led the army? Ravenna or Seraphina?

None of the soldiers challenged him or Sisu as they approached, the wariness showing in their eyes and in the way that they placed their hands on their weapons. Miska's own hands tightened in the ruff on Beringer's neck, his familiar now his only weapon against an attack. He could not use magic and his hunting knife would be useless from so high up on Beringer's back. Still, the fact that no one challenged them was potentially a good sign.

A whisper brushed against Miska's mind, the sound only inside his head and yet startling all the same. He had grown used to it after all those moons of communicating with Cavaris, but for some reason this startled him. His fears were catching up with him, it seemed. Miska jumped, the straps holding him onto Beringer's back happily keeping him in place. His legs dangled uselessly at his side.

Be not afraid. It was Cavaris, the dragon's mind reaching out to him even though he was nowhere in sight.

Does she...? Miska couldn't finish the thought, even in his own mind. The response he received was more of an impression, a feeling than a true reply. Weariness, sadness, acceptance. Miska's heart dropped in his stomach.

She lives. She has prevailed. But I think the cost has been too great.

A line appeared in Miska's vision, pulsing gently white, the urge to follow it pressing on his mind. He started Beringer along the line, Sisu following suit, though the larger man seemed to watch the soldiers around them with more uncertainty than Miska. Miska could not bring himself to say the words out loud, could not bring himself to tell his friend that they had won, but that Ravenna might be lost for it. So he followed the line until it stopped. And then he wished that he could leap down and run to Ravenna, scooping her in his arms and holding her.

She knelt on the ground, her back a bloodied mass, her wings completely limp at her sides. She had new scratches and gouges in her skin, the bleeding stopped but the damage done. On her lap, she cradled the head of Seraphina, the other woman's body limp in death. Ravenna ran her hands over Seraphina's hair, smoothing it, rubbing away blood where it had stained. All the while, she wept. Cavaris stood over her, his hands folded neatly in front of him. And in almost a perfect circle, soldiers gathered, whispering with each other as they stared at the sylph and their dead Queen.

Beringer moved around so that Miska could see Ravenna's face clearly. He called out to her. She lifted her eyes, no longer empty pools of ice, masked by stone. All the barriers had gone. She was open, her pain more than visible. It nearly broke Miska's heart.

"I know she meant us harm. I know she meant to sweep across this place like some great hand, conquering everything in her path. Do you know why she was doing it? She did not want to be forgotten. She did not want to be nothing more than the wife of a warlord, insignificant in her power and scope. She wanted what her brothers were going to have. She wanted history to always remember her, she wanted people—all the people—to know her name. She did this because she was afraid." Ravenna's mouth moved so slightly that Miska had to stare and block out all other happenings in order to understand her words. And what he understood frightened him. "Wings, Miska, she was so *afraid.*"

"I fought her in battle, my lovely Ravenna. I faced her and I saw that she revelled in the bloodshed. She lusted after it. Do not feel sympathy for her, or regret that she is dead. You have saved us all from a monster."

Ravenna shook her head, the movement stilling something in Miska's breast. He scrambled with his fingers at the ties that held him to Beringer. A moment later, Cavaris and Sisu had moved to help him, Sisu lifting him from the bear's back and carrying him to where Ravenna knelt. Miska dragged himself with his arms the last few inches until he could reach out and move Seraphina's body, laying it off to one side. He held out his arms and Ravenna crawled into them, seemingly heedless of the wounds on her back.

"Can you heal her? Her wings..." Miska looked desperately at Cavaris, who simply blinked and shook his head, though he seemed to hold some sympathy for the weeping sylph.

"Unfortunately, I cannot. If I were to do so, then the bargain that had been struck to cede control of Seraphina's lands and her inheritance and her army to Ravenna, it would all be void. Whatever injuries she garnered must be hers to bear." The dragon stepped forward and reached out, as if he wanted to put a hand on Ravenna's head, as if he wanted to provide some sort of assurance to her. But he hesitated and pulled back. Miska could have sworn that he saw a flicker of pain in the dragon's red eyes, but it was gone so swiftly that he could not be sure. Sisu pulled out some cloth and his water skin, wetting the fabric and starting to dab at the wounds on Ravenna's back. She did not flinch at his touch, just lay her head on Miska's chest and wept.

"You did not do anything wrong," Miska said. "You *saved* us. You saved your people. My people. You took one life to provide a future for generations to come. Can you honestly say that it was not worth it?" He brushed his hand over the sticky feathers on one of her wings, coming away with dabs of blood on his fingers. Ravenna took three breaths, holding each one for a few moments before releasing it. Then, she pulled back from Miska and looked him in the eyes so that he could see her response.

"I don't know. I would have done it again if it meant saving my people. But I held her against me as the life went out of her. I felt her heart stop. I felt her terror at going into the unknown. All of her efforts, all of her ambitions, snuffed out with a single squeeze of my arms. And what is left to me now? I will be forever known as the killer, as someone who took a life to save those she cared about. I will always be a warlord with blood on my wings. That is what history has in store for me. And it terrifies me almost as much as that terrified her."

Miska brushed a strand of hair out of Ravenna's face, tucking it behind her ear. He kissed her forehead gently and then pulled back so that she could see the emotions he held for her, so that she could see everything as he spoke, as he did with so many others. So that she could see as he saw. "This is but a moment in time. You are not stuck here, in spirit or in actuality. You have the ability to make something more of your life. To become remembered for something other than a single act. I will be with you the entire time. You are not alone. You are not stuck with blood on your wings and death in your hands. If you never want to fight again, then don't. Make peace. Change the world. But don't you dare think that you *have* to be anything. You can be whoever you want, Ravenna. Warrior, philosopher, anything."

He kissed her forehead and felt her trembling beneath him, still grieving for what she had done. He pulled her close and wrapped his arms around her shoulders, mindful of her wings. "Now, your family is waiting for you back at the encampment. Lenore wants to see you; she will have had her child when we get back. Desarra...misses you, even if she's being stubborn about it. And we have a new life to start. So what do you say? Will you start a new life with me?"

Ravenna closed her eyes and took in one more breath, this one shuddering through her body and causing her wings to tremble, though only slightly. "To be with you? To lay down my swords and only ever fight with word and pen? To *finally* have peace? Always, my love. Always."

Miska nodded and kissed her firmly, letting his head rest against hers. "I have been waiting so long for you to say that."

Ravenna pulled back and reached up to brush her hand along Miska's bearded jaw. "I will never forget what I did here. I'm always going to be afraid of what this means. Of how easy it was to kill. But...I think I am ready to face what the future holds."

For the first time in too long, Miska smiled and did not worry about the consequences. He just held Ravenna and finally felt right with the world.

CHAPTER TWENTY-FIVE

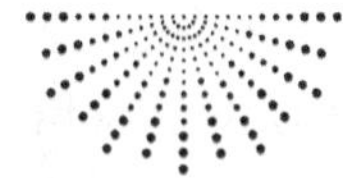

"Two more movements and we shall be done with the whole set," Ravenna said, her voice tense. Beside her, standing in the garden oasis of the Red Palace, his teeth set in a grimace and his wings trembling as he held them in the Dalketh pose Lands in Tree, Crispin struggled. One moon had passed since everything happened, and still Ravenna could not get the feeling out of her head of strangling the life from someone. It was entirely different than killing them with a blade, though her hands and wings did not suffer for blood from that. Even as she went through the Dalketh with Crispin every morning, trying to retrain her wings into doing as she asked of them, trying to heal her body as she healed her mind, the shadows haunted her.

It was meant to be a glorious time. Only the day before, Lenore had received a missive from the Salusian Empire. As Davorin was technically the only remaining heir to the Empire, and his mind was like a child's, focused on drawing and dancing and playing, Lenore had petitioned the Emperor for control of Davorin's assets. The Emperor, ageing and bitter and disappointed with everything that life had granted him, agreed. He wanted nothing more to do with the Red Desert or the Salusian

Empire or any of it. He had lost all of his children to their pursuits of power and ambition, there was little point to him trying to retain control. He would not even venture to the Red Desert for Erowain's official declaration as Lenore's heir, as the Red Prince.

The sylphs were free, no longer burdened by the past or the present, able to fight or to live in peace as they chose. Those that were able had returned to Shinalea, leaving Ravenna, Crispin, Desarra and a few others behind. They would all return once their official alliance with Lenore had been declared. Ravenna had not yet decided whether she would be going with them.

She moved her arms and forced her wings into the final position of Dalketh, the right wing weaker than the left and both unable to move as she wished them to. She would never be able to run through the forest again, to fight as she had done with wing and sword. It seemed that fate had decided she should give up fighting in any case. What use was going back to Shinalea as a broken warlord, as the one responsible for so much death? Miska was here, too. He had been working with Warra to figure out a means of mobility while his back healed. If it ever healed.

"I should go speak with Desarra before the fete. She does not particularly like leaving Elyria with the human nursemaids. I shall have to convince her, because having an infant at the sealing ceremony will not go well." Crispin spoke the words hesitantly, as if he needed permission to go see to his mate, as if he could not manage on his own. Ravenna had noticed that he was tentative of late. Since losing the ability to fly, he seemed to mistrust the very ground beneath his feet, as if that would be taken from him, too. He did not talk about the impending return to Shinalea, not with Ravenna, and from what she could tell, not with Desarra or anybody. He was not the only one whose wings had been injured in the various battles, but his was the only injury so severe it would keep him from flight for the rest of his life. If Ravenna did not return to Shinalea with him, he would be the only flightless being on the island apart from the infant Elyria.

"You will regain full range of motion in your wings. They may never be strong enough to carry you in the sky, but you can run and you can dance." Ravenna lowered her own wings to her side, trembling with relief as she released the aching muscles in her back. They hung limply, not folded neatly as they would have been, but tired, weak. She did not seem to mind her own injuries, seeing them more as a burden to bear for all that she had done. She reached out and touched Crispin on the shoulder. He flinched away.

"I don't mean to be…cruel, but how could you possibly know what it means to lose flight? I was a Lord of the Wind. Flying was *everything*. To feel the currents between my feathers, to figure out how to dive through clouds and to speed through storms, it was the best thing of my life. Now what am I? I'm not meant to be an Intellecti. I don't think I have the patience for it. What else is there?" He tried to wrap his wings around himself and failed, the exertions from going through the Dalketh too much for such casual movement. Ravenna pretended not to see the tears listening at the corners of his eye, knowing that despite all of this he still had some pride.

"Do you remember when I was a girl and we were learning the Dalketh for the first time? You and Desarra ran out into the forest to go practice flying, and I wanted to go with." Ravenna gave a weak smile at the memory, curious as to why she felt nostalgic at the thought of learning her faults for the first time.

Crispin shook his head. "I remember…I don't know. I was too caught up in my own world, and everything that I was doing to remember what I thought was an annoying pest. Things have changed."

"*I* remember. I ran after you and Desarra and found you at

the edge of a gully. I asked to play with you, and you told me that if I could fly, then I could." Crispin's skin darkened, a flush. So he did remember. "You pushed me into the gully. Or Desarra did. And no matter how hard I tried, no matter how good I was at the Dalketh, I couldn't get my wings to fly. It was that day that Tacitus told me that I would never fly. That the dreams of a young sylph female of being accepted, of soaring through the wind and becoming the best flyer, they were dashed. What was I if not a sylph able to fly? I was never going to be able to relate to you. I would never understand what it meant to have nothing but wind holding you up."

"Ravenna..." He took a step back, eyes widening. She shook her head, feeling the brush of her braid against her sore back.

"The point is, I know exactly what it is to have something you wish, something you want more than anything in the world, something you love, to be torn away from you. And yet no one would say that I am worthless. *You* define your worth. If you do not wish to be an Intellecti, then do not. Find a different way to be connected to the sky. Map air currents around the island. Teach the Dalketh to the youth. Train falcons or something to be messengers between Shinalea and the mainland. There are options to you. Don't forget that."

She would have said more, would have happily explored the future with Crispin, but they were interrupted. Sisu stood at the window leading into Ravenna's chambers, gesturing to her. Without a backward glance over her shoulder, Ravenna turned walked towards the man, deciding that it was probably better Crispin figure out his future on his own, or with Desarra. There was no telling whether or not Ravenna would have a place in it.

"Lenore wishes to speak with you, to inquire as to your plans." Sisu folded his arms behind his back, clasping his stump in his right hand. The movement in the loose desert clothing that showed off his bulk, made him look even more of a giant than he did while wearing the furs of Hullgard. He seemed out of place in the desert, but he never stopped smiling or smirking. And he never gave up on Miska, or Ravenna.

"*You* do not wish to inquire as to my plans?" Ravenna asked. She was not sure whether the tone was teasing more if she was just becoming more sure of herself, despite the shadows that touched her mind.

"My girl, I have no more right to determine your plans than to determine those of your sister. You were raised well without me, and you have become a magnificent woman. Female. Whatever you choose to do with your life, you will do it well. I just ask that you don't forget that you have others to stand by you, others that need your support as much as you need theirs. And if you ever happen to be in Hullgard, why then I shall teach you how to hunt." It was the most that Ravenna had ever heard him say at one time, and it was perhaps precisely what she needed to hear. She smiled at him, genuinely. He returned the book and they walked through the Red Palace in silence, nodding acknowledgment of the guards and the servants who had started to return to the palace, making things feel almost as normal.

Almost.

"And when you're done here," Sisu said as he led Ravenna to the doors of the library, "go see Miska. He and that healer of yours have come up with some ingenious ideas."

She nodded acknowledgment and entered the library, breathing in deeply the smell of tomes—books. Raised an Intellecti, she had become a warrior, but she would always feel at peace amongst the tomes. Well, almost always. Perhaps finding Lenore and her sister sitting there, two queens staring each other down, was not so peaceful.

"Ah, Ravenna," Lenore said, rising from the chair where she sat. She had regained much of her graceful figure after her pregnancy, and she looked now even more the regal queen than she had when Ravenna first met her. Her hair was bound back in its multitude of tiny braids and she wore a flowing dress fit for magnificence, in a deep burgundy red. Desarra, sitting opposite her at the table, wore a dress styled much like the one that Ravenna had worn to her first ball so many moons ago. The straps went over her neck, leaving the back low to accommodate her wings. It was a deep grey, speckled with tiny gems that shone like starlight.

"Both of you do realise the fete does not start for another several hours," Ravenna said warily. "The sealing ceremony, to bind our people in alliance, will only take a few minutes. Surely the two of you do not need to be so well attired until then?"

"I did not wish to spend the afternoon away from Elyria," Desarra said with a sniff. She winced, then shook her head. "Look, Ravenna. I know things have been complicated since…"

"Since you sent me off with the verdict that I would be forgotten?" Now it was Ravenna's turn to wince at the tone of bitterness in her voice. She had not blamed Desarra, thinking her reaction perfectly valid, but apparently the sting had not yet been forgotten. "All of that is passed. Soon you will return to Shinalea and there will be no need to worry about my legacy. Only yours."

"So you do not mean to return to Shinalea?" Lenore asked. Was that a spark in her eye?

"I have not yet decided," Ravenna said. "I shall go wherever Miska goes."

"But —"

"I thought —"

Lenore and Desarra looked at each other, either trying to decide who would speak first, or apologising silently in some unspoken language. Ravenna sighed and stepped forward, sitting on a stool at the table, trying to hold back a groan as she let her wings relax further. She was too tired to deal with this nonsense just then.

"If you have something to say, then say it. If you have an

opinion on what I'm going to do with my life, then I ask you to keep your silence. It is my life. I am beholden to no one but Miska. And Allora. And Beringer." Almost all she had heard over the last moon was people trying to figure out what would be next. Once Lenore's power was reinstated—with control over Southron and all of the kingdoms of the Salusian Empire, from coast-to-coast reaching up to the Iron Mountains and down to the plains of Southron—Ravenna had been the target of great whispers. Everyone seemed to want to know what would happen to her. Where would the legendary warlord go next?

"That is precisely why I think you are so important," Lenore said carefully, almost mincing over her words. She sank down in the chair and smiled at Ravenna, reaching out and grabbing her hand gently. "You do not belong to any nation, and yet you belong to all of them. You have interacted with people from Hullgard, from the Salusian Empire, from Southron, and are respected by all. You are well versed in politics and philosophy, and you have enough clout to your name to be dangerous without ever having to pick up a sword again. I think...I think you might be the perfect ambassador."

"Ambassador?" Ravenna raised her brows. That was an option that had not occurred to her in her deliberations. A strange one.

"I told you that it would not be a welcome option. Ravenna's place is with her people, so she can live her days in peace." Desarra looked at Ravenna with a slight smile, perhaps silently trying to fumble through an apology once more. She had tried to do so several times during their stay at the Red Palace, but she seemed unsure of the words, of herself.

"And what of Miska? And Allora and Beringer?" Lenore asked, squeezing Ravenna's hand. "Would you so quickly allow humans to come to Shinalea?"

Desarra nodded. "I have already made the offer to Miska to join the Intellecti. He would be able to explore and to learn and to teach. Where else would a human sorcerer go? Anywhere he resided in the human lands would seek to claim favour from him. The sylphs are not now numerous enough to even consider such a thing. I have...I've also made the offer to Cavaris."

"Des," Ravenna said. She took a breath and tried to start again. "Des, it is not your place to try and rebuild my life for me. I appreciate you offering such an honour to Miska, and I am sure that Cavaris would be pleased to live a life of quiet study, but would you have us be so far from our friends, from places that we have grown fond of, from the world? Would you isolate us again?"

Desarra closed her eyes, a faint tremor moving through her feathers. She opened her eyes and fixed Ravenna in a desperate gaze. "I know that I have not treated you well, but I cannot imagine the future without you. Ravenna, you are my *sister*. You are one of the few people that believed in me after I took the crown. You have stood by me no matter what, and you have never tried to pretend to be something you were not. Perhaps it is I that am the imposter, the one who should never have been given the crown, but as you said, it is done. And I shall spend the rest of my life trying to serve our people, to move forwards from everything that we have lost. We are so reduced in numbers. The Stormbringers..." Desarra scoffed and shook her head. "Even if we are to teach our people about Dalketh as a means of fighting, the Stormbringers are not numerous enough to go to war again, not for some many generations. We have to try a different way. One that does not forget what we were. And I would give anything for you to be part of that."

It was Ravenna's turn to reach out and grab Desarra's hand, squeezing gently. "I love you too, Des. And I absolutely want to be part of this. Of all of this. I have done so many things in the last cycle, it is difficult to try and reconcile that with who I am, what I was. The reality is that I have a wing in both worlds. And

I will not abandon either of them. Lenore…I will happily take the role of ambassador, so long as I can spend some time in Shinalea every cycle. And Des, I shall happily come and try to help make our society into something greater. But both of you must understand that my home will always be with Miska and my family."

"We would expect no less," Lenore said. She leaned back and stretched, fighting a yawn. "Now, I really must go see to the final preparations for this fete or ball or whatever. And then I must put Erowain to bed. I shall see both of you in a while."

Desarra rose as well, leaving Ravenna to stand, her movements slow and stiff after cooling down from her exercises. "I am going to go help Crispin prepare. Did you know that he preens just as much as any female?"

Ravenna chuckled. "That does not surprise me in the slightest."

She followed her sister out into the hall, off to find Miska, to talk with him about her plans and to see what he would want to do. She imagined that Allora would be there, questioning Warra on every decision that the healer made to try and help Miska or to fashion one of those wheeled chairs. Allora was nothing if not precocious, and she did not seem to mind one way or another whether Miska could walk or Ravenna could beat her wings. She just lived her life as fully as possible, Beringer trailing in her wake. Even when Allora went to go play with Davorin, the madman usually left to his own devices in his chambers filled with toys and drawing materials.

Ravenna was just about to turn into the corridor that led down to the healer's rooms when she paused. There he was. Standing there, his hands held before him uncertainly, his fingers twining and untwining as he tapped his foot. Davorin looked nervous, even a little sad. Ravenna wandered over to him and put a gentle hand on his shoulder. "You look disconcerted. What is wrong?"

"Everyone is going to leave, aren't they? I asked and they said that all the angels were going to fly away. That I would be left alone, and then Lenore would forget about me." Davorin turned and looked at Ravenna, his eyes guileless, his expression full of the innocence of childhood. A grown man, once a tyrant, concerned with little more than his own ambitions, now afraid that he would be left behind, that his friends were going away. That he would have no one to play with.

"Everyone leaves, Davorin. Now or later, everyone must make that journey alone. That does not make the connections that we forge along the way any less valuable. You shall not be forgotten. You shall not be alone. I promise you that."

A smile, filled with joyous sunrise and pure contentment, spread across his features. For once, the scar between the wings on her back that Davorin had given her, so much more insignificant than any Seraphina had meted, did not twinge. She did not feel any anger or fear or disappointment. She moved in and wrapped her arms around Davorin, squeezing him tighter when he tentatively returned the gesture. She pulled back to look at him.

"Never alone." Davorin nodded, and slipped out of her grasp, skipping off to go back and play in his room, no longer afraid. Ravenna watched him for a moment, grateful that he could be spared any of the shadows that hunted her, that followed her in the night. Maybe someday, she could achieve that level of peace. For now, she had a future to embrace.

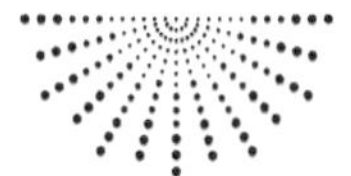

Ravenna had discovered something in the cycles that she had been ambassador to the Salusian Empire, or what was left of it: she hated rain. Sure, it rained fairly frequently on Shinalea, but those were pleasant drizzles compared to this deluge that made the roads all but impassable with mud. The horse she rode was not terribly pleased with the situation either, and both would have been happier if she stopped at one of the roadside inns and made her way back across the Independent Kingdoms later. But Ravenna had been gone from Shinalea too long. Her ambassadorship to the Independent Kingdoms and the remnants of the Empire had her traveling many moons out of the cycle, but this time she had been almost a complete cycle away from home. Away from Desarra. From Crispin. From Miska.

Ten cycles. Could it really have been so long? The world had changed so much and so quickly since then. The Salusian Empire had fallen apart. The death of its Emperor and Lenore's distance had it falling into a military-ruled country, and two cycles after that had become overrun by riots, eventually, under threat of invasion by the Red Desert, putting the government into the hands of a senate voted in by the people. Between that, the reinstating of many kingdoms formerly controlled by the Salusian Empire, and Lenore taking charge of the Red Desert and rebuilding, the region was both prospering and in constant chaos.

Southron had fallen back into the hands of warring tribes, their brief unity under Seraphina's lead disintegrating as soon as Ravenna and Lenore granted them their freedom. The Red Desert had become a political bastion in the region, building up its army and using its vast reserves to deal with squabbles between small kingdoms, to reinstate leaders or to select new ones when the old had been poor. Hullgard remained as enigmatic and silent as ever, the only news that Ravenna had of the place her occasional encounters with Sisu when he ventured down from the mountains to visit.

Ravenna urged her horse onwards on the South Desert Road, the main thoroughfare that now linked many of the small kingdoms together. She had gone from the wet winter of the Salusian Empire to the monsoon season of the desert and was thoroughly tired of both. Her wings lay at her side beneath a weatherproof cloak, the feather brooch she wore at her throat the only sign of her station. Ambassador. Not only for the Red Desert, but for Shinalea as well. Ravenna travelled between all of the kingdoms, sometimes spending more time in one than another. Her hand in returning the region to some semblance of independence had made her a valuable asset to all humans. She was considered a neutral party, the Stormbringer reputation preceding her. So she travelled, spreading peace instead of war, turning her swords into the feather symbol that she wore.

Finally, she came upon an inn nestled at the edge of the Red Desert, a short distance's ride from the sea. Places like this had sprung up over the last ten cycles, catering to travellers between regions, even those humans that were allowed to venture to Shinalea to learn from the famed Intellecti and their new

University. A place of learning. Led not by Kratos or the Council that did their best to enact Desarra's rulings in the Aerial City, but by Cavaris. He had decided that teaching those who came to seek knowledge was perhaps the best way of guiding the younger races without incurring such pain. Strangely enough, Miska taught at his side.

"Room for the night, dearie?" a buxom woman asked as Ravenna dismounted her horse at the entrance to the inn. Behind her, a young boy ran out to take the reins of Ravenna's horse.

"Is there another ferry to Shinalea this night? I'm eager to get there." Ravenna stepped under the eaves of the building, shaking her wings underneath her cloak to shed some of the water. Part of her regretted that she would never be able to move them as freely as she had done in her youth. They would never unfurl fully and many of the Dalketh movements were beyond her. But her fighting days were gone, and her need to run through the forest to find calm were just as far behind her. Now, she had purpose and family to keep her spirits high.

The woman considered, looked out at the grey horizon, hidden by fog and rain. "There is meant to be one, but I doubt it will sale in this weather. Fog is dangerous enough in the day. At night, everything becomes opaque. But, it's the wrong time of year to be going for recruitment at University. And them sylphs are mighty particular about those they let on their island."

Ravenna twitched back her cloak far enough so that the woman could see the feathers of her wings. She blushed furiously and muddled through an apology to Ravenna, assuring her that she meant no disrespect. "You need not apologise. I know full well how particular they can be. I spend so much time in the human lands that going back is always a bit of a shock. But they are growing more accustomed to strangers."

Ravenna resigned herself to another night on the road, though she would happily have paid extra fitment the fairy men would take her to Shinalea. Still, winter weather there was always complicated. When the innkeeper woman clicked her tongue and made a humming sound in the back of her throat though, Ravenna allowed herself to smile.

"It is possible that they will be making a last run for the day. Not but this morning did a couple of potential new students say they were heading to the University. You can always go down and check to see. If not, then return here and we'll give you a room and a bed and a hot meal." Before the woman could even finish her offer, Ravenna was back in the saddle and racing towards the coast. If there was even the slightest chance of her getting home that night, then she would take it. Besides, there were still some hours before sunset, not that you could tell with this wretched drizzle.

Her horse's hooves slipped slightly as she urged it and towards the pier. There. At the edge of the pier, the boat. It was the flat bottomed barge that often carried supplies or trade goods to and from Shinalea. This time it carried two humans, a male and female, looking just as miserable as the weather. The boat man saw Ravenna coming in urged her on words. She slipped off her horse's back and let it on to the boat, smiling widely.

"Just-in-time, Mistress. We were casting off. I expect that you have all of your papers in order?" The boatmen didn't bother to wait for Ravenna to show any traveling papers, just undid the ropes mooring the barge to the pier and shoved off, his crewmen taking to the oars to push them into open waters.

"They've been expecting me," Ravenna said. She tapped the brooch at her neck and the boatmen's eyes widened.

"Ambassador. Yes, suppose they would be expecting you. Have you heard the news of the outside world? What am I saying, of course you have. You're better set to tell us the news than anything." Ravenna chuckled and shook her head.

She knew precisely how long this boat ride was and that

there was plenty of time for telling stories. The University students glanced at her with sideways gazes, unsure whether they should converse with her or keep to themselves. That habit would be quickly taught out of them if Cavaris had anything to do with it. He didn't much care for people who had no ability to communicate. Though, there was politeness to consider.

"What would you like to hear?" Ravenna asked. Beneath her cloak, her wings shuffled as if they could sense the approach of her homeland. She tried not to get over eager, knowing the wait she still had in store.

"I heard tell that Lord Davorin finally died. That the Red Desert held a great funeral for him." The man's words brought a whisper of sadness and Ravenna's mind. She pushed it away. It was inevitable that he would die eventually, likely far sooner than many of his peers. Lenore had cared for Davorin all of these cycles, having the best doctors attend him, letting him play freely in the gardens. Ravenna had wanted to entertain him on Shinalea, but Lenore desisted. Ravenna had visited Davorin several times over the cycles, always taking time to look at all his drawings.

"Yes. Lord Davorin is dead. His madness finally drove him to injure himself. He fell into a sinkhole and cracked his head. Queen Lenore and Prince Erowain stood vigil. A great tomb was built for him." Ravenna tried to relay the facts without adding any emotional inflection to her voice, without indicating that she was personally saddened by the fact. She still had the scar between her wings where Davorin had cut her open. She still dreamed about being in chains. Yet the greatest part of her mourned for him. A man so determined to conquer the world, laid low by his own doing.

The boatmen shook his head and clicked his tongue. "There is a man no one will mourn. Many still remember how cruel he and his brother were, before the reckoning."

Ravenna took a deep breath and nodded. "He was no hero.

Many described him as a monster. But to be fair, that man died ten cycles ago. The one that died only a few moons ago was little more than a child. In the sense of understanding, that is. He will be mourned."

The boatmen looked as though he wanted to ask more questions, but one of the oarsmen called something out to him and he ducked his head before scurrying away. Ravenna sighed and patted the horse at her side. It whickered and shook its mane of the droplets of water that had gathered there. Ravenna grumbled and turned to sit on one of the benches beside crates of supplies and food. The potential students continued to watch her, whispering amongst themselves. Ravenna could answer all their questions right there. She could inform them that they were accurate in their guesses, that they recognised her from her descriptions. Instead, she closed her eyes and tilted her head back so that the fine mist beaded on her face. Better let them have a bit of mystery.

She was shaken awake some time later, the sun well on its way to touching the horizon, the mist dissipated to create a fairly pleasant evening for the season. Before her, beyond the boat man's inquiring figure, mottled green and red in the dying sun, was Shinalea. Home.

Ravenna stood and stretched, old wounds aching from the damp. Beside her, the students chattered amongst themselves, their energy invigorating. Ravenna grabbed the reins of her horse and let it to the edge of the barge where they would be offloading. Would Miska be waiting for her? Would Desarra?

The barge jolted as it touched land, bottom scraping along the shallow sands on the beach that Ravenna had abandoned so many cycles ago, her hands bound, the nightmares that were humans taking her away. Now, it was a place of welcome. The only shadows that remained were her memories.

"Fare thee well ambassador," the boatmen called as Ravenna walked onto the beach, leaving her horse behind her. The students started whispering again, following after Ravenna as she moved on to the island. One of them, the female, was even bold enough to clear her throat and address Ravenna.

"Pardon me, ambassador?" She asked. Ravenna turned and fixed her in an icy stare, one eyebrow quirked upwards, mouth curled in amusement.

"You seek to know how to get to the University. How to get to the Stone Tower. Very well. Follow me," Ravenna said. She knew full well that one of Crispin's falcons was probably already winging its way back to its master, informing him of the new arrivals on the island. Had the students wanted to wait, then in a few minutes time, someone would be flying down to meet them, ready to introduce them to the island to Shinalea and all its ways. To the place of art and philosophy, of thinking and learning. Fighting.

Ravenna might not have held the sword for nearly ten cycles, but the art of Dalketh was alive and well. It was taught by many of the sylphs that she had originally taught. So far, the Storm-bringers hadn't needed to be used except as a show of force, or on special occasions. They did not need Ravenna to be their Warlord. They needed Desarra instead. The Philosopher Queen they called her, after she had started including the Intellecti into many of her political conversations, after she had started learning and taking as many courses as she could. After she had adopted a human child with her own. Whatever Miska had told her all those moons ago—something he never would say to Ravenna—it had worked.

Ravenna led the newcomers onto the path from the beach and ignoring the stares that pierced her cloak from behind. They wanted to ask many more questions, but Ravenna was far from eager to play nursemaid to some curious students, though curiosity was a trait she admired. Finally, the young female gathered enough courage again to start to ask Ravenna a question. "If you please, ambassador—"

"Hail the conquering hero, returned from cycles away!" The voice sang through the trees. In the quickly darkening light, it was fairly easy to spot the one figure who held a torch, her white blonde hair reflecting the oranges and reds of the flickering flame. She squealed and ran forwards, thrusting the torch into the hands of one of the students and then wrapping her arms around Ravenna.

Ravenna laughed and squeezed her back, spinning her around. "Allora!"

Allora squeezed Ravenna tighter, and the sylph could feel her heart-daughter's smile through their hug. "You're back. We weren't expecting you for another week. But then Crispin's falcon came and told him that you were here, and I had to come down to see you. Miska wanted to come, but his chair has been having problems with the mud. That, and some of the more ambitious students have decided to see if they couldn't engineer him something better. They've been taking it to pieces for days."

Allora broke her hug with Ravenna and pulled back, taking the torch back from the startled student. The young male blushed as Allora flashed him a winning smile and Ravenna laughed, shaking her head. "Don't tease them. Your father will be after them if they so much as look at you funny, no matter that he cannot actually walk."

Allora waved her hand dismissively, winking at the now thoroughly nervous student. "I missed you. No one else teases me like you do. Well, Elyria and Meritus try, but they haven't quite gotten the knack of it yet. And I don't think Auntie Desarra appreciates me trying to corrupt her youngling's. Crispin always approves."

"He would, considering he taught you most of it. Now, how have you been? I have heard politics and civil disputes and border skirmish arguments and trade agreements and nothing else for moons. Tell me something fun. Something of home."

The path before them opened up into a slight clearing,

where the new buildings of the University has started to take form. After it had become relatively well-known in the region, Cavaris and Miska had worked with some of the builders from the Aerial City to design a more complete set of buildings than just the Stone Tower. The Intellecti did not love having students under wing at all times, and the more students they had, the more space they seemed to need. Cavaris loved it, and Miska did too, though he would not admit as such when students were doing things like tearing apart his mobility chair.

"You're going to take me with you next time, aren't you?" Allora asked. Ravenna turned to her heart-daughter and raised her eyebrows. Allora huffed. "Miska said that I could only go if you let me. I had to be proficient in Dalketh, which I am. I had to be able to hunt without Beringer's help, which I can. I had to be able to speak all of the different languages, which I have been practicing. Please, take me with you next time. I want to see the world."

"You have already seen more of the world than many people," Ravenna pointed out. Allora sighed dramatically and shrugged. She pulled Ravenna towards the main building, the Stone Tower that had been her home for so many cycles. The place where everything had changed for Ravenna. It had been updated, expanded. The tomes were now housed in a library the likes of which could be seen only at the Red Palace. This was where she shared rooms with Miska, when she was on Shinalea. This was where Cavaris lived, when he was not off flying in dragon form.

"That was when I was a child. And besides, you and Miska didn't let me do anything fun but stay in the encampment. I know, I know, it was for my own good, I was only six cycles old, blah blah blah. All I do here is run around from Intellecti to Aerial City. I have already had the training, and I want to meet more people. More than just sylphs and students. I want to go on an adventure."

Ravenna paused just before the steps to the Stone Tower.

She wanted to tell her heart-daughter that adventures were sometimes overrated, that the dangers and the nightmares that followed in their wake were perhaps better left avoided. But, there was something in a Allora's eyes that told her she already knew this. She knew what scars would remain after such a thing. And she wanted it anyways. For all that Ravenna was haunted by shadows, for all that each laugh reminded her of pain gone by, she understood. She had changed so much from her adventures. She learned how to live and how to love and what it meant to really be. "Very well. My next journey, you may come with."

Allora squealed again, dancing in place. She threw open the Stone Tower doors and dashed inside, running to meet with a man in his chair. Miska grunted as she ran into him, her arms wrapping around his neck. "She said yes!"

Miska tore his eyes away from Allora's mouth and turned to Ravenna, raising his brows in question. Ravenna gave a wing shrug, the fabric of her cloak moving as she did so. She threw it back and spread her wings, revelling in the feeling of that slight freedom. Then, she moved forward and wrapped her own arms around her mate's neck. She did not say anything, knowing that he could not read her mouth at that angle. She could have communicated with him through her mind, a connection having been forged between them some cycles ago when Miska perfected that particular magical art, but there was something more profound about simply touching her forehead to his and breathing in his scent. They stayed like that for a few moments, just quietly taking in the other. Allora coughed pointedly beside them, and Ravenna slowly pulled back.

"Do you have to do that now?" Allora asked drily, her mouth twitching and a smile.

"They recognise, as well as the you do dear child, that such moments are precious." Ravenna turned to face Cavaris, the dragon looking exactly the same as he had ten cycles ago, hands folded neatly into his robes, his obsidian horns gleaming in the torchlight, his eyes flashing. She had aged. Miska had aged. Time marched along with all of them, and yet Cavaris remained the same. Still, they had many cycles together to look forward to and the dragon seems to be content with that. Sometimes though, such as moments like this when Ravenna returned and greeted Miska with her whole heart, she recognised the pain in the eyes of her friend.

"Hello Cavaris," Ravenna said. She stepped forward and wrapped the dragon in a hug, her wings extending around them as far as they would stretch. Cavaris returned the gesture, his claws patting her back, magical energy surging through her where they touched, brushing away the weariness from her travels. "You will be pleased to note that things are going well in our fledgling region."

"I never doubted it. Did you give my message to Lenore?" Cavaris asked. Ravenna's smile faded, and she nodded. She hadn't known what the message meant when Cavaris gave it to her so many moons ago, but after Davorin's death, the condolences had been much appreciated.

"We have some new students, it seems," Miska said. Ravenna turned from her greetings to Cavaris and noticed the two humans cowering in the entrance to the Stone Tower, their eyes wide, flicking between Miska in his chair, Ravenna with her wings, and Cavaris. It seemed that knowing legends existed did not make witnessing them any less magical. Or terrifying, if one were to judge by the expression on the female's face.

Cavaris step forwards, extending his hands to greet the newcomers. "Welcome to the University here on Shinalea. We are a place of learning and exploration—"

Something shifted. The world started to shake, the ground beneath Ravenna's feet becoming unstable. The stones in the floor seemed to undulate and move as if a wave had turned them to water. The walls around them vibrated, small chunks of stone falling from the ceiling. Miska and Cavaris both extended their hands, the shield of magic appearing above the heads of everyone there. Allora fell to her knees, hands above her head. The students cowered together. Ravenna spread her legs in a familiar Dalketh position, hands twitching towards her back where she kept swords no more.

As swiftly as it had begun, the shaking stopped. Cavaris and Miska lowered their shields. Ravenna turned to her mate, checking him for damage, for ridges or pain. Miska shook his head; he was all right. Ravenna turned then to Cavaris, his mouth hung open, his eyes wide and almost afraid.

"An earthquake?" Ravenna asked. Cavaris shook his head, gazed still unfocused, hands starting to tremble.

"Perhaps. This island is not known for such tremors, but I have not…ah…made a great study of such things." Cavaris seemed shaken, though it could have just been the dust floating through the air.

"We need to go see to the University, to the Aerial City. We'll check if there's damage there," Miska said firmly, moving his chair towards the entrance to the tower, rolling past the new students as if they were not there. They gaped at him, obviously still shaken.

Ravenna snorted, then followed him. "If you wish to do well here, you should learn that *nothing* is going to stop him from doing what he wants."

"Oh, really? And what about yourself?" Allora walked up to Ravenna, brushing dirt off of her clothes. The damage to the tower seemed minimal, and there were no screams of terror, so Ravenna allowed herself to thread her arm through Allora's, moving at a slow pace.

"I have earned that right," Ravenna replied. The students' eyes widened and they scurried after her. Allora just laughed. Ravenna, too, smiled. Earthquakes, dragons, politics, even rain, nothing could diminish her pleasure. She was home.

* * *

Cavaris watched the mortals exit the Stone Tower, so ready and eager to help those who might need it. He had already sent out tendrils of his magic through the island to see if there was significant damage. He had found none, just as expected.

The shaking of the ground, that was not due to some fault in the surface of the earth. There was no expectation of damage, only a warning to those who knew what it meant.

Miska had not felt the magic that flowed through the quake, and for that Cavaris was grateful. These particular mortals had earned their right to a life of their choosing. Not the mess that was surely to come. This event was not caused by anything so simple as a natural phenomenon.

No. No this was something different. The fractures and reality that were caused all those cycles ago, during that momentous war, they finally broke through. The dragons were awakening.

End, The Wing Cycle
Onwards to The Fire Wars

ACKNOWLEDGMENTS

The end of a series, the end of a story, is always a bittersweet occasion. I am absolutely thrilled to get this story out to the world, but a little sad to say goodbye to these characters. However, this is not the end! There will be more books in this world and you may even see some of these characters again.

But there is more in this series and these books than my stories and my characters. There are people behind the scenes who made The Wing Cycle what it is. I should like to thank Michael Evan who helped with editing and publicity, Fay Lane who made the covers for these books, and most definitely all who have read these books. You have made all of this possible and I cannot thank you enough.

ABOUT THE AUTHOR

E.G. Stone is an independent author who has been writing, quite literally, since the age of six. Since then, E.G. has improved rather a lot and has written (so far) twenty-two full-length novels, various short stories, a screenplay, snippets of poetry, and various blog entries that may or may not make sense. E.G. enjoys writing in many different genres. The favourites are science fiction, mystery (preferably of the murder variety), adventure, fantasy — basically anything where the world isn't quite what you would expect. When not writing, she is off musing about the workings of languages, both real and created, or wandering around and experiencing new people, places and things. E.G. reads voraciously, perhaps to the point of slight-insanity. She also is enjoying making a go of this writer thing full-time. Weird, nerdy, perhaps a little crazy, she is having a grand old time writing, reading, reviewing, interviewing, and causing trouble.

ALSO BY E.G. STONE

Speaker of Words

The Wing Cycle:
The One Who Could Not Fly
To Never Hear the Song
The Forsaking of the Blind

Pestilence and Plague: An Anthology of Stories about the Virus

www.ingramcontent.com/pod-product-compliance
Lightning Source LLC
Chambersburg PA
CBHW021135110726
47900CB00002B/359